MY UNEXPECTED
FOREVER

Guaranteed Tears by Eric Heatherly
© 2012 Eric Heatherly/Psychobilly Music/ASCAP
Ry Bradley
Edited by: Esperanza Lumm at Second Gaze Editing
Cover Designed by: Sarah Hansen at © Okay Creations

❀ Created with Vellum

For Yvette

CHAPTER 1 - HARRISON

THE MUSIC SHEET DOESN'T MAKE ANY SENSE. I'VE BEEN over it a hundred times or more and it's still all a blur. I know the lyrics and the beat, but everything I put down is a mess. Liam is expecting something from me by the time band practice starts in an hour, and I'm not going to be able to deliver. My mind is consumed with thoughts of love and lust and there isn't jack shit I can do about it.

I rip my ears buds out and move away from my computer. I can't do this, not today. Not after seeing her last night. I hate that I can't tell her how I feel. I hate that when another man looks at her, I feel nothing but murderous rage. I want to be the *only* one looking at her.

I'm a fool to think she wants me, with my full-sleeved tattoos and rocker lifestyle. I know I can offer her more than those other men. A stable home, financial security and a man who will worship and kiss the ground that she walks on. But I'm not the one you can take home to mom or to the school PTA meetings without being stared at. I know she doesn't want that. Enough people stare at her now.

I pull out a clean sheet of paper and write down more

lyrics. More touchy-feely shit that I wish I could tell her. Instead, I show up almost daily with something to offer her; coffee, lunch, or a free lawn mowing job because I can't, for the life of me, get it through my head that I'm nothing more than just a friend to her, and that's all I'll ever be.

I write down six words before tearing the paper up. I know why Liam tasked me with putting the music down for these songs, but they're mine. I hadn't planned on sharing them with the band. I think he's trying to get back at me for all those things I said about him falling in love when he returned home for his buddy's funeral. Now that it's my turn, he's sitting back and laughing his ass off. I ought to write some heavy shit. The head pounding scream-your-lungs-out shit that I sometimes think about. Either way, we need new songs and we've all been taxed with producing something.

But no, that isn't who we are. We've skyrocketed with Liam's heartfelt ballads and rocking personal stories that make women fall in love with us. They all think we're tortured souls and in need of companionship. Little do they know that Liam has only written about one woman. Hell, even I didn't know about it until he upped and left Los Angeles for the quiet, mundane life of Beaumont.

I can't blame him. I've done the same thing. This is the best place to raise Quinn. He'll go to school with Noah, and when Liam and I have a gig, Josie will take care of him. She's really filled the role of mother for Quinn and for that, I will forever be thankful to her. That and she gave my best friend a whole new life and we've since had a string of number one hits, putting us back at the top of the charts.

Now, if I could just get the one I'm infatuated with to just look in my direction. I'm firmly stuck in the friend category, though, and I don't know how to get out of it. I'm afraid to tell her how I feel because the look on her face will break me. I know she doesn't want me the way I want her, and I'd rather be her friend then not have her in my life at all.

I put my ear buds back in to try this one more time. I picture the things I want to do to her. The way I want to hold her. How I want to be the one she comes home to at night. Be the one that she turns to when she needs consoling on the anniversary of her husband's death. I want to be the one that the twins need when someone dares to break their hearts.

Imagining a life with her is as easy as breathing. I just have to find a way to make it happen without putting too much pressure on her. I hope that time is my friend and that someday she'll look in my direction and realize I'm someone she can trust to take care of her. That she'll know I'd never hurt her or the girls. That she will see me for me and know that Quinn and I would fit perfectly into her life.

I push away from the desk and head to my drums, bringing my laptop with me. I need to pound out some anger and frustration and maybe something will transpire that is usable. I close my eyes and let my sticks guide me. My beat starts off hard and steady. I'm beating the drums in front of me, releasing this pent up energy.

Her face flashes before my eyes, her voice inside my head. I instantly calm down and work out a rhythm. I hit record on my laptop and play the sound through. It's slow, smooth. Definitely something Liam and I can work on.

Jimmy and Tyler knock on the window, alerting me that they're here. Tyler is our new soundboard guru and he's been spending time with Jimmy in Los Angeles for the past week getting to know him. I stop the recording and take off my headphones to open the door for them. When I do, she's coming down the stairs talking on her cell phone. Her eyes meet mine briefly. I can't tell you if I'm smiling or not showing any emotion whatsoever, her presence alone makes me turn into a fool. It's times like this that I'm thankful she works for us. It gives me every conceivable excuse to be near her. It's so easy to fake a conversation about music and what gig we have coming up or what our deadlines are. The funny thing is, I know all of this, but act as if I've forgotten or can't find my phone to look it up.

Jimmy, or JD as we call him as he tells us it suits his 'rock star' lifestyle, slaps me on the shoulder as he passes. He's chuckling and muttering something to himself. Liam is trudging down the stairs before I can shut the door and turn on the light to let Katelyn and Josie know we are working.

I hate the way Liam looks in the morning. No, I shouldn't say that. I'm happy for him. He's with the one woman he loves and they are happy. Sickeningly happy; he's paid his dues and deserves this. The pride I see in his eyes when he looks at his son is the same way I am when I look at Quinn. They are the best of us, no matter how much we screw up.

"JD, my man," Liam says as they man hug. "I didn't hear you come in."

"Linda let me in. Tell me, how much did you have to pay her to leave her cushy job at the hotel to come here to take care of your sorry arse?"

Liam laughs. He made it a few months before he started looking for a housekeeper. He didn't want Josie having to take to care of the house by herself so he asked his former maid, Linda, to move to Beaumont. He's in the process of building her a nice little house behind his and he bought her a car.

"Let's get to work. Katelyn is working on booking some

new bars that she heard about, so we need to work out the kinks." Liam straps his guitar on and starts tuning.

"I worked this out before you guys got here." I move over the laptop and press play, watching JD and Liam as they listen to the melody. Liam smiles and looks over to the lyrics we've been working on. JD moves to the keyboard and hits a few keys and I add in the beat from my drums. Liam signals to Tyler to start recording. He strums his guitar and sings into the microphone as JD and I play along with him.

When I look up, Katelyn is watching me. Not us, but me, before she turns and is out of sight. For one brief moment I have a sliver of hope that she might feel the same way.

CHAPTER 2 - KATELYN

I set the phone down, resting my head in my hands. I know I can do this. I just have to convince myself that Liam didn't make a mistake in hiring me. What was I thinking when I opened my mouth at Christmas, saying I could be their manager? I fear I've bitten off more than I can chew, but Liam has confidence in me, even if I'm only booking 4225 West in small bars.

They laugh – the bar owners – when I call to book a gig. They ask if I'm joking, and I assure them that I'm not. I tell them, repeatedly, that the band is trying a different angle, more family friendly and want to give back to the fans that have made them so popular. Still, I can hear the humor in their voices when they agree to a booking and the small fee is figured out. What they don't understand is that with a bit of advertising, they will clean house at the end of the night. 4225 West isn't asking for a large percentage; they just want to play and want to do it without the bright lights shining in their faces.

My phone rings, startling me. I almost spill my coffee when I reach for the handset. My hand steadies the cup before there's a mess everywhere. I don't know where all these jitters are coming from... okay, yes I do. I know exactly what or who is setting me on edge. I just choose to ignore it. I can't focus on my children and career with the distractions that face me daily. I need to get through... I don't know what. He's my boss. That's what I keep telling myself, whether he's actually the one who signs my check or not. I work for him.

I pick up the phone on the fourth ring, clearing my throat and taking a deep breath before saying hello.

"Is this Katelyn Powell?"

"It is," I say, pulling my pad of paper closer to me to take notes.

"This is Christa Johnson and I represent an artist known as DeVon. He's an up-and-coming artist that we recently signed. His debut single releases next month and we're interested in getting him some attention. I'm calling to see if 4225 West would be willing to work a small tour with him?"

"What type of music? He sounds more hip hop with a name like DeVon." I write down his name and scribble *research* next to it. I haven't heard of him, but that doesn't mean anything. When it comes to music, I'm pretty much in the clouds.

"You'd think, right? DeVon is actually blues with a rock vibe. It's very funky with a kick. We think that with the success of 4225 West, DeVon will not only gain some fans, but will learn from the veterans and how they run a tour."

Veterans? I know I'm not a veteran when it comes to tours, but the guys are. Me? I'm just the person behind the desk trying to find places willing to pay them.

"Do you have venues set up?" This is important. How much work am I going to have to do?

"About fifteen, but we'd like thirty."

I can arrange the remaining venues. This will be good experience for me. "Where are you looking to tour?"

"Ideally, we'd like to hit the younger crowds, so Miami, New York City, Seattle."

"And when would you like to start?"

"We're hoping for August."

August? One month before school starts. Not that I need to be on tour with the guys, even though Liam will want me there. I'm sure Josie and Noah would go and Harrison would probably take Quinn as well. The band has a new CD coming out and this would probably be a huge benefit for them. Thirty stops, is that enough?

"August really doesn't work for us. What about July and we'll tour for forty-five days?" I throw that number out there, hoping I'm doing the right thing. Liam has given me full reign to do whatever I see fit, but I still question every-thing. He rolls his eyes most of the time or tells me to ask Harrison, and that's really not going to happen.

"We can do that."

"Great." Christa and I spend the next hour on the phone hashing out the details. I take copious notes and she promises to email the contacts from the venues she's already booked. We agree that I will take the lead, as 4225 West will be the headliner.

I look out my window to see if the red studio light is still on. It's not. I gather my notepad and pen and head out to the studio. The guys are standing around Tyler, laughing. This is good. This means they've recorded something they like and are happy. I like happy.

Liam kisses me on the cheek when I walk up to him. He puts his arm around me, pulling me closer. He's been like this since he moved back. I'm not complaining. I love him like a brother and he's been there for us, helping out more than I could ever thank him for.

"Katelyn, did you meet Tyler?" Liam asks as he points to Tyler who nods.

"Yes, Jimmy brought him in to fill out his paperwork. Did you guys get something recorded?"

"No," Harrison says sharply. I look at him and immediately wish I hadn't. He's staring at me, or Liam's hand, which is still resting on my shoulder. I'm not quite sure. Either way, his piercing green eyes are looking at me. His expression is stoic, almost hard.

"Well listen," I say. Liam drops his arms and moves so he's standing in front of me, leaving just enough space for the other guys to hear what I'm saying. We're talking business now; he's being serious. This Liam sometimes scares me. "I just got off the phone with a manager whose client is releasing a CD. His name is DeVon —"

"Is he a rapper?" Harrison asks, interrupting my spiel. I don't know why he does that, but it makes me want to slap my hand over his mouth.

I shake my head and continue. "DeVon is a blues artist with a bit of a rock kick. They're looking to build his fanbase and asked if we're interested in a tour. I figured with the CD about to come out, we could use the publicity, so we're doing a forty-five city tour starting in July. You guys will be back in time for the kids to start school."

"You guys?" Jimmy questions.

"Yes. I'll stay here."

"No, you'll be coming with us." Liam says. "Book a tour bus. Harrison can help. He has some connections and knows what we'll want. This will be fun."

Harrison and I stare at each other. The black beanie that he always wears is mocking my imagination of what his hair looks like. I've only seen him without his hat through pictures, never in person. I'm the first one to look away because I can't take the intense way he looks at me. Or maybe it's because I can't understand the way I look at him. Or the way I want to know more about him.

Liam kisses me on the cheek before heading upstairs. He declares it's lunchtime before I have a chance to say anything. Jimmy and Tyler move faster than I've ever seen them before, leaving me with Harrison.

"Should we go into your office?"

I look up quickly, expecting him to smile or change his expression, but he doesn't. I remind myself that this is my job and he has the answers I need to get my job done; and as much as I don't want to sit in my office with him while he leans over me, it has to be done.

I nod and lead the way. I count the steps to my office and then to my desk; twenty, twenty-one, twenty-two. He pulls out my chair. I make the mistake of looking at him as I sit down. The slight turn of his lip tells me that he's happy to be here. He beat me into my office and I don't know how. Was I really walking that slowly?

He pushes in my chair slightly and leans over me. I try not to breathe in his cologne. I don't want to know what he wears, but he smells good. I lean away, closer to my screen, and he leans in too. I wonder if he knows what he's doing to me. Doesn't he know I'm trying to avoid him? That we can never be anything?

Harrison tells me what site to bring up and I do. Except my fingers aren't working and I have to type the web address repeatedly. He moves his fingers over mine. I pull them back instantly, afraid for him to touch me. My hands rest in my lap.

"Sorry, I was just trying to help."

I nod and realize how stupid I'm being. We can be friends, right?

He brings up the website and walks me through how to order a custom charter. He says that they've used this company before and to call and ask for Larry; he'll make sure we get what we need and in time. I write down what he tells me and he laughs. I turn slightly, but think twice and focus on my paper.

"I think I can take it from here."

"Katelyn?"

The sound of his voice, the way he says my name, low and sweet with just enough mystery, makes me look up at him causing me to mentally kick myself.

"It's lunchtime and Linda doesn't like to leave out food for too long."

He's right. I slide my chair back. He moves one-step back giving me some space. I was hoping I could follow him upstairs, but he doesn't move or lead the way. He waits for me.

I feel stupid for feeling like this, but it's too soon after Mason. In fact, nothing will ever happen with Harrison. I know how he feels, but it just can't. Not only because I love Mason, but because he's not my type. I would never date a man who is covered in tattoos, wears a beanie and shorts all the time. He's the quintessential rocker and doesn't fit my life.

I don't care that the way he looks at me makes me feel wanted.

I don't care that the way he looks at me makes me feel desired.

I don't care that the way he smells makes me want to crawl into his skin until I'm enveloped in his scent.

I don't care because he's not Mason.

CHAPTER 3 - HARRISON

I PICK UP A SLEEPING QUINN FROM LIAM'S GUEST
bedroom. I left him here early this morning after we
finished loading the tour bus. It didn't make much sense to
wake him just to bring him back a few hours later. He's used
to this life, the constant touring, late nights and hotel food.
He's had a nanny before, but she traveled with us. I didn't
want to be away from him for more than a day.

Katelyn offered to stay home, but Liam was adamant
that she comes with us. Said she needed to learn the ropes.
She balked, but when he tossed out words like family vacation and Disney World, she agreed. Now I can't get the
vision of Katelyn in a bikini out of my mind.

I have a hard enough time, literally, when she's
dressed in her work clothes. Always a skirt, the length
changes, but one only notices that if they are paying
attention, and I am. All the time. My imagination is
running wild and I have to fight every urge I have to
reach out and touch her. To feel just the smallest amount
of her skin against mine. The casual brushes of my hand
against hers; or when I lean in and her hair tickles my

space, day after day and night after night, never apart unless we have different errands to run. Our friends are together, keeping us together. Sometimes I wonder why I moved to Beaumont. Was it because of the instant connection I felt with her on the first night we met? I tell myself it wasn't. That moving here was for Quinn and the band and to have an easier life. That having her here is just an added bonus.

When I hear her shut the girls' door, I pull my beanie down. I know she's standing next to me. I'm sulking like a child, a habit I've picked up from Quinn. He loves to sit in our recliner and pull his hat over his eyes, ignoring me until I give in. I always give in. I don't want her to see the confusion in my eyes. The desperation I hold for her. I don't want her to know she has me by the balls and can string me along like a puppet.

I want to move my hat, but she'll move as soon as I do, so I stay still and pretend to sleep just so she'll stand there longer. I feel the chair move as if she's leaning over it, trying to figure out if I'm truly asleep or not. Her breathing is normal, in and out. Her perfume is strong. I know she put it on before she came here. If I was standing behind her, I'd breathe in deeply just so I can smell her coconut and lime shampoo, a scent that I now love because it reminds me of her.

"What are you doing?" It's Josie. I know I should show them I'm awake, but I'm curious about what they are going to say. I've officially become the lowest form of a man. I should be ashamed of myself. I'm not. I'm evil and desperate for a sign on how to get through to her.

"I was just putting the girls in their bunk."

"And now?"

"Now... I'm... I don't..." I'm trying to slow down my

breathing, but the fact that Katelyn is stumbling over her words excites me. Do I do this to her?

"You know it's okay to date. Mason would want you to move on."

I want to jump up and kiss Josie right now, I do. Even if it means Liam would kick my ass, it'd be worth it.

"It's too early."

"It's been a year."

"No it hasn't. It's been ten months. That's two months shy of a year. Besides, you waited for three when Liam left you."

Josie sets something down and moves closer. At least I think she does.

"Liam left me, Katelyn, he didn't die. I waited because I prayed he was coming back. There's a difference."

"You don't know what you're talking about."

Silence follows. Now would be a good time to let them know I'm awake, but I'm far too chicken to do that. I'm curious if they are having a staring contest like kids do in elementary school. You know the type that if you smile first you lose. I never lost. Probably because I was never invited to play, but I watched from a distance and wondered how people, especially kids, could hold a straight face for so long.

"Hey, the bus doesn't pack itself."

Oh thank god Liam is here. He'll get the ladies moving and out of the way so I can wake-up.

"Sorry, we were just talking." I hear lips smacking against each other and cringe internally. Liam is a lucky ass bastard.

"I just need to grab our luggage and we'll be ready to go." God damn it. I forgot about her luggage. Instead of helping her, I'm sitting in his chair feeling sorry for my rejected ass. What the hell is wrong with me?

"You can wake-up now, they're outside."

Busted. I lift my beanie and look at Liam. He's shaking his head with a smirk plastered to his face. He forgets that I'm older than him.

"What the hell are you doing?" he asks in a hushed tone.

"Clearly feeling sorry for myself," I say, rubbing my hands over my face. I readjust my beanie and stand.

"She'll come around."

I shake my head. "I honestly don't think she will. I'm not her type."

"I've seen the way she looks at you and she talks to Josie about you. If you weren't getting under her skin, she wouldn't freak out every time I tell her she needs to work with you."

"You do that shit on purpose?"

"Of course I do. You're both my best friends and I want to see you happy. I think you'll make her extremely happy. She just needs to open her eyes."

Liam slaps me on the back and heads off the bus. I follow and see Katelyn at her car, her arms full. I walk back over, my hands in my pockets, stopping in front of her.

"Can I help?"

She looks at me, her lips turn upward slightly, but it's enough for me. I reach for her bags, loading them onto my arms and take her stuff to the bus. I'm going to be a gentleman this time, though. I leave her bag on the chair and quietly put the girls' bags on their top bunk.

When I close their door she's standing there, close enough to touch. She looks up at me. Her eyes move over my face, down my arms and back again. I can't tell if she's happy or not.

She raises her hand. I hold my breath, anxious for what

she's about to do. Her eyes move back and forth over mine, questioningly. I want to nod or tell her yes that she can touch me, but I'm afraid to speak. She drops her hand all too soon for my liking.

"Thank you, Harrison."

I swallow hard at the way my name rolls off her tongue. "You're welcome, Katelyn."

I turn and walk into my small room and throw myself onto the bed and will the instant hard on away.

This is going to be long-ass tour.

CHAPTER 4 - KATELYN

"Mason, how did you get here?"

"What do you mean? I walked."

"Is it a long walk?"

"What are you talking about? I walk from school to home all the time."

"But you're..."

"I'm what? What's going on Katelyn, why are you moving away from me?"

I look at the distance between the both of us and move closer. He extends his arm, his hand reaching for mine. My reaction is automatic, like I've done this a million times. I have. For as long as I can remember, I've always been holding his hand. My palm slips into his, he holds my hand tightly. I look down at them, our wedding rings shine as they reflect off the sun.

Sun? I thought we were inside.

I look around. Flowers and wheat surround us. We weren't here before.

Mason wraps his arm around me, pressing his lips to my ear. I hold him there, afraid to let go.

"It's time, Katelyn."

I'm afraid to know the answer, so I don't ask. "Stay."

Mason pulls back and smiles. I've missed him so much. The girls will be so happy to know he's back. That he's come back to us and everything has just been a nightmare.

He pulls my hand to his mouth and kisses my wedding band and engagement ring.

"I'll love you no matter what."

He's gone just like that.

"Mason, come back."

"Please. I can't do this without you."

I run, looking for wherever he went. I look down. Everything is black. I'm barefoot and bleeding.

"Katelyn?"

I jump when he shakes my arm. I know who it is by his voice. I sit up, adjusting the book I was reading in my lap. I move my matted hair away from my face. I can't believe he's standing next to me, staring. I'm a mess.

He hands me a tissue. I look at him questioningly.

"You were crying."

I take the tissue from his hand and wipe my eyes. I haven't dreamt of Mason in months and never like this. They've always been about the accident and how it plays out in my mind. This dream... it means something else, but what?

"Thank you," I say, clearing my throat. He stands and nods, heading back to the chair he was sitting in until he woke me. I look out of the window, the passing fields flying by as we travel down the highway. I don't know where we are, but all I can see is a random farmhouse every now and again.

Harrison clears his throat loudly. My kneejer"k reaction is to look over. He rubs his hand over his black beanie. It slides back and forth slightly. I watch intently, waiting for the tiniest hint of his hair. I wish he'd take the hat off, but he never does. If I had any nerve, I'd rip the sucker from his head and run. Burn the thing when he's not looking.

The beanie moves only inches, nothing telling. He glances over, catching me staring. I can't look away, even though I should. I look over my shoulder for anyone to rescue me. There's no one. I'm alone with him.

I've known this man for months. We've had dinner. Work together almost daily. When we aren't working, we are around each other, so why for the love of God can I not sit in the same general vicinity without needing someone else in the room? I'm a professional. He's a professional. We can be adults.

Right?

I turn back, catching his eye. He shakes his head, turns and looks out the window. I open my mouth to say something... anything, but nothing comes out. I don't understand why I can't talk to him. It makes no sense, this way I'm acting toward him. I'm sure he's a decent human being, regardless of the tattoos on his arms. It's not just his arms though, his leg too. He has something on his calf, but unless I bend down to look or ask him, I'll never know what it is.

I could drop a pen the next time I'm standing near him and get a good look. How long does it take to pick-up a pen and mentally take a picture? Longer than I have, because he's always aware of me. It's like he's a magnet and I'm the piece of metal he wants to attach to, which is just silly because magnets are attracted to other magnets and I'm not a magnet.

When he gets up I jump, dropping the book I have resting in my lap. My gaze follows him down the aisle. He enters the girls' room, and before I can get up and find out what the hell he's doing in there, he's out and holding Elle in his hands. She's clinging to him, her arms wrapped tightly around his neck. Her face squished into the front of his shirt.

He stops in front of me. "She was crying."

I look from him to my daughter and down the aisle. He heard her crying, but I didn't? What does that make me?

I reach for her, but she clings to him. She whimpers lightly, which breaks my heart. She's upset and would rather be comforted by him than me. I don't get it.

"I can hold her for a while until she's asleep again," he offers. His voice is incredibly soft and caring. I nod, even though it pains me to do so. She needs her mother, not him. I'm the one who takes care of the girls. Me. Yet, it looks like Harrison has been holding her from the day she was born.

Watching him sit down with her, he moves with such care and ease. He reclines his chair, nestling Elle across his chest. I get up and cover them both with my blanket. He smiles so softly, as if this gesture was the nicest thing anyone has ever done for him. He closes his eyes, his arms wrapped tightly around my baby. I wonder if he knows that he's holding half my life in his hands.

I pull her hair away from her face and feel her forehead, testing for a fever. Maybe the driving is getting to her, making her sick. This is their first road trip, unlike Quinn who has done this many times. The girls have never gone anywhere.

"She feels fine, must've been a bad dream," Harrison says this without opening his eyes. I hate to admit it, but he's a natural. All I can do is step away and watch him keep the demons at bay.

"DO you think we should wake them?"

The sound of young voices, those of the other children, ring in my ear. I open my eyes slowly. Six pairs of eyes stare back at me. One set, in particular, has her arms crossed over her chest. She's without her football and I wonder, if for one moment, she realizes she's not holding it. I refuse to call attention to that fact. Maybe she needed this trip more than the rest of us.

I stretch and quickly surmise that sleeping in a chair is painful. I remember why I was sleeping here and look over to see Harrison and Elle still covered and sound asleep. She looks like she hasn't moved an inch and by the looks of his arms, he has a death grip on her.

"Do you know if we are stopping soon?" Quinn asks. I haven't seen much of him since we took off. He and Noah have spent a majority of their time in Liam and Josie's room playing video games.

"I'm..." I sound as if I have a frog in my throat, which makes them all laugh. "I don't know, but I'll find out. I'm sure you guys are hungry. Just think, after the first stop we'll be staying in hotels most of the time."

"Yes!" Quinn fists pumps. "You guys, the hotels are so awesome and they bring you all the food you want. My dad doesn't care if I jump on the bed either."

"Yes I do, I just never catch you doing it."

Quinn's head whips around. I'm not sure if he's in trouble or not. Harrison winks at him, causing Quinn to smile so wide he shows his missing teeth.

"How do you wake her up?"

"Like this." Before I can say anything, Peyton slaps Elle so hard that she starts crying. Harrison stands and moves Elle away from Peyton's fury. I pull Peyton aside.

"What is wrong with you?" I'm trying to look at Peyton,

but can't take my eyes off of Harrison and Elle. He's holding her, rubbing her back where her sister hit her.

She crosses her arms and looks away.

"What's going on out here? You'd think we were travelling with a zoo?" Liam says.

He and Josie join our early morning circus. Josie takes Elle from Harrison, who doesn't look happy. Liam ruffles Noah and Quinn's hair all while Peyton glares at me. I take her hand in mine and walk her down the aisle to my small bunkroom. Whoever said travelling by tour bus was easy is so mistaken. Our rooms are barely wide enough to fit a twin bed and one of our bunks has two grown men in it.

"What's going on, Peyton? Why did you hit your sister?"

"I felt like it."

"That's not a good enough answer and you know it's not okay to hit."

"Elle hits me."

"Peyton —"

"NO! You always take her side. She hits me all the time and you never do anything about it because she's your favorite and I was daddy's favorite and he's gone so I have no one." She yells at the top of her lungs, loud enough that everyone on the bus hears her. She has tears running down her face. I reach for her, but she hits my hand. She doesn't want me to touch her.

The door opens. Liam is standing there. He looks at me and then to Peyton. He picks her up and holds her in his arms. A moment later, his door shuts. I step out and try to listen, but he's whispering to her. I can hear her crying and I can't do anything about it. I can't comfort either of my children.

Josie wraps her arms around me, holding me close.

"We're stopping soon. Everyone is just cramped and not used to being cooped up for so long. She'll be fine."

"What if she's not?"

"Then we'll figure it and go from there. Maybe the girls need to see a therapist or something when we get back. They might want to talk to someone who isn't their mom."

"Elle had a nightmare last night. I didn't even hear her crying, Harrison did. He went and got her and when I tried to take her, she wouldn't let go of him. He fell asleep in the chair with my baby wrapped in his arms and all I could do was sit there and watch another man hold Mason's daughter."

Josie pulls back and looks at me, her hands resting gently on my cheeks. "Mason would approve of Harrison, Katelyn. You should give him a chance."

She walks away, not waiting for answer, but I give her one anyway. "I can't."

drinking myself into a stupor. People make stupid decisions when they've been drinking.

"Well, you were that night."

"What's your name?" *I'm quickly realizing that I've made a mistake letting her into my house.*

"Alicia."

"Alicia, what?"

"Tucker. Alicia Tucker. We met about ten months ago."

I'm not stupid. I can do the math. I know it takes nine months for a baby to do its thing.

"Looks like you've been busy since we met." *This comment causes her to rip her sunglasses off her eyes. If looks could kill, I'd be dead right about now and she'd be cleaning out my checking account.*

"We met ten months ago after one of your shows. I was backstage and we went to the bar. I bought you a drink and you brought me back here."

"Okay." *I'm not sure what else to say. I can only imagine what happened when we came back here and sad to say it, but it wasn't memorable.*

"Anyway, this..." *she points to the carrier on the floor.* "Is yours."

The last two words hang in the air. I heard her loud and clear. I don't need her to repeat herself. I look at her and the carrier. The baby is mostly covered, except the face. I don't know if it's a boy or a girl. I really don't care. This chick is nuts. I always wrap my junk.

"What makes you think he's mine?"

"Because we slept together and I got pregnant."

"Not possible. I don't drink so I can avoid situations like this. I always wrap my junk. Your kid isn't mine."

"It is."

"It? Do you not know what you gave birth to?"

She rolls her eyes and places her hands on her hips. I stare at her, not willing to give an inch. Her phone rings. She takes it out and looks at it, smiling. How can she be smiling? This isn't anything to smile about. She's blaming her mistake on me. She pockets her phone and looks at me.

"Listen. I had a crush on you. I went to your show, got backstage and met you. I bought you a drink and we ended up here. I'm sure you're smart enough to figure it out."

"What are you thinking about, dad?"

I blink a few times, wondering why I was remembering the day he came to me.

"Not much, bud. We should probably get going." He nods and climbs off the bed. I watch as he moves around the room with ease. He's so used to this life and I sort of hate that for him.

WE ARRIVE at the venue in time for sound check. The artist who is opening for us finishes as we arrive. The kid shakes our hands, raves about our music and goes on and on about how thankful he is. I leave Liam and Katelyn to talk to him, although I want Katelyn to come with me. I could show her how to play the drums, while she sits on my lap. I hate what she's wearing. Her skirt is shorter and her shirt is one of our band shirts. I want to tear it to shreds so I can get to what she's hiding underneath and that skirt would look fine on my floor or up around her waist.

I start my sound check, playing a few of the first few bars of our songs so Tyler can figure everything out. This will be his first major gig and I'd like to make sure it goes off without a hitch.

Liam finally joins us on stage and starts going through

his list of requirements. He sings the first verse of each song on our set list for tonight. For the most part sound check goes fairly well. It was Tyler who didn't like the way a few of the songs sounded, but the adjustments were made and we finished in time for the doors to open.

I walk out front and check in with Luke at the merchandise table. I hadn't had an opportunity to see everything that Katelyn ordered for our shows. We have the standard band shirts with our new album cover, keychains, lanyards and five different images of me, Liam and JD. This is new, usually it's just been Liam on the images, but now it's all three of us. I have to say I like that she's included JD and me.

I look up when my name is called. A few girls start coming toward me, but it's not them who catch my attention, it's Katelyn. She's looking for me.

I can't help but grin from ear to ear as I walk toward her.

CHAPTER 6 - KATELYN

I SHOULD HAVE AN IV DRIP OF COFFEE INSERTED DEEP into my veins today. I don't know if I can do this. Liam made everything sound so easy and yet here I am about to jump off a cliff because I haven't a clue as to what's going on.

At first, when I opened the dressing room door, I thought this was normal. This being red roses everywhere. We are talking on every surface. I thought this venue was just being nice. A bit over the top – yes – but ass-kissing nice nonetheless.

That was until I heard the yelling, followed by the breaking of glass. I've never been in a violent home. My father dotes on my mother, who would rather have something on her body lifted than to raise her voice. And Mason, he never raised his voice unless he was yelling at the TV. So this bone-chilling sensation running down my spine is rather unnerving and honestly, I'm a little freaked out and afraid to open the door.

I breathe in deeply and try to center myself. If it's Peyton or Elle yelling on the other side of the door, I can handle it for the most part because I know what is causing their turmoil, but Liam... I can't fathom.

The sight before me is pure anguish. Liam is throwing vase after vase against the wall, a string of profanities accompanying each shattering vase. Josie has her hands up begging him to stop. And me... I'm standing in the room not knowing what to do.

Jimmy runs by me, stepping in front of Liam and pushing him back into the chair. Josie rushes over to him, crying. She holds him like something has hurt him purposely.

"Katelyn, go and find Harrison," Jimmy says, heavily, clearly out of breath.

I look at Liam and Josie; neither of them are paying attention to me and then back at Jimmy who signals for me to go. I turn and leave, holding my clipboard to my chest, while I try and figure out where in the hell I can find Harrison.

I search the stage. I ask Tyler if he's seen him. I knock on DeVon's door; he's not there. The bathroom turns up nothing. He's not in the greenroom with the kids, but Quinn says he likes to see what the fans are buying. Lovely. I take Quinn's advice and finally head out to the concourse and see him immediately. You can't miss the beanie, it doesn't matter what color it is, I'd spot it anywhere.

"Harrison," I say, not loudly enough. I guess I'm secretly hoping he won't hear me and I can go back to Jimmy and tell him to find Harrison himself, but he turns, as do the heads of the women near him. He's probably getting their phone numbers for later.

He keeps his head down when he walks toward me. For the briefest second I want him to look up so I can see his green eyes. Or are they blue today? I shake my head. I can't believe I even know that about him. That's crossing so many lines. I don't think I'll ever be ready to cross any line, especially with him.

Harrison stops in front of me. His hands are pushed into the pockets of his cargo shorts. He's wearing black combat boots today, they are unlaced and if this was Peyton I'd be on my knees tying them up for her. His black nondescript shirt accentuates his defined biceps. He's not built like Mason. Mason was muscular, always working out. He didn't need to flex to show off his muscles, they were there for everyone to see. Mason would have never covered his body in ink. Not like Harrison. I can't see the skin on his arms without seeing ink. No, Harrison is nothing like Mason.

At the last moment, he looks up and I wish he hadn't because now I don't know what to say. His eyes, they're baby blue with a hint of green today and are being overshadowed by his long eyelashes. I can't look at him; when I do, I can't think and I need to think.

I shake my head and rub my temple.

"Are you okay?" he asks and I wish that he didn't. I don't want him to talk, not right now.

"Jimmy said to get you. I don't know what happened, but Liam, he's upset and throwing the vases against the wall."

Harrison looks down the corridor and back at me. I know he's curious, but I don't have the answers for him. I've honestly never seen Liam like that and only read about divas and their dressing rooms. I didn't expect Liam to be one.

Harrison motions for me to go, but I shake my head. I don't want him behind me. I fumble too much when he's around and I don't know why. I certainly don't want to snag my heel on a step and fall on my face. I'll gladly walk behind him.

And now that I'm behind him, I wish I wasn't. I'm staring. I can't help it. Once again the tattoo on his calf is begging for me to look at it. My mind wants to know what it is, but my mouth is definitely not going to ask. If the two of those would get in sync I'd greatly appreciate it.

We arrive at their dressing room. Harrison doesn't knock. I suppose he doesn't really have to, does he? He swings the door open with a, "What the fuck are you doing?" blurting out too loudly for my taste.

Jimmy is leaning against the wall, shaking his head. Liam is sitting in a chair with Josie rubbing his shoulders. I'm not sure I'd be touching him if I was her, but there she is, standing by her man.

"Why are there roses in here?" Harrison is looking at me like I know the answer. I shrug and look at everyone else in the room.

"Why did you add roses to the rider? Didn't I tell you, no flowers?" This time it's Liam speaking. There is so much venom in his voice and, for the first time since I started working for him, he's my boss and not my best friend. He's angry and hostile. His face is red and his temples are throbbing. I know how he feels.

"Wh-what?" I stutter. Jimmy rolls his eyes. Harrison just looks at me. Liam throws his hands up in the air and jumps out of the chair, causing Josie to fall back a bit.

"The rider, Katelyn. Why did you add flowers?"

"I didn't."

"Let me see it!" Liam stalks over, his footsteps heavy and solid. This is a different Liam, this is Liam Page, the performer and I'm not sure I like him at the moment.

I fumble though my file, looking for the rider that I

faxed over before we hit the road. My file drops, spreading my papers out all over the floor. Liam sighs and starts muttering a string of curse words that bring tears to my eyes. I will not cry in front of him. I have a feeling this will be my mantra.

I get down on my hands and knees and start gathering the papers. Now that they are all out of order, I'm not going to be able to find anything. My hands are shaking so bad. I hate this. Why is he suddenly being an asshole? If Mason was here, he'd kick his ass for yelling at me.

Mason pushes Liam up against the locker. Josie screams before I realize what's happening. I'm grabbing Mason's arms, but to no avail. He's much too strong for me. Liam doesn't push back. He's letting Mason hold him there.

"What the fuck, man?" *Liam spits out.*

"Don't what the fuck me, you rat bastard. I saw you yell at her."

"She deserved it." *That comment earns Liam another slam against the locker.*

"Baby, come on, let him go. It's no big deal," *I plead.*

"Did he yell at you?"

"Yes, but —"

"No buts, no one yells at you, except me."

I push Mason as hard as I can, causing him to lose his hold on Liam who easily slips away. "What the hell? Only you can yell at me? Is that what you think, Mason Powell?" *I push him again and again. My small hands beating on his chest.*

Mason looks over at Liam, who has his face buried in Josie's neck. I know he's laughing, I can see him shaking.

"I didn't mean it like that, baby. Come on, you know I'd never yell at you."

"I can't believe you were willing to beat up Liam —"

CHAPTER 7 - HARRISON

I TOUCHED HER.

She let me touch her.

And I stopped.

Why did I stop?

I have no idea.

My steps are heavy. My ears pound as I walk away from her. Every fiber in my being is telling me to go back. Go back into that room and hold her hand. A simple graze of my fingers against hers would suffice. I'm not asking for much.

Although I know I am.

She's not ready.

She may never be ready.

Is that something I can live with? Maybe, I don't know. I've never felt this way. All I know is that touching her for that one brief moment, having her hair glide along my knuckles and the look in her eyes when I did it; I felt like I could do anything, all because she didn't move away, she didn't look away. She stayed and allowed me one solitary piece of herself and now that moment will burn into my memory until I can do it again.

Liam is pacing when I find him.

"What the hell was that?" I ask him. I don't like the way he spoke to Katelyn. Yes, being on tour is stressful, but this time it's supposed to be for fun. We are supposed to be showing our families what our lives are like away from home. Treating Katelyn like she did something wrong is going to make her want to quit, and I can't have that.

Liam looks up at me with impatience and a self-accusing look. He shakes his head, rubbing his hands over his face before he lets out a frustrated scream. The only thing preventing everyone from hearing him is the fact that DeVon is on stage performing.

"I can't believe I yelled at Katelyn like that."

"What was that?"

"Sam all over again."

"I figured, but this isn't Katelyn's fault. She doesn't know about the things Sam used to do and if she did, she surely wouldn't do them without asking us."

"I know." Liam moves toward the wall and leans back. "Remember that first gig we had? God we opened the door and they were there, every square inch was covered."

"I remember."

"What's all this?" I stand behind Liam and JD, surveying the room. We knew when we signed with Moreno Entertainment that we'd get the star treatment, but this may be over the top. "Did we ask for this?"

Liam turns and looks at us, we both shake our heads. I'm a guy. Simple things amuse me. I definitely don't need a room full of roses... so many in fact that you can't see the furnishings.

"Sam thought it would be a nice touch," Mr. Moreno says. He's a short, pudgy man. He sort of reminds me of a gangster, always wearing a fedora that covers his balding head. He's never without a cigar hanging out of his mouth, even though I've never actually seen him light it. He looks at Liam and winks.

"I don't think we like it," Liam says and JD and I nod. I'm not a flower guy. I mean I'll send them to my mom, but can't say I want them stinking up my place. The room looks like a funeral home – a red one to boot. Red roses cover every available inch, leaving barely a space for us to sit down.

"Can we go someplace else, Mr. Moreno? This isn't us," I say.

Mr. Moreno rubs his portly belly. "But my Sam did this for you, Liam. She said you'd like it."

I hear Liam sigh. He pinches the bridge of his nose and shakes his head. "4225 West doesn't need or want this. Can we please have it cleaned out or go to a different room?"

Mr. Moreno pats Liam on the back. He doesn't pay attention to us. I mean why should he? Liam is the talent behind the band. I'm just a lowly house-band drummer that he asked to come play with him when he got signed and JD joined after answering an ad in the paper. For Moreno Entertainment – Liam is their prize.

"My Sam did this especially for you, Liam, I think you'd want to accept her gift."

"Mr. Moreno, with all due respect to you and Sam, this room is supposed to be a place for us to relax before going out to perform. I know for me, and I'm assuming for Harrison and JD as well, we can't center ourselves in this room when the over-powering scent of flowers is trying to kill us."

Mr. Moreno chuckles, his belly bouncing up down as his menacing laugh carries on. Liam looks at us, we both shrug.

We don't know what's going on, but from the sound of Mr. Moreno, we aren't going to like the result.

"Liam, you're young and new to all of this. It's best you let me decide what you like and don't like. Sam is merely trying to show her appreciation and make you feel comfortable. I suggest you repay her in kind."

Mr. Moreno walks out, leaving us in the middle of the red funeral room. There isn't any place for us to sit down, let alone hang our coats.

JD starts walking around, pulling the cards from each bouquet.

"Good Luck, Liam. Love, Sam."

"You're the best, Liam. Love, Sam."

"You'll be amazing, Liam. Love, Sam."

"Dude, did you sleep with her?" I ask. Liam shakes his head.

"No, and maybe that's the problem. I've rebuffed her advances. I just want to keep things professional and earn our way to the top."

"Yeah, well, I think Sam is making it very clear that the way to the top is by shagging her." JD says as he drops the cards on the floor.

Liam starts picking up the vases and moving them into the corner. He stacks them on top of each other, breaking the flowers underneath. JD and I follow and soon enough we have a minimal amount of space to sit down.

"I'll take care of it." That's the last thing Liam says before we start going over the set list.

We've been down this path before in the early stages, just after we signed with Moreno Entertainment. Liam and I were so new to this side of the industry we didn't know what to expect. JD said his dad was a total diva when it came to his dressing room, but never to this extreme.

touching. I wonder if she realizes how close she is to me. I'm tempted to let my hand fall to my side and seek out her fingers, if anything, just to brush ours together to give me enough of a jolt to last me though my set.

The lights go down and that's our cue. I'm to go out first, but I'm not budging. I don't want to leave the shared space with Katelyn. Liam puts his head back and rolls his neck. He's ready. I know I must move.

"Good luck, Harrison," she says. I'm not sure how I can hear her over the crowd, but I do. I feel the smallest of pressure on my back. I turn slightly and look at her. She allows us the briefest of eye contact before turning away. That's enough to spur me into action. I brush past JD and Liam, who both slap me on the back, and turn left and count my steps. One, two, three, four and turn right. Another five and I'm sitting on my stool. I spin once before pulling my drumsticks out of my back pocket.

I hit the cymbal and the crowd roars. Even through the darkness I know JD and Liam are on stage waiting for me to get things started. I raise my arms above my head and bang my sticks together for a count of five. My sticks slam down on my drums and the lights come on. The fans scream just as Liam and JD starts their riffs.

It's pure magic.

MY ARMS ARE SORE. My t-shirt drenched in sweat. My feet kick the dozen or so water bottles that clutter the floor around my drums. The fans continue to chant, even though we've done three encores. I'm the last to leave the stage. I don't acknowledge the crowd the way Liam and JD do. I slip out as quietly as I can. I'm seconds behind the curtains when the lights come on. The groan of the crowd is loud and I can't help but internally fist pump. Even without Moreno Entertainment, we still have it.

I swing open the door to the kids' room and Quinn jumps into my arms. A piece of me will die when he's too big to do this. Right now, I wrap my arms around my boy and hug the shit out of him because he still wants this.

"You were awesome, Dad."

"Thanks, buddy." I set him down, but he doesn't leave my side. He's tired. I can tell. It takes a while to adjust to our longer nights. I'm thankful we are doing this tour during the summer because I'm ready for him to experience school the way I did, except for the parts that I didn't like.

Cold hands clamp around my leg. I look down to find Elle looking up at me. I smile at her, only to be rewarded with the biggest smile I've ever seen. Who knew after one sleepless night that we'd be friends? I crouch down so that I'm level with her. Quinn stands tall, my hand set on the back of his leg so he can more or less hold me up. I'm too exhausted to trust myself not to fall over.

"I saw you throw your sticks lots a times."

"You did? Did you remember that I was doing it for you?"

Elle nods. "Peyton didn't care though. She didn't watch the show."

"It's okay. Maybe she'll watch next time." I look over at Peyton, who is standing in the corner with arms crossed over her chest. She looks up, her face stoic, when the door opens again. Noah runs up to Liam and Josie, and Elle waves at her mom. It doesn't go unnoticed that neither girl is running to her. I can see the heartbreak roll over her face. I want to pull her into my arms and tell her that everything will be okay, but that would be crossing so many lines that I know she's not ready for.

Instead, I do the only thing I know I have a little bit of power over. "I think your mom missed you. Maybe you should go see her," I whisper into Elle's ear.

Elle looks at Katelyn and says, "You think?"

I nod. "Yeah, I think so."

Elle takes off and launches herself into Katelyn's arms. I stand, pulling Quinn's hand into mine and look at Katelyn, offering her my sincerest apologies. I want to help her, but I'm not sure if I can.

CHAPTER 8 - KATELYN

WHEN THE BAND TOOK THEIR FINAL ENCORE, I FELT like I could finally breathe. As the guys left the stage I wanted to clap like I was fan, but held back. I'm so proud of Liam, and seeing this side of him is amazing. He performs with such confidence, just like he did on the football field. I have no doubt he could've done either and been successful.

Liam and Jimmy pass me as if I'm nothing more than a common employee. I know that I am, but it still stings. I can't forget that I'm at their beck and call, not the other way around. I wait for Harrison and I hate that my body shivers in anticipation that he'll be close again. It shouldn't feel like this, my body belongs to Mason. *I* belong to Mason. The lights go on and still no Harrison. I look out and see people moving out of their seats. I take a deep breath and step out onto stage, ready to face Harrison and encourage to him to get back stage. I look at his drum set, empty. He's already gone and I missed him.

Why do I care that I missed him? I don't. Or maybe I do and I can't bring myself to admit that, when he's in the room, the chaos doesn't exist. That watching him hold Elle

I push him slightly. "You're incorrigible."

"You love me."

"I do, more than anything."

I wish I had a camera at the time to capture those moments between Mason and the girls. I'm not sure I ever thought to take a picture when they were climbing all over him or sitting on his lap while he was scouting. So many memories that I've missed and I'll never get back or be able to show the girls just how great their dad was.

I'm relishing the fact that she's letting me hold her for so long. I don't want to put Peyton down. I want to cuddle with her until she feels safe enough to open up. Josie's right, the girls need to speak to someone about what they're dealing with. Clearly, I'm not enough, and I need to be okay with that.

I sit down on the couch and immediately regret it. She's out of my arms faster than I can ask her to stay. She goes to Noah and sits down. He doesn't acknowledge her, but Quinn does. I can't hear what they are talking about, but Peyton smiles and Noah rolls his eyes.

The bus roars to life and the kids all cheer. They should be sleeping, but tour life doesn't allow for normal hours. We'll drive for a few hours before getting to our hotel, where we'll stay for a few days and take the kids to Disney World. This will be a first for Noah, Peyton and Elle. This was something Mason and I had talked about many times and I hate that he's not here to share it with us.

Liam sits down next me and hands me a bottle of water. "I'm sorry for yelling at you earlier. I get a bit stressed and the flowers, they set me off."

"It's okay."

"No, it's not," he says as he shakes his head. I watch as he downs the bottle of water in one gulp. I've always wondered how he and Mason could do that. I'd choke if I tried.

"It is. I just don't want to be fired."

Liam laughs. "I couldn't fire you if I wanted."

"Yeah, why's that?"

He looks around and his eyes land on Harrison who is talking with the kids not a few feet away from us. "He'd kill me."

I shake my head. I know Liam and Josie think he'd be a good fit for me, but I don't. We have nothing in common.

"You need to stop."

"Stop what?" he asks nonchalantly.

"Trying to fix us up. He's not my type."

Liam leans back and puts his arm on the back of the couch. He grins so brightly when Josie comes down the aisle. He loves her just like Mason loved me. I can see it in the way he looks at her.

"Am I Josie's type?"

"Of course."

Liam looks at me questioningly. "Seriously? Look at me, with my tattoos, motorcycle and music. This is the not the Liam that she fell in love with. That Liam was a football star. He woke up every morning and ate some gross protein shit. He worked out during and after school. He was football. Now look at him. He's the exact opposite of who she fell in love with."

"What's your point?"

"My point is that you fell in love with Mason when you were fifteen. He's all you've ever known. Who's to say that he wouldn't have gotten a tattoo when he entered the NFL? Would you have loved him any less? Probably not, I'm guessing. Thing is, Katelyn, love doesn't know the way someone looks. Love knows the inside of who that person is.

CHAPTER 9 - HARRISON

I'VE NEVER WANTED TO BE A FLY ON THE WALL UNTIL tonight while watching Liam talk to Katelyn. I wanted to know what he was saying. I tried not to lean forward and listen, but I caught myself doing just that a few times. When Josie sat down and started talking about inconsequential things, I wanted to kindly ask her to be quiet so I could maybe hear what Liam was saying.

But I didn't.

The bus is quiet. I hate quiet. I need noise to feel at ease. Everyone's gone to bed except for me and JD, although being asleep in the chair is close enough. I pull out my phone and push the button for GPS. We are a still a few hours away from our hotel, but there's not enough time for it to matter if I sleep now or later. The plan is to take an early morning nap at the hotel before we hit the theme parks in the afternoon.

I'm excited about going to Disney, mostly because I'm looking for any excuse I can get to be close to Katelyn. I know she's struggling with Peyton. I've racked my brain trying to think of ways I can help, but short of finding a spell to raise the dead, I'm no use. Not that I'd actually do that. I thought that Quinn might be the answer, but he's never known his mom, so it's hard to say he's been there.

A door shuts quietly behind me. I turn and see Katelyn coming down the aisle. She's dressed in an oversize t-shirt and for my sake I hope she has shorts on underneath, because all I can see are her legs and they are very bare. I have to bite the inside of my cheek in order to keep my mouth closed.

I wish I knew how to talk to her in a way to get her to open up. Since moving to Beaumont, I haven't given another woman a second glance. With Katelyn, I'm not only giving her a second one, but a third, fourth and fifth whenever she's in the room. I could live a day without water if I was granted the permission to just stare at her.

I can't look up and make eye contact with her, even though it's probably the right thing to do. My eyes follow the steps she takes as she passes me. I wonder if she's sleep walking or if I'm even awake. Maybe I'm dreaming and she's not really here - standing in my general vicinity - half naked.

I swallow hard when she sits down and tucks her legs underneath her. Does she not see me sitting here? Of course she doesn't, I'm invisible. I need to find a way for her to see me, the real me on the inside and not the graffiti'd man she sees when she looks at me. I see the way she looks at my arms. I have no doubt that the wheels are turning in her head wondering why someone would cover their arms with ink. All she has to do is ask and I'll tell her. I'm an open book once you crack my cover.

I clear my throat, but that doesn't get her attention. What the hell? "Hi," I say loud enough to cause JD to adjust in the chair. I wish he'd wake up and leave now that she's here. I want to bask in her presence without an audience.

"Hi." Her reply is soft, quiet. Is she afraid to wake up the log-sawing machine?

I look over at JD and shake my head. "Sorry. He's not usually like this."

"It's okay."

At least she's answering me. It means that she's actually awake, although I'm not sure I am. I look back at her and see that she's rubbing her arms. She's cold. I get up and go to the closet and pull out a blanket. Sitting down, I unfold it and lay it on top of her.

"Thank you."

I nod. "Why are you up?"

She looks up at me. Her eyes are sharp. "Do you want me to leave?"

I swallow hard, catching myself from squeaking out an answer. "No, not at all. It's just that it's late, or early depending on how you look at things. I thought I was the only one still functioning."

"I couldn't sleep. What's your excuse?"

This is the most she's spoken to me since I've met her. "I have a hard time unwinding after a show, especially when I know we're stopping soon."

Katelyn looks at me but doesn't say anything. No acknowledgment or anything. The awkward silence follows. It shouldn't because I have so many things I want to ask her. Actually that's not true. I know what her favorite color is, her favorite food and how she takes her coffee. I've paid attention these past few months, learning how she functions and what makes her tick.

I don't know what to do or say. This is where I fail. This is where I've had my status as a drummer work to my benefit. Most women I've gone home with don't care about what's on my mind or how I like my coffee. They aren't looking for a meaningful conversation. They just want one thing.

I don't want that with Katelyn. I don't want her to be someone that I just bring home when the urge is there, because with her even breathing, the urge is there. I want to know her, inside and out. I want to learn how to fall in love with her as my partner.

I can't keep staring at her or off in to space. I don't know how to proceed. I don't want to push her into talking to me. I pick up my book and flip to the page where I left off. The words blur in my mind. I'm not going to make heads or tails of these pages as long as she's sitting one cushion away from me.

Katelyn adjusts and lets out a long sigh. I close the book, setting it back down on the floor.

"Do you want to talk about it?"

She shakes her head. "I don't know how you do it."

"Do what?"

"Raise Quinn by yourself."

I turn and face her, but keep my eyes focused on the outside. "Sometimes I wish I wasn't raising him by himself. I know there are things that only a mom can do, but I try to be both. I've read a lot of books on how to be an effective parent and provide him with the right tools, but it's hard. I'm the only parent he knows. Our situations are different. He didn't lose his mom the way you and the girls lost Mason."

"Where's his mom?"

I shrug. "I don't know."

"How can you not know? Doesn't she call?"

I shake my head. My finger starts playing with my lip as

CHAPTER 10 - KATELYN

I WANT TO KILL JOSIE. OKAY, MAYBE NOT KILL, BUT maim in the worst way. I don't even think she means well. I think she's evil and cold-hearted because all I want to do is sleep. I don't think that's too much to ask, but apparently my presence is required at dinner, which according to her will be followed by dancing. I don't want to dance. I have no one to dance with. Does she really think I'm going to bump and grind with some stranger?

I drag my brush through my hair angrily. This is the last thing I want to do. A night of sleep in a hard hotel bed ranks higher than a night out. I balked at first, told her there isn't anyone to watch the girls, but of course she had a babysitter all lined up. There is no getting out of going out, no matter how hard I try.

Slipping into the red cocktail dress she had sent up, I step into a pair of over-priced peep-toed shoes, also a gift from her. I want to wring her neck. She knows how I feel about gifts, especially when they are expensive. I really want to send them back to her with a giant 'no thank you', but I don't want to look ungrateful. I know she does this because she loves me and Liam encourages her. Both of them together are going to cause me to go gray long before I'm due.

Today was supposed to be the beginning of an epic three-day adventure. When we pulled into the hotel, the kids were so worn out all they wanted to do was lay by the pool. Jimmy was all too happy to take them, only for me to find out that he used my girls as a single dad ruse to pick up chicks. In hindsight, I should've listened to Harrison when he told me not to let the girls go, but who is he to tell me such a thing? I sent the girls on their way to a smirking Harrison and a laughing Liam. Jerks.

Now my girls are lounging in the "kid" room, as Liam calls it, with a highly paid babysitter, all giddy about babysitting Liam Page's son. I'm sure she's telling the world on her many social networking apps instead of actually watching the kids.

I look in the mirror and touch up my make-up. I'm stalling. Maybe I'm dragging out my arrival so they'll think I've ditched and spent a childless night holed up with a good book. Josie won't let that happen though.

With a deep and reserved breath, I make my way up to the top floor. Who knew Disney would have an adult area in their kid-themed hotel? The décor is black and polished. I could probably see my reflection clearly if I wanted to stand there and stare. Music is thumping, but it's not loud in the restaurant area. A hostess leads me to my dinner party. The party that I plan to poison before the night is over. I round a corner and my eyes are immediately drawn to him, sitting with his arm resting on the back of booth. His leg is half hanging off the bench. He's wearing dark jeans and a dark hoodie and his head is covered, like always. Why does he do that? It makes me think that his head is scarred or to take the edge off. I'm so tired of feeling like I'm about to fall off the side of a building.

"What is it?" Harrison asks as he tips his beer back.

"Well, we've set a date!" Josie squeals. My mouth drops and Harrison starts laughing. He reaches over the table and high-fives Liam. I scramble to get out of the booth so I can hug Josie.

"I'm so happy for you," I say into her ear as we hug. I wish Mason was here to see this. He wanted nothing more than for her to be happy, even if it meant she was marrying Nick. I'd like to think he'd be happy that she's marrying Liam because they are meant to be together.

We sit back down and I wipe a few happy tears that have fallen. I can't wait to see Noah in a tux. He's going to look so handsome and dapper.

"When's the big day?"

"We want to get married right after Christmas, but we're keeping this among friends," Liam answers without taking his eyes off of Josie.

"Well that doesn't give us a lot of time to plan, doesn't it?" I say as the waitress sets down our dinner. Liam and Harrison dig right in. I shake my head and pick up my fork, twirling a piece of pasta.

"Will you be my matron of honor?"

"Of course," I say as I cover my mouth in that awkward you caught me with my mouth full moment.

"What about you man, can you stand up for me?" Liam asks Harrison.

"Yeah, man," Harrison says with a nod. Why does everything have to be so simple for them? They didn't even look at each other. It hits me like a ton of bricks that if I'm the matron of honor and Harrison's the best man, that means we'll be walking down the aisle together. We'll have to share a dance. Is that why they brought us here tonight, to test our ability to dance together? I pick up my drink and finish it, signaling to the waitress that I need another. Liam catches my eye. I shrug. I don't need any comments from the matchmaking duo that can't take a hint.

As we eat, we talk about the wedding. Josie wants something outside and Liam wants a big party afterward. They both agree that 4225 West will not play at the reception. Liam says he wants to enjoy his bride and not worry about putting on a performance for anyone.

Harrison returns his arm to its previous position, resting comfortably on the back of the booth. I feel myself shifting. My body wants to sit in the nook he's created, and for the life of me I don't understand why. I'm not attracted to him. We are opposites and the tattoos... I can't. I try to slide away from him without drawing too much attention to myself, but he notices. He shakes his head and removes his arm. My heart pounds and tension fills my body. I shouldn't care.

"I'll be back," he says as he throws his napkin down on his half eaten plate of food.

"Where's he going?" I ask. Liam turns his head as we both watch Harrison walk away from the table.

"I don't know," he says with a shrug. He picks up his beer and takes a sip, watching Josie the whole time. I try not to watch Harrison, but I'm curious. He stands at the bar and it doesn't take a minute before a tall leggy blond is standing next him. Harrison turns and leans against bar. The woman moves closer. Too close if you ask me. Clearly they don't know each other. She leans in and laughs at something he says. Her hand rubs along his chest and it doesn't seem to bother him. He looks at our table briefly and catches me staring.

Harrison raises his eyebrow as he pulls her hand into

his. He carries his beer in his other hand as he leads them to the dance floor. I look away. I don't care that he's going to dance with her. It's none of my business. He's single and free to do whatever he wants.

I signal the waitress again and order a round of shots for the table. When they arrive, only Josie does one with me. I don't know why I ordered four. It's clear that Harrison has left us to our vices for the rest of the night. I down my second as my eyes find him on the dance floor. The woman is draped all over him as they dance. His hand is on her ass. He's pulling her to him and each time he does, her head falls back. Her hands rub up and down on his chest. My mouth drops when she slides his hoodie off and pushes her fingers into his dark locks that are cut short on the sides, but left longer on top. Not too long, just enough to grab a hold of. I've been waiting months and she's known him for thirty-seconds and is already touching him. He says something to her causing her to nod as he takes her hand and leads them off the dance floor.

"Where's he going?" I ask again.

Liam laughs. I turn and glare at him.

"What's your problem, Westbury?"

"You, you're my problem, Powell. That man likes you and you ignore him. Now you're pissy that he's found someone to give him attention. Either friend-zone him or let him in, but I've seen the teeter-totter you keep him on and it's not fair."

"I don't like him."

"Then don't like him. No one is saying you have to, but don't lead him on. Don't get up in the middle of the night and talk to him like you want to get to know him."

"He told you that?"

"Yeah, he did," Liam throws down some money on the table. "I'm outta here. Are you coming?"

Josie nods as she links hands with Liam. "Night, sweetie."

"Night," I mumble as they walk off, leaving me at an empty table.

I get up slowly on shaky legs. I have to steady myself against the edge of the table. I've definitely drunk too much. I slip off my shoes and attempt to walk in a straight line back to the elevator. The car I get in is full. I step on and wait for my floor. I'm sure these families are wondering what kind of trash I am. Drunk and shoeless in a resort hotel, riding the elevator at god knows what time of the night. I can't get the image of Harrison and that woman out of my mind. The way he was holding her to him, it was rough and sexy. And she touched his hair; hair that I've been dying to see. He just let her do whatever she wanted as I sat there and watched their foreplay unfold on the dance floor.

I step off and stare down the hall. My steps are slow as I pass his door. I stop and listen. Would he really bring a woman back to his room with Quinn in there? Of course he wouldn't, but Quinn isn't in there, he's in Liam's suite with the babysitter.

I startle when a door opens. Harrison stands there with his hoodie on, covering his hair again. It's zipped half way down so I can see multiple tattoos on his chest. He's changed his jeans for khaki shorts.

"What are you doing?"

I shrug. "Shouldn't you be busy?" the words are out before I can stop them. I don't know why on earth I'd ask such a brazen question. It's none of my business what he does. He looks sad that I've asked him and I feel my body sigh in relief. Why is that?

"She got to touch you, take your hood off and when I tried, you moved away."

She was watching. This should give me hope, but it doesn't. It hurts that she saw me with that woman. If this was last year, I would've bedded her and never thought about her again. That all changed the night I met Katelyn. One look at her and I knew.

"Because I want you to know me."

My answer isn't enough for her. She turns and walks out into the hall, toward her room. I step out, leaning against the door jam and watch her walk to her room. She stands at her door. Her hand comes up to her face and across her cheek. Fucking great, I made her cry. She doesn't offer me a look before entering her door. The click echoes down the hall, effectively ending the best and worst minutes of my life.

I sit down on the couch and stretch out. I don't know what else I can do to get her attention. Maybe I should stop. I should take her walking away from me as a sign. But I'm in too deep. Too far gone to give up, and I don't know if I can be her friend anymore. Something has to give.

I rub my hands up and down my face before screaming out in frustration. Life isn't supposed to be like this. I've waited for the right one to come along, and when she finally does, she's so torn up after losing her husband that I don't stand a chance in hell.

I should've known better.

I should've...

I search frantically for a piece of paper and a pen, finding one in Quinn's backpack. Sitting back down, I clear the coffee table of his games and start writing.

I shoulda known better, but my
heart trumped my mind from the
day I met her

I know I shoulda known better,
but my heart trumped my mind from
the day I met her, I knew she was
hurtin I knew she was the hurting
kind that type of heart breaker, it
aint nothing new it takes one to
know one, I know I ve broke a few.

I set my pen down and read over the words. I like how
they are coming together, how she's bringing this out of me.

I like to drink to get drunk, its like
a bullet
She s like a drink that I need to
feel like a gun needs a

I get up and pace. My fingers play with my missing lip
ring. Sometimes I wish I still had it, but Quinn would've
yanked it out when he was younger had I kept it. I read the
lyrics that I wrote down. My chicken scratch is barely legi-
ble. School definitely doesn't prepare you for stardom.
Maybe if I paid more attention in handwriting class, I
wouldn't groan internally each time I'm asked for an autograph. I stop and play the air drums with the lyrics running
through my head.

I have to scramble back to the couch when the next
verse works its way into my subconscious.

she's raising twin daughters who are six. What else does my son say?"

"That she makes you smile and that one of her daughters really likes you." Quinn must be talking about Elle because Peyton doesn't like anyone right now, unless their name is Liam. It makes me feel good that Elle has taken to me. I would never want to replace her dad, but wouldn't mind being a part of her life. Right now, Elle's the only one willing to let me in.

"She does make me smile, but she also irritates me so much. I'm afraid to show her the real me because she definitely looks down on all my tattoos and the rejection... I'm not sure I can take any more." As soon as the words are out of my mouth, I regret them.

"Any more?"

I take a deep breath and push my hood off. "I kissed her tonight."

"That's good, right?" Yvie sounds too happy. I want to be her kind of happy someday.

"It was, until she pulled away. I moved too fast and probably scared her away."

"Ah big brother, I'm sure she'll come around. Once she gets to know you, she won't be able to resist you. I know that for a fact."

"Do ya now?" I ask, trying not to laugh at her enthusiasm. "And how's that?"

"Because you're the most amazing person I know and anyone would count themselves lucky to be loved by you."

I can't help but smile. "I love you, Yvie."

"I love you too. I gotta go. I'll call in a few days."

"Be good."

"Ha, you're one to talk. Go snag your lady."

"You're funny."

"I am." My sister hangs up. I lean back and stare at the ceiling. She's been studying and working extremely hard to land a lead on Broadway and she's finally done it and I couldn't be more proud. Now, if I could get my life in order, maybe the James family can finally be in sync. The only problem with mine is that I haven't waited a year – the predetermined mourning period according to Cosmo, and now I'm stuck in limbo and don't know what to do to get out of it. Obviously my kissing powers did nothing for her.

CHAPTER 12 - KATELYN

I lean against the closed door. As much as I wanted to slam it and send the message that I'm not interested, I didn't. My head bangs against the wood in frustration, not because he kissed me, and not because I didn't pull away the moment his soft lips touched mine; but because I liked it and wanted so much more.

The way he held me to him like I was the most fragile object he's ever touched? Mason never did that. The way he looked at me like I'm the most fragile being he's ever seen? I can't remember if Mason did that. Was it because we started dating so young he didn't have to learn to be romantic? I know Mason loved me, I've never doubted that and I don't want to compare them, but I can't help it.

"Who are you looking at?"

"Mason Powell," I say without taking my eyes from him. The school year has been good to him. He's gotten bigger, more muscles. It's hard to believe for only a freshman, well almost a sophomore.

"Why?" Josie asks.

I shrug and close my locker. We have cheerleading try-

outs today. I'm not nervous, but I know Josie is. We've been waiting all year for this. We missed the try-outs before our school year started so this will be our chance.

"Do you like him?"

"I don't know. Maybe. He's cute, don't you think?"

I follow Josie's eyes as she looks at him. When she cocks her head to the side, I roll my eyes and pull on her arm, leading us away from the group of football players.

"If you like him, you should ask him out."

"No way," I reply as we walk into the gym. "He'll never go out with me. I'm not his type."

"Why do you say that?" she asks as we start stretching.

"I've seen the way he looks at Candy. She gives all the guys the one thing I'm not willing to."

Josie shrugs. "Maybe he'll look at you that way too some day."

"Yeah maybe, but I'm not willing to put myself out there, ya know? I mean, what if he makes fun of me? He's this big time football player and everyone says he's going somewhere. He doesn't have time to date. He's probably like those guys we see on those stupid afterschool specials we are forced to watch. He takes the unsuspecting girl on a date, they go parking, nine months later they are expecting and he wants nothing to do with the girl and the whole town hates her."

"You're so dramatic, Katelyn. Seriously, if you like him, hint or something." Josie moves into a split and pops up quickly. "Oh I know, drop your pencil in front of him and bend over, that will surely get his attention."

"Not going to happen."

Josie shrugs and goes quiet. All I can think about now is Mason looking at my ass and now I'm self-conscious that it might be fat or too flabby for him. I'll have to start some butt crunches or something, like my mother does to firm it up.

together, and now here I am with our girls and standing in front of me is a man who, I have a feeling, would move into the role of dad without hesitation, if given the chance.

The girls and I walk forward. Elle lets go of my hand and walks right up to Harrison. I try not to show any emotion when she slips her hand into his. Quinn doesn't seem to care, so why should I? Peyton lets go next, leaving me to stand awkwardly in the middle of the entrance to Disney World by myself. Josie shoves me lightly when she walks by. I want to kick her. Tackle her to the ground like I did when we were in kindergarten. Childish, yes, but the look in her eyes tells me enough. She knows Harrison is watching me. I know it too because I can feel his eyes on me, even if they are covered by dark glasses.

Harrison steps forward and onto the path that will lead us to the most magical place on earth. I check on Peyton, who is firmly attached to Liam's hand, just as Elle is with Harrison. He looks back at me, clearly waiting for me to follow. He doesn't need words, it's like I can read him already.

Two bodyguards with two more in front of Liam flank me. If it were just the guys out today, we wouldn't need them, but with the kids out, the security is required. The guys also don't want to sign autographs today, which is understandable. Jimmy comes up behind me and puts his arm around my shoulders. It doesn't escape my attention that Harrison's already somber expression turns even bleaker.

It's nice to be out as one big family. People stare and point, no doubt recognizing the guys, but they ignore them. This is our day; a day to be away from our jobs and their public life and to give the kids some fun.

Jimmy runs ahead and scoops Peyton up, throwing her

over his shoulder. She laughs, and the sound brings tears to my eyes. Harrison slows down and walks next to me with Elle on his other side. She hasn't let go of his hand, nor has she stopped talking, and Harrison hasn't missed a word, even though he's looking at me every few seconds.

It's only a matter of minutes before my camera is out and both girls are wrapped in Mickey Mouse's embrace. Noah jokes that Mickey is for babies, earning an ear flick from Liam.

"Go stand with the girls, I'll take your picture." His warm hand covers mine. His lips are dangerously close to the ear. My tongue is thick, no words willing to form as I hand him the camera and walk over to my girls. I bring them both into my arms, kissing them both on their cheeks before posing for what will surely be our Christmas card. We didn't send one out last Christmas, so maybe we'll do it this year.

"Thank you," I say when Harrison shows me the picture. He stands next to me, his chest pressed against my shoulder. I should step back and remind him that we can never be anything more than co-workers, but doing that might be rude and presumptuous. He's just being nice right now.

Jimmy, I've determined, is the biggest kid of all of them. He races the boys and Peyton to the lines so they can start riding, even though it clearly says *no running*. I've never been one for rides, so I've gladly accepted the photographer role.

I'm surprised when Harrison appears. I thought for sure he'd be with Quinn. For a brief moment I worry about Elle, but remember that Liam and Josie are there and neither of them would let anything happen to her. Harrison stands next me, his body brushing up against mine. Today he's wearing a baseball cap and it's starting to bug the shit out of me.

I try to adjust my body so that we aren't touching, but fail in my attempt and end up creating just enough friction to cause the hairs on my arms to rise. If he notices, he doesn't say anything and for that I'm thankful.

"Do you want to talk about what happened?"

I shake my head. "It was a mistake."

Harrison sighs. He hangs his head and turns slightly to look at me. "It didn't feel like one to me."

I don't have an answer and I think that upsets him. I look down at the manicured garden in front of me, fearful of seeing his expression. My eyes start to water and for what? Nothing can happen between us, he knows this.

We hustle from ride to ride and even though I'm not riding them, I'm exhausted from the stories that Peyton and Elle are telling me. Peyton is having a blast. Seeing her smile gives me hope that she's turning the corner in her mourning. Not that she needs to be rushed, but I miss my little girl.

"Mommy, I'm tired." Elle pulls on my t-shirt to get my attention. We're in one of the many gift shops looking at souvenirs. It's also a great place to cool down from the beating sun.

"Are you ready to go back to the hotel?"

"No, can you carry me?"

"Elle, there's no way I can carry you. You're too big."

Elle leans against me, grinding her face into my side. This is typical Elle – she's the child that loves to nap – whereas, Peyton can go all day. I play with her ponytail, contemplating what to do with her. I don't want to ruin her day, but carrying her is out of the question.

"Excuse me, where can I rent a wagon?" I ask the clerk behind the counter.

"What do you need a wagon for?" I turn to find Harrison behind me. He gazes down at me. His eyes are soft and forgiving, showing no mention of our earlier conversation.

"Elle's tired. I can't carry her, so I need something to put her in or we need to go back to the hotel."

Harrison nods. He bends over and says something to Elle before he picks her up from behind and places her on his shoulder. Her face beams as she steadies herself.

"We won't be needing the wagon," he says to the clerk who shrugs. I stand there stone-faced as he walks out of the store, ducking when they get to the entrance, with my baby on his shoulders.

"Hey, is that Harrison James?"

"No," I say as I leave.

"Harrison?" he stops and faces me. His sunglasses are covering his eyes again and it makes me wonder if Elle did that for him. "You don't have to carry her, she can walk."

Harrison looks up at Elle while she looks down at him. They smile at each other as if they are sharing their own secrets. "Princess Elle, I'm your Henchman, what say you?"

I smile and laugh at the way Harrison is talking to her.

"Take me to my palace and I shall feed you for the night," Elle says in her princess voice. Good lord, he fell right into her game.

"We're good, Queen Katelyn." Harrison winks as they walk off. He starts to gallop, giving us all the sound of laughter. I seek out Peyton, wondering if she's jealous. If she is, she's not showing it. Between Jimmy and Liam, I think they have her missing piece filled nicely as well.

"Looks like I'm by myself," I say to no one.

CHAPTER 13 - HARRISON

WALKING DOWN THE RAMP FROM THE HAUNTED Mansion, I try to eliminate the big ass grin that has taken over my face. Taking Katelyn on this ride was a total ploy because I wanted a chance to hold her and knew by listening to her talk that this would be the perfect opportunity. But making out with her twice, within a ten-hour span, definitely ranks high on my list of accomplishments. After she left my room in the early hours of the morning, I thought her walls would be up. That she'd be closed off and attached to Josie all day. So, when she started walking with me – when she would touch me without thinking about it – I knew she was letting her feelings come through.

I don't know if she realized what she was doing. She'd brush her hand down my side after giving Elle water or the she'd grab my shirt to change my direction. I caught every single moment. These weren't friendly gestures, at least not in my book. Most important, though, was the way she asked if I was hungry and that was the only time I couldn't hide my reaction. She knew I caught the underlying meaning and I tried to play it off for her sake, but inside I was rejoicing.

I purposely chose a table that sat five. I wanted to see what we'd look like as a family and the picture in front of me was one any man would be proud of. Now that I've seen it, I want this even more.

Liam is standing at the exit when I come around the corner. I look over at Katelyn, who is now back to completely ignoring me, fucking perfect. I reach for my sunglasses and realize that I had turned my baseball hat backwards. I'm damn lucky that I didn't lose them on the ride. Not that it would've mattered, kissing her is so worth the cost of replacing them. I turn my hat around and stop in front of Liam who's watching Katelyn as she walks by and up to Josie and the kids.

"What's with her?"

"She got scared."

Liam laughs. "I can't believe she even went in there. Mason could never get her on a ride during the fair. He tried enough times though."

"Yeah, it was fun," I say, rubbing my cap back and forth.

Liam and I walk behind the girls. Noah and Quinn are a few steps ahead of them. Josie is holding Elle's hand and Katelyn has Peyton. The picture from earlier – the five us – holding hands like a family sticks in my mind. No one balked. Not even Peyton, who I thought for sure, would refuse to be silly. It felt good to be like that.

"Are you serious about her?"

My steps falter with Liam's questioning. We've never discussed women before, except for Quinn's oven, but he knows that I'm interested in Katelyn. I've not exactly hidden how I feel.

"I am," I reply confidently.

"How serious?"

This time, I stop so I can look him in the eye. I know I don't have to answer to him, she has parents for that, but he's her friend and he's fiercely protective of those he loves. "For a brief moment today, I saw us as a family and it didn't scare me, it made me happy."

"You can't dick her around. She's not one of those that you can date for a few months and push aside when you're bored."

"Where the hell is this coming from?" I scoff. "You've known since the moment I met her that I wanted to be something... anything to her. I haven't been with anyone since the night I was blessed with shaking her hand." I shake my head. "Fuck, man, seriously? You think I'm going stick my dick in her and bail? Why, because she has two kids, or because she's still dealing with losing her husband? Or, because every time I think we are getting close, she fucking shuts me out?" I stuff my hands in my pocket and kick a pebble on the ground. I thought I'd made my intentions pretty clear, but apparently not.

I walk away from Liam before I say something that I'll regret later.

"Quinn," I yell out. He stops and turns. He's such a happy boy. I'm lucky to be his dad.

"I'm going back to the hotel to pack. You can stay or come with me."

"I'll come back with you."

I nod and walk away from the group without saying anything. I'm tempted to look back at Katelyn, but I don't want to see what expression she might have now. If its relief, I'd be done for. She's my own personal rollercoaster, and right now I'm feeling a bit sick from the jerking back and forth.

Quinn and I walk back in silence. He stays right next to me as we navigate the crowds. I want to take him back to the others so he can hang out with Noah, but I am happy that he's come with me. Sometimes I just need to spend time with my boy. He calms me. Keeps me centered and gives me something to get up for each day. Without him, I'm not sure where I'd be.

He sits down on the couch when we enter the hotel room. We don't have much to pack - a few bathroom things - but that's it. I needed to get away from Katelyn and her cold shoulder and Liam with his preaching. Where the hell does he get off? I've never been close to the player he was before he reconnected with Josie.

I sit down and pull Quinn into my arms. Sometimes I just need to hold him. One day he's going to push me away. Not sure how I'll react when that happens, but until then, I'm going to be a sap and enjoy every minute I can with him.

"You told Aunt Yvie about Katelyn, huh?"

He shrugs.

"You're not in trouble."

"Okay."

I try not to laugh. I never want him to think he can't talk about his feelings with Yvie, even if he's ratting me out.

"Do you like Katelyn?" I'm curious how he feels. If he doesn't like her, maybe I shouldn't even pursue anything with her. I've never brought a woman home before, not that I'm bringing Katelyn anywhere, but clearly he sees something between us. I've always kept Quinn separate from my love life. I don't want him to get attached to someone that isn't going to stay around. Liam's right in the aspect that I haven't dated anyone longer than a few months because I get bored, but with Katelyn, it's different. From the moment

I saw her eyes, I knew she was the one for me, the one that is going to make my life complete. I made a change in my life because of her. I really can't see myself doing something to screw it up.

Quinn snuggles into my shoulder more. I rest my head on top of his. "I like her a lot."

"Yeah, me too, buddy."

"Is she going to be my mom?"

I'm taken aback by his question. He's never asked me about his mom and if he's asked Yvie or my mom, they haven't said anything. If I ever see his mother again, I don't know what I'd do. Who drugs someone so they can get knocked up, only to abandon their child the way she did? She didn't know jack shit about me as a person. She carried him for nine months and just left him in my living room with nothing. No clothes, food or even diapers. I had a lot of growing up to do when he arrived.

"Do you want to meet your mom? I'll find her if you want to know who she is."

Quinn pulls back and looks at me. "No, but Katelyn would make a good mom. When you're working and Josie isn't home, she makes me and Noah lunch and she cuts the crust off my sandwich, even though I don't ask her to."

I start laughing and ruffle his hair. "Is that what makes a good mom? What if she's evil and makes you scrub the floor with a toothbrush?"

Quinn smiles. "I don't think so, Dad."

"No?"

He shakes his head. "I think she's a good mom. Noah loves her and says nice things about her and she makes you smile even when you think no one is looking. I see you smile and I like that."

He's right. She makes me smile. "Can I tell you a secret?"

"Yes."

"I like Katelyn, a lot, but sometimes I feel that I can't be enough for her."

"Why? I think you're a great dad."

"Quinn, you make being a dad the easiest thing I've ever done, but that's not it. I don't think she likes my tattoos and I'm very different from her husband."

Quinn rolls his eyes. He's far too smart for his age. "I think your tattoos tell a story, maybe she should learn to read."

I lean back and study my son. "You're right, maybe we can teach her."

"I think she needs her own so she'll like everyone else's." Quinn gets up and heads toward the bed and starts packing, reminding me of the fantasy I had of Katelyn with ink on her body. The thought of seeing something delicate, in a place for my eyes only, arouses me. I have to push those thoughts away. It's never going to happen if I can't keep her walls down for longer than a two-minute haunted house ride and some stolen kisses.

THE BUS IS quiet as it speeds down the highway to our next stop. Only a few more shows and we'll be done. DeVon seems to be having fun, although confused as to why he's not traveling with us. For one, there's no room, and two, this is a family trip for us. Katelyn made it clear to his manager that he'd be on his own, though I do feel bad for the kid. His first time on any type of tour and only sees us during sound check. For the most part, he seems nice, just lost. I suppose that has to do with his manager being glaringly absent from the tour, which I find extremely odd.

Once again, it's a sleepless night for me. I tried lying down, but my mind is swimming. Since we've returned to the bus, she's avoided me. I don't get it and I'm starting to get frustrated. I get the chase is supposed to be there and that I need to be patient, but is it too much to ask for a simple smile or a brief acknowledgement?

I pull the song lyrics from my pocket and unfold the scribbled out piece of paper. I hate song writing with a passion. My words don't flow as easily as Liam's and I'm not easily moved by situations in my life that I feel the need to jot everything down. Music – yes – I can add a beat to just about anything he throws at me, but not words.

"What's that?"

I fold the paper haphazardly before Liam can see what it is. I clutch it in my fist and look out the window. We've had misunderstandings before, like the time he was with Sam. That relationship, as short as it was, screwed up the dynamic of our group. He became withdrawn and she became more of a bitch. It didn't take long for JD and I to ditch him and just do our own thing, and at one point, I started looking for a new gig.

But this is different. He knows how I feel about Kate-lyn, so the outburst in the park is completely unwarranted. I've never been clearer about my intentions than I have with her.

"It's nothing," I say as I slip the paper into the pocket of my hoodie.

He sits down next to me and sighs. "I'm sorry about earlier."

"All right."

"No, it's not all right. I was wrong. Here I've been

harping on Katelyn to let you in, and then I jump your shit and accuse you of trying to use her. I was wrong." He turns and faces me, but I continue to stare out the window. "I'm scared for the both of you. I've only seen her love one person and you... you're so shut off from females after Quinn that I don't know what to expect.

"But, I see the way you look at her and that's the way I look at Josie. Like you just know she's supposed to be in your life. I've all but begged her to give you a chance – to get to know the Harrison that I know - but I'm not sure if she can."

"I'll wait."

"For how long?"

"As long as it takes, I guess. I don't know, Liam. I'm trying to be respectful and give her the space she needs. These past few days she's acted like she wants things to progress, but then she shuts down and I'm back to the drawing board."

I get up and start to pace as much as the bus allows. I hate talking about my feelings. If this was anyone else, I'd clam up, but I know that he has hers and my best interests at heart.

"I want to do right by her, Liam, I do. But if she doesn't want me, I'm not going to keep chasing her. I respect her too much to keep on forcing myself in her life if she's not interested."

"Does she know how you feel?"

I run my hand through my hair, pulling my hood off. "I don't know if she does, she hasn't asked and it's not like I'm going to offer up my feelings on a silver platter. Rejection isn't an emotion that I like to experience."

Liam stands and pats me on the back. "For what it's worth, I think she does like you, she's just afraid to open up." I watch as Liam disappears behind his door. He doesn't realize how lucky he has it, knowing that there was one girl for him. I want that. The only problem is the one I want belongs to someone else, and there isn't a single thing I can do about that.

CHAPTER 14 - KATELYN

Walking into the greenroom, which ironically is not green, Harrison is asleep on the couch. Since being on tour, I've learned that he doesn't sleep much on the bus. How he functions on very little sleep is beyond me. Although, after being on the bus and in different hotels, not only does my back hurt, but the bags under my eyes are getting harder to cover. I long for a solid night's sleep in my own bed.

I contemplate waking him, but this is giving me an opportunity to really digest what I see. I've told myself over and over again that it's the tattoos that are turning me off, but what if that's not the case? The art on his arms is so intricate, not pieced together like Liam's, who has what I'd call sporadic tattoos, Harrison's tell a story. I just don't know what that story is and as much as I want to ask, I'm afraid that he'll take it as a sign that I'm interested.

I want a moment where I can trace the ink, discover the hidden secrets and figure out if this is what's keeping me away, or if I'm not ready to move on, and do all this without him knowing. I don't want to give him hope if that's what he's looking for. I also don't want to be just another conquest. I'm not like the woman he picked up in the bar. If he's looking for someone just to bed, I'm not it. I can't be. Those days where I could be carefree ended when I committed myself to Mason at the age of fifteen. Never have I thought about being with another man until the other night, when Harrison kissed me. Never have I felt such power from another person.

I move closer, the carpet quieting my steps. His body is splayed out with his t-shirt lifted so I can see more ink on his side. As luck would have it, a skullcap covers his head similar to what Mason would wear when he'd go to the gym. I'm starting to think that he owns stock in a hat company or that something is wrong with his head and he's hiding it. Yet, I know that's not the case because he let that woman touch him, remove his hoodie without any reservation. When I tried, he shied away, saying he wanted me to know him.

What does that even mean?

My shins collide against the couch. I hold my breath, waiting for him to move, waiting for his eyes to open and find me staring at him like a stalker. My eyes appraise him. His dark stubble from a few days' growth mocks me, as if it knows that this is one of my favorite things about a man. I allow myself to take in his form. His stomach shows the dark swath of hair, leading to a place I should never think about because he's not my husband, but I can't help it. He intrigues me, even though I'm not willing to admit these feelings out loud. Can I go the rest of my life being this way, not willing to let another man in? Is this what Mason would want for me? Josie and Liam are insistent that Mason would be okay with Harrison, but how do they do know? Is this something Liam and Mason discussed before he was taken from our lives? Mason and I never discussed whether we should find happiness with someone else if one of us was to die early. What if it was me, would Mason move on a year after I left this world?

I'd want him to. My girls need a mom, so why is it okay for me to accept that Mason would move on, but not myself?

Harrison shifts slightly and before I can move, his hip bumps my leg. His eyes open cautiously, probably wondering what he just hit. I take a step back and start to stumble. He reaches out and grabs my arm to steady me, keeping me from falling on my ass. His hand slides down my arm until his fingers are linked with mine. He pulls me forward until my knees hit the couch, but that's not close enough for him or for me.

I don't know what I'm doing. I feel out of control, as if someone else is making my body move. I lean forward and trail my fingers down his arm, over the ink. It's the first time I've touched a tattoo and I expected his skin to be raised, not smooth. Harrison watches my every move without saying a word. His skin pebbles as I move up and down his arm, as does mine. He's not even touching me and I feel excitement. When I look at him, his eyes are steady on mine. A smile plays at my lips and I hate it. I hate that he can do this to me when it shouldn't be like this.

He sits up, his hand cupping my face. I lean in as if it's automatic for me to do something like this. His thumb glides gently over my cheekbone, his fingers threading into my hair. I look at him and know what's coming next and I'm so powerless to stop it, because as much as my heart doesn't want to kiss him, my body wants him.

He bites my bottom lip, bringing me to his mouth. I sigh, urging him on. My hand cups his cheek, my fingers pushing under the hat he's wearing, feeling his short hair against the pads of my fingertips. He pulls me closer, our chests touching. Everything in my heart is telling me to stop, that this isn't right, but my body is telling him yes, I want this.

Harrison wraps his arm around my waist, leaving no space between our bodies. He moves me so I'm sitting on his lap. My hand roams down his chest, my fingers finding their way under his shirt. His breathing hitches when I touch him. He places kisses along my jaw, nibbling my neck as my hand explores his chest. The soft kisses and dangerous bites he's giving me drive me crazy. This shouldn't be happening. I shouldn't feel like this in another man's arms.

But I do feel like this and I can't help but want more. Crave more.

"Harrison," I say, barely above a whisper.

He pulls away, resting his forehead against mine. Our breathing is heavy with anticipation. It could be so easy to fall into his arms and forget the heartache I've been dealing with, but I can't, in good conscience enter into a relationship with him.

"Please don't tell me to stop, Katelyn. I can't. I can feel that you want this as much as I do."

I shake my head without breaking our contact. Why doesn't he understand that I can't be anything more to him? I need to remove myself from the situation. Keep things professional between us.

The ringing of his cell phone causes me to pull away. I move, keeping one of the couch cushions between us. He pulls out his cell phone, only breaking eye contact when he looks the screen. He silences it and looks back at me.

"We need to talk."

"Why?" he asks.

"Because this can't happen between us."

Harrison leans his arms on his knees and sighs. "So you've said, yet you're the one in here watching me while I sleep, touching me and encouraging me to pursue this with you. You got jealous when I left the bar the other night with a woman. You acted like we were something at the park. I don't get you at all."

His cell phone rings again, before I can respond. He silences it.

"I *want* to get you, Katelyn. I want to understand what goes on in your head and be there when you need someone. I can be that person for you."

"How do you know?"

"Because I do." He gets up and starts to pace, only to be stopped by his cell phone again.

"Shouldn't you answer that, it must be important?"

"No I shouldn't and it's not important. You're important. You're what matters right now," he says as he drops to his knees in front of me.

"I can't."

"Can't or won't."

"Is there a difference?" I ask.

"Can't means there's something physically holding you back from me and I know that's not true. I can feel it when you kiss me and just now, the way you were touching me, exploring with your hands.

"Won't means you won't give in to temptation, but we already know that's not true. You've let me kiss you. You've let me hold you against my body. Neither of these are valid reasons.

"I know you've lost your husband. I know every day is a battle for you because you miss him. I'm not trying to take

"What have you done?" Liam asks in an incredulous tone.

"What are you talking about?"

"This." Liam holds up a piece of paper and shakes it.

I walk over and pull it out of his hands. It's the contract for the venue. As I read it my stomach drops.

"I... I... don't —"

"You're right, you don't. This is bullshit, Katelyn, aren't you paying attention?"

"I am," I say with a shaky voice.

"What is it?" Harrison asks.

"Seems Katelyn has doubled booked us for the rest of the tour. We are supposed to be in Colorado and Seattle tomorrow night."

"How is that possible?" Harrison stands and walks over to take the paper from Liam. He reads it over, looking at me for answers that I can't give. I never set any dates in Colorado so I'm not sure how they ended up with a contract.

"Says we lose ten grand if we don't show."

"Yep sure does."

My heart drops and dread takes over my body. An error somehow on my part just cost the guys ten grand.

Harrison looks from Liam to me, and I know this time he's not coming to my defense. I've ruined any chance of having him in my corner when I told him that I couldn't be with him. He hands me the contract and leaves the room, followed by Jimmy and lastly, Liam. I jump when the door slams shut and don't even bother stopping the tears when they flow.

CHAPTER 15 - HARRISON

I LIE ON MY BED, WITH MY HANDS BEHIND MY HEAD, replaying the last few days over and over in my head. Now that the tour is over, albeit cut short, reality is jumping up and down, reminding me that school is about to start, that I have to be a responsible parent. My circle of friends, people I've depended on for so long, are living their lives in L.A. while Quinn and I live the high life in Beaumont. I shouldn't have to remind myself that this is what I wanted. I just thought things would be different.

Hell, I don't know what I thought, but definitely not this. I'm not gonna lie, I want her in my bed at night. I want to wake up and find her cooking breakfast for our kids. I want to come home at night and have everyone gathering around the table for dinner. But that's not going to happen. She's made herself very clear and I can't continue putting myself out there for the rejection. A man can only take so much in his lifetime.

I look at the clock and sigh heavily. This year I'm taking Quinn to buy his school supplies. Usually my mom, or Meghan, his nanny, has done it and now it's my turn. It's time for me to grow up, I guess. I get up, get dressed and slip into my boots, looking down at my attire. I know Katelyn snubs her nose at the way I look. I've seen her do it and that's fine. I'm not going to change for her or anyone. I like my t-shirts, khaki shorts, beanie and either my boots or Vans. Hell, I've been known to wear Chucks before. Aren't those supposed to be considered high-class-guy-fashion or something?

I knock on Quinn's door and open it, sticking my head inside. He's sitting in his beanbag chair playing in his Xbox.

"Wanna go school shopping?"

"Sure," he says as he powers down his console. It's a proud dad moment when he doesn't argue or roll his eyes. I know those days are coming and honestly, I don't know what I'll do the first time he smarts off to me. He walks ahead, his clothes matching mine, everything except for the hat. He likes to keep his hair styled, something I never did at his age.

Quinn is nothing like me. He's confident and self-assured, making friends easily. I was shy and awkward, always alone, never fitting in. I thank my lucky stars that he's different from me. I'm not sure how'd I'd handle things if he had a childhood like I did.

We walk to our car; the non-descript family car that I bought when we moved here so we wouldn't draw unwanted attention with something flashy. I still have my motorcycle in the garage, but haven't really taken it out much, aside from a few rides with Liam. I'm trying to live a normal life, one away from the balance in my checkbook, and give Quinn a quiet life, which is why I let Meghan go and didn't ask her to move with us. Quinn has spent far too much time in her care because of my job, and now Liam's provided me an opportunity to be home more.

Driving into town, I can't help but look over at him while he watches the scenery pass him by. He's well adjusted and acts like nothing bothers him and I want to believe that, but sometimes question if he needs something else, mainly a mom. Not that I'm going to run out and get married, but maybe bringing Meghan here is an option.

I pull into the parking lot of the mall and look around at all the other parents taking their kids shopping. Now I know why I never cared when my mom took Quinn shopping. This place is nuts.

"Grandma sent me a list of things she usually buys you. She didn't tell me the mall would be like this, though."

Quinn starts to laugh as he gets out of the car. I follow, locking it behind us. "It's not so bad. Grandma always bought me ice cream though." He looks up at me and bats his eyes.

I shake my head. "Of course she did," I say as I throw my arm around him. We walk toward the lion's den, the James men, brave... and incredibly stupid.

Quinn walks from store to store with me following behind, carrying his bags. I never knew my son was such a shopper; that definitely has to be Yvie rubbing off on him. I can't remember a time when I'd step foot in a shopping center. They scare me. People just stare at me. We manage to get everything on my mom's list and then some.

"Hey, Dad?"

"What's up, bud?"

"Are you and Katelyn going to be boyfriend and girlfriend?"

I put the boots back on the shelf and try to compose my thoughts. This is exactly why I've never brought anyone home. I don't want Quinn getting attached to anyone. Kate-

shoulder, looks at me. His toothless smile making my steps just a bit faster. For months I've held him in my arms, waiting for this moment. Praying that a simple piece of paper will confirm what my heart feels, that he's mine.

My mom sits. I choose to stand behind her, near the door for a quick escape. My palms sweat and my heart races. I think I'd rather listen to him cry for hours than sit in here and wait for a short man with beady eyes tells me my fate. My mom looks over her shoulder and reaches for my hand, holding it for reassurance.

"Mr. James," he says as he shuffles paper back and forth on his desk. Shouldn't he be ready? He called me and asked me to come in. You'd think everything would be in an orderly fashion. "I trust your day is going well."

"It's fine," I reply.

"Okay, well I have the results here and also another matter we need to discuss."

I roll my neck, trying to loosen up my nerves. He picks up the stack of papers and taps them against his oversized desk. He knows I'm paying him by the hour, that's why he's stalling.

He leans back in his chair, holding a single sheet of paper in the right light so I can see print, but I'm unable to make out the words.

"In my hand, Mr. James, are the paternity results that you requested."

"Okay," I say, trying to control my shaking leg. I want to reach across the desk and rip that paper out of his hand and read it. Quinn squeals, catching my attention. I rub my hand on top of his head, his baby fine hair standing on end. He puts his chubby hand in his mouth and start sucking.

"The child known as Quinn James is yours. You're ninety-nine point nine percent his father."

I bend over and let out the breath I had been holding. My mom rubs my back as I fight back the sob that is threatening to take over. Five months ago when he showed up, I didn't want him, but now I'd never let him go. He's my son.

"I have more news," my lawyer says. I stand up and give him a slight headshake for him to continue. "Miss Tucker has been located," he says as he turns back to his desk. I freeze at the one name that can change anything. He sets his hands in front of him, his fingers forming a tent much like my guidance counselor at school when he'd speak to my mom about me not being social enough for his liking.

My lawyer may be pissing me off, but he's been very upfront with my rights. Alicia can come back and take Quinn from me. All she has to do is claim some type of depression shit and I'd lose my son. He says the courts side with the mothers first and listen to the father's later. I don't want that.

"And?" I encourage him to continue. I need to know. I need to hear the words out of his mouth.

He extends his hand, holding a piece of paper.

"What's this?" I ask.

"Miss Tucker has signed away her parental rights. Quinn is yours and available for adoption by your wife when you choose to marry."

"I'm never getting married," I mumble as I read over the document saying she's relinquishing all her parental rights. "He's mine?"

"He's yours, honey," my mom says. She's crying into my shoulder, but I know they're happy tears because I'm shedding them as well.

"He's mine."

"Do you miss Meghan? If you do, I can call her and see if she'll move here." Maybe moving away from all the women in his life wasn't the smartest thing to do. I didn't think he would need them. Maybe I don't know what an eight-year-old needs.

"No, it's okay. I just..." he shrugs again. I reach forward and still his hand with mine. He looks up. I raise my eyebrow, waiting for him to answer me. "I like Katelyn. She's nice to me."

I sit back and study my son... the matchmaker, who knew? I like... no I fucking love that she's nice to him and nothing would make me happier than for her give us a chance. I look out into the courtyard and watch a few people while I compose my thoughts. Dads and moms with their kids all getting ready for school, and here I am living the single life because I'm afraid to love anyone, except her. There's something about her and I don't know if I can say it's just one thing. I love her hair, her eyes, or maybe it's the way her lip curls when she's really happy. She doesn't know that I watch her like I do. That I take in her presence every chance I get.

I don't know how to answer my son. For the first time ever, I'm going to clam up and keep my thoughts to myself for fear of what I might say. "Come on, let's go to Noah's. You can play and I can work for a bit."

Quinn cleans up and carries the tray to the garbage can. He walks a bit slower. He's either tired or thinks he's done something to upset me. I bump him lightly, earning a grin, one that hasn't changed from when he was a baby.

I CAN'T GET Quinn's comments out of my head. Pounding on the drums doesn't do anything to alleviate my stress either. Every time I close my eyes I see her beneath me and hate that it's all in my imagination. I need to get over her, to move on and get her out of my system.

The song that I had been working on during the tour is on replay in my mind. I pull the lyrics out of my pocket and pick up a pen. I know Liam has written songs about Josie and continues to do so. He says it's one of the best things about them. He writes and sings to her and she's instantly dropping her panties for him. Not that I want Katelyn to do that... right away, but it would be nice for the hot and cold to stop. I feel her heart race when we're together, I know she wants it, but refuses to see that we can be anything more than what we are. Maybe if she doesn't want to see how I feel, my words can convince. Maybe if she hears words from my heart about how I feel, those are from me and meant for her, she'll stop and think about what we could be together.

"What are you working on?"

I spin on my stool to find Liam picking up his guitar. There's no point in hiding the lyrics from him any longer, not if I want Katelyn to hear them. I hand him the paper, he takes it and starts moving his head up and down. He can already hear himself singing the words.

"When did you write this?"

"That night after the bar."

"This is really good. Want to give it a go?"

"I don't know. It's about..." I shake my head and pick up my drumsticks. "I like her. Quinn likes her. I don't know what to do."

"She'll come around and if she doesn't, move on. Her loss."

He strums his guitar and starts with the first line. He writes down some notes and starts over until he's found a melody that will work.

"Why the change of heart?" I ask.

twenty-nine years old worrying about a job. A year and half ago everything was so much simpler. My biggest concern was wondering what I'd make for dinner. We weren't well off by any means, and we lived paycheck to paycheck, but it worked. We didn't fight or struggle with making our minimum payments. We just lived.

I roll over and look at the clock. It's after midnight and Mason still isn't home. There's a pounding sound coming from the living room. I get up slowly, realizing that I'm still in my clothes from earlier. Tonight's game had been two hours away. A team trying to make a name for themselves asked if we'd come play them. Mason, never one to turn down a game, obliged happily as did the rest of the team. They loaded up the bus, plus two additional ones for fans and made the trek. The girls and I went, but left early because it was cold.

I walk out into the living room, its dark, but blue lights flash through the window. The pounding starts again. It's the front door. Mason probably locked himself out.

"Crazy man," I mutter. I open the door and am met by Paul Baker, the local police chief. "Paul, what are you doing here this late?"

"Hi, Katelyn," he says as he tips his hat. I push the screen door open and look out into the driveway for Mason's truck. It's not there. I try to keep the feeling of dread from creeping in, but it's there. Something's wrong.

"I need to take you down to Beaumont General."

"What for?" I don't give Paul a chance to even tell me why before I'm asking.

Paul takes off his hat. His eyes are red showing evidence that he's been crying. "Mason's been in an accident. You need to come to the hospital."

My knees buckle. Paul catches me before I hit the

ground. "I got you. Come on Katelyn," *he says as he rights me.* "Call Josie, tell her to come and sit with the girls. They'll be okay until she gets here. Roberta will sit outside. We gotta go."

I nod and walk on shaky legs to the phone. It takes me four times to get her number right. The phone rings and goes to voicemail. I hang up and try again. "Hello?"

"Josie, I need you to come watch the girls. Mason... he's had an accident and I need to go. Paul's here."

"Okay I'll be over." Josie hangs up, but I stay on the phone listening to the buzzing sound. Mason's been in an accident. An accident. The word plays over and over again in my head, but I'm not grasping the meaning. What kind of accident? Paul's hand presses down on my shoulder and the other takes the phone from my hand. He sets it down so gently I barely hear it click.

"Come, Katelyn we need to go."

"Is Mason alive?"

Paul doesn't say anything as he guides me out of the house. He shuts the door behind me and pushes me toward his car. The blue lights blinding me the closer I get.

"The girls..."

"They'll be fine. Roberta is right there, see?" I follow the direction he's pointing and see another police car sitting in front of my house. My neighbors are standing on our property line in their robes and slippers, holding hands. I don't want to know what they're thinking when Paul helps me into the front seat and pulls out of the driveway.

We drive through the empty streets and even though he's speeding, it feels like the fifteen-minute drive is taking an hour. My hands are wringing in my lap. My stomach turns and threatens to empty itself all over the floorboard that my feet rest on. Paul turns into the almost empty parking lot and right up to the emergency room entrance. I look out the window at the sliding glass doors and see a few people walking around. Everything looks calm inside, yet everything inside of me is burning and on edge.

Paul opens my door and holds my hand until I'm standing. Everything is moving in slow motion. I hesitate at the door, afraid to cross the threshold. The last time I was here was to give birth to the twins and something is telling me that I'm leaving here by myself. He nudges me, his hand guiding my back as we walk through the quiet halls. A door clicks and we are in the center of the action.

"Mrs. Powell," I look at the doctor standing in front of me. His blue scrubs look clean, fresh out of the laundry. I nod, unable to find my voice. Paul motions for us to sit down. I can't move. I shake my head. I need to know what's going on.

"Where's Mason?"

When the doctor looks at me I know. He doesn't need to say the words. My hand covers my mouth and my head starts to shake back and forth. Paul's arm comes to rest on my waist holding me up.

"Mrs. Powell, if you'd like to see your husband I can take you to him. He doesn't have much time left. I'm sorry. We've cleaned him up and he looks like he's sleeping. The machines are keeping him breathing, but he can't breathe on his own and he has very little brain activity."

"He's alive?"

"At the moment, yes."

The doctor turns and I follow with Paul beside me. He pauses at the door separating me from my husband.

"What happened?"

Paul clears his throat. "He was sitting at the bottom of the hill, waiting for the light to change when an eighteen wheeler came behind him. The truck's brakes gave out at the top of the hill and he couldn't slow down. The driver said the light changed, but by then he was already too close and hit Mason. He says he honked, but you and I both know Mason probably had the radio turned up, so he probably didn't hear him."

Paul takes deep breath. "As soon as he hit, Mason lost control. He hit the wall before jumping the guardrail and hitting a tree."

I don't acknowledge Paul or the doctor. I push the door open. My hand covers my mouth as a sob takes over my body. My husband... my school sweetheart lays before me with a white sheet covering his body. His arms are down at his side. His face... his beautiful face is bruised and covered in cuts. I can't tell if this is my husband or not. I take tentative steps to his bedside and run my fingers up his arm. I bend slightly and look at his shoulder, unable to control myself, I lay myself on top of him and cry. This beat up man is my husband and he's dying.

"Mason," I say over and over again waiting for a sign or some type of response to show me that the doctor is wrong. My husband is strong. He can pull through this. He just needs to know that I'm here and that I love him. I cup his face, lean in and kiss his lips. They're cold and uninviting. I run my hand over his hair. He has an appointment tomorrow morning so he can get a trim. Every six-weeks like clock work.

"Mason, baby, please wake up." I plead with him. "Open your beautiful eyes for me." I lay my head on his chest to feel his heart, but it's so faint.

"Katie?"

My head pops up and I see Mr. Powell standing at the end of the bed. I forgot to call him. He looks at me with such

I think about Peyton and Elle and how I don't want them to grow up. How I need them to stay just the way they are so I don't forget what it was like to have their dad around. I need Peyton to always love football, to keep Mason's spirit alive on Sundays and for Elle to be the princess that her daddy said she was going to be. I think that is the only thing that is going to keep me afloat.

CHAPTER 17 - HARRISON

GROCERY SHOPPING. I HATE IT. AND ONCE AGAIN, I'M asking myself why the fuck did I move so far from my mom or not bring her with me? What the hell was I thinking? Right, I wasn't thinking with my brain, but another member of my anatomy; because I thought I could win the affection of the hottest chick I'd ever come across and look where it's gotten me. I'm in the grocery store, looking at a million different boxes of cereal, standing next to my son who can't make up his mind on which one he wants.

Quinn stands next to me with one arm across his stomach and his other resting on top of it. His hand is almost cupping his chin as if he's deep in thought about what cereal is going to make his first day of school better. Who knew that buying breakfast food was so challenging?

"What do you want?"

"I don't know," he says with a shrug.

"How can you not know?" his response confuses me. This kid eats cereal every day and he doesn't know what kind he wants? This is exactly why I paid my mom to do all my shopping.

"Grandma says that I need to eat well because I'll be getting up early and breakfast is the most important meal of my day."

I look at him and roll my eyes because that is exactly what my mom texted to me last night after I asked her to send me the grocery list. My mom helped us get settled in Beaumont, but returned to Los Angeles when we went on tour. Big mistake. I had forgotten how nice it was to have her around. She was my personal assistant until this big move.

"Mr. James?" I turn at the sound of my name and find a tall woman with long blond hair, pushing a cart full of food, behind us.

"Yes?"

"I'm Monica Lowell... from Quinn's school... his teacher. We met at the end of the school year when you came in and registered him."

I look at her for a moment before her words set in.

"Oh yes, hi." I extend my hand and shake hers.

"I see you're getting ready for school to start."

I look at our barren grocery cart and compare it to hers. I need a lot more food. "Yeah we just got back from being on tour, need to replenish."

"Quinn, are you ready for school?"

He shrugs, which I'm starting to think is his new thing.

"I'm sure he's ready." Quinn looks at me briefly before turning back to the cereal selection. Maybe he's not ready for public school.

"Well, it was nice to run into you guys. I'll see you in a few days."

"Bye." I watch her as she walks down the aisle. My head bends slightly when she bends over to pick something up.

"She likes you."

"What are you talking about?"

"I can tell. She makes those eyes."

"What eyes?" I ask.

"The same ones Josie makes at Liam all the time. Noah teases her about it. He says they're the sexy eyes."

"You guys watch too much TV," I say as I push the cart away. "Pick a cereal and let's go."

I head to the next aisle and find his teacher there as well. She looks and smiles when she sees me. I wink, even though I don't mean to, and the result is an instant blush. She fumbles with the box that she had in hand and I can tell she's embarrassed.

I try not to laugh and have to turn away so she doesn't see the shit-eating grin on my face. Quinn's right, maybe she does have a crush.

"Oh ouch."

I turn back around and find Monica bent over rubbing her head. "Are you okay?" I ask as I walk to her.

"Fine," she responds is a raspy voice. This is the same voice that Elle uses when she's trying not to cry. I reach for her hand and pull it away from her head. She's got the makings of a nasty goose egg forming.

"What did you do?"

"It's stupid. I'll be fine. The shelf and I had a disagreement."

"It doesn't look fine. You need some ice." I move her hair away from her face and study her wound as if I'm suddenly a doctor. I'm closer to her than I want to be, but I feel responsible for what she's done to herself. I don't intend to flirt with her, but it's nice to be flirted with, so I inadvertently return the gesture.

"Dad, look who's..."

My head snaps to Quinn's voice and behind him is

travel, just as long as he always came back." Josie toes the ground before taking a deep breath. I'm not sure where she's going with this, but I'll gladly lend her an ear if she needs one.

"Anyway, when you decided to move here, it made his decision easier. So I thank you, Harrison. Because of you, my son has his dad home for more nights."

"I didn't do anything. I like it here."

Josie smiles and leans in to give me a hug. I wrap my arms around her and look up at Liam. He's shaking his head. Josie steps back, she looks around before looking at me again.

"You'll find happiness here."

I shrug. "I'm not worried." It's not exactly a lie, but if I stress about it too much I'll let my productivity suffer and I can't do that. My drums can take a beating before I let the band down. "I'm going to head up with Liam. I'll see you later." I lean in and kiss her on the cheek. Liam is one lucky son-of-a-bitch.

I climb the ladder and am greeted by a beer being tossed at my head. Liam snickers as I fumble the catch, almost losing a full one. The other guys with him laugh and make small talk. A few I've met, others are new. I sit next to Liam. My legs dangle over the edge. I look down and question my sanity and the stability of this walkway. If this tower is still used, how often are they doing repairs? I pop the cap on my bottle and down my beer. The thought of drinking enough so I don't feel any pain is a pleasing thought, but tomorrow will suck and that's not fair to Quinn.

I let my bottle sail into the back of a truck at the same time I see Katelyn walking across the field toward Josie. She's dressed in those stupid daisy duke shorts that my sister likes, and even though she's about a foot shorter than I am, her legs go for a mile long until her strappy sandals come into view. What the fuck is wrong with me? I shake my head to clear my vision, but that does nothing for me as my eyes watch some dude come up to her and give her a hug. His hand lingers on her back longer than it should. She doesn't move his hand or step away from him. They stand there talking to Josie like they're some couple.

Is this who she wants to be with, some slack wearing, tweed sport coat type of guy? How boring is that? I reach for another beer, popping the cap and downing this one just as fast. I throw it hard, hoping to catch her attention. I don't and it pisses me off. I should've known she was coming here tonight. If this is their tradition why would she stay home? These are her friends, not mine.

I reach for my third, catching Liam's eye in the process. His eyebrow is raised and he's smirking. I hate when he smirks. It usually means something's on his mind and I'm about to hear some insightful bullshit from the great Liam Page.

"What?"

"Nothing man. Just haven't seen you drink that fast in a long time. Josie's my DD tonight you can crash at the house if you want."

I pop the top and set my beer down between my legs. Tonight is supposed to be fun, the last hurrah before summer is over and the adults have to focus on their kids, yet all I want to do is get drunk and create havoc. I haven't felt this wound up in a long time. I lean against the rail and look out over the crowd. I try not to seek out Katelyn, but my eyes gravitate toward her, no matter how hard I try to stare at the other scantily clad women that are here. I could go back to the way I was before I moved here – keeping a woman on standby for a few months at time – no connection, no emotions.

But that's not what I want.

I want her.

Everything in me is saying give up; that I don't need her, but I do.

I need her like I need to breathe.

"So," Liam says breaking my reverie. I take a long pull off my beer and look at him. "I'm thinking the four of us hit L.A. for a combined bachelor/bachelorette party."

"You're having a party?" Why on earth would he want to do this? He's got the perfect woman on his arms and he wants to fuck it up with a night in L.A. where all the groupies are.

"Why wouldn't we?"

"I don't know, because you're not single."

"Nah, it's not like that. Josie wants to go to L.A. and we have an awards show coming up. Let's take the girls."

I shake my head and start peeling the label off the bottle. "You act like Katelyn and I are together and were not. Hell, we aren't even speaking right now."

"No, but she's Josie's... whatever you call it and you're my best man. This is like wedding law or some shit. I don't know. I'm just trying to make her happy."

"Whatever, man. L.A. and awards shows are a mistake, especially with Sam being there." I down the rest of my beer and throw it to the bed of the truck. "But if that's what you want, fine."

The only exciting idea about going back is that I'll be able to sleep in my own bed. Yvie moved into my apartment when I left and she'll be on Broadway with her show.

"I'm going to take off," I say as I get up, patting him on the shoulder.

"I'll come down with you."

Liam and I descend the rickety ladder one at a time. I'm going to suggest an alternative place to hang out. I'm not sure the ladder is going to hold many more of us. I'm sure it was fine when they were teens, but some of them have put on a few pounds since.

We walk... well I walk, Liam struts to where Josie and Katelyn are. The douche that was touching her is still near her, but with his back turned. How can any man turn his back on her, I'll never understand.

"So baby," Liam says as he wraps Josie in his arms. She giggles, and while that used to make me cringe I'd give everything to hear Katelyn do that as a result of my arms. "We're going to go to L.A. for our dual parties."

"What if I wanted a stripper?"

My mouth drops. Katelyn stifles a laugh behind her hand. Liam's face turns red as his mouth open and shuts. Josie stands there with her eyebrow raised and her arms crossed. Oh this will be good.

"You..." Liam looks down at the ground and takes a deep breath. "Okay," he says when he looks back at Josie, who looks like she's about to crack under pressure.

"Don't tease him, Josie."

Liam looks from Katelyn to Josie. His eyes close slightly. "You messin' with me, Jojo?"

"Maybe." She winks.

"You guys are too much."

"They're in love." Katelyn says mockingly.

"Oh yeah, are you suddenly in love with the stiff there?" I nod to the guy behind her. He doesn't hear me, which is a shame. Katelyn's face falls and I instantly feel like an ass. "Yeah I'm outta here." I turn and walk away.

"No, but your hostility tells me that you're interested in someone."

"I am not." I break my gaze from him and look down at my hands. They're clutched, my nails digging into my palms. "I can't..."

"Why not?"

I roll my eyes. "It wouldn't work. He's not my type."

"There is no *type* when it comes to love, Katelyn."

"Sure there is. I love Mason and this man, he's nothing like Mason."

Dr. Brooks leans forward. "Are you trying to replace Mason?"

"What?" I scoff. "No, that's absurd. No one can replace him. Why would you ask me something like that?"

His hand moves his pen across the paper. It sounds like a bird walking across the desk. I sit up and try to make out what he's writing down, but his arm moves to cover my angle.

"Finding someone to spend time with doesn't mean you have to fall in love. It means you have companionship. Someone you can lean on and who understands and accepts what you're going through. This person can be a friend or a lover. The important thing is to not let the passing of Mason close you off from what you need. Everyone needs someone, Katelyn."

He pushes his chair and walks over with a tissue extended to me. I didn't even know tears had fallen. What if he's right? What if I can let someone in and still love Mason?

"I'll see you next week." He sets his hand on my shoulder. "It gets better, if you allow it."

MY HEART STARTS BEATING RAPIDLY AS SOON as I hear the mower start. I don't know why he's here. After last night – the way he acted – I thought he'd bail on me. I close the photo album and slide it under the couch. I don't know why, it's not like I plan to invite him in. I never do. I'm not even sure he'd come in after yesterday. But if he did, and I'm not saying he would but maybe he needs to use the bathroom, I don't want him seeing me sitting here pining over my dead husband.

I lean forward a bit to peer out the sliding glass door, but don't see him. Each time he starts in a different place. Mason always started in the back. He'd mow in a square, moving the girls' toys out of the way each time. My yard is no longer mowed in a square, but straight lines. I know this because I've spied on him, even though I tell myself I need to stop. I need to focus on the girls and not the man who is mowing my lawn in place of my husband.

Luck is not on my side today because he's starting in the front and my curtains are closed. If I had any nerve I'd go throw them open and see what he's wearing, not that I've seen him in anything except shorts, t-shirts and a stupid beanie. If I had an ounce of courage, I'd rip the thing from his head before he could stop me so I could see what he's hiding. And why, why is he hiding under those stupid things?

"There is no type when it comes to love." The words replay over and over in my head. What if Dr. Brooks is right? Can I be strong enough to let Harrison into my life without reservation? I don't know if I can. I also worry about what Mr. Powell would think. I know that my mother would never accept Harrison. He doesn't fit her stereotypical poster boy for her daughter, but my daddy, he wouldn't care, as long as I'm happy.

Christmas last year hangs in my closet. I can't bring myself to throw them out.

Each time Harrison walks by, he's closer. His pattern has changed. Maybe he's done this every time he's out here and I just haven't noticed.

I'm looking now and I'm not sure I'm going to be able to stop. There's something that pulls me to him, and as much as I don't want to admit it, he makes me feel; and not the same way that Mason did, but different.

He shuts the mower off. He lifts his shirt and I can see his toned stomach and the dark patch of hair extending into his shorts. I try not to stare, but I can't help it. He's beautiful in his own unique way. I know why women flock to him. He's easy on the eyes. He wipes the sweat from his forehead. His hand moving under that god-awful hat he's wearing. I'm starting to think he wears it just to piss me off. If he is, it's working.

He's watching me, waiting to see if I'll run away. Maybe I need to heed Dr. Brooks' advice and find a companion. I'm just not sure Harrison is the one for me. There's too much that I can't wrap my head around where he's concerned.

I take a step closer. He does the same thing. Both of us are taking steps until we're in front of each other. He stands so much taller than me that I have to look up at him.

"I'm sorry about last night."

I didn't expect those words to come from him. His voice is soft. I can hear the remorse in the tone.

"Me too, I was out of line."

"It happens."

Harrison and I stand close enough to be able to touch, both of us looking at each other. No words are exchanged, but I do smile and am rewarded with one of the most brilliant smiles I have ever seen. One that if I'm not careful, I could get lost in for days.

"Mommy."

Harrison's head snaps up before I can turn around. Peyton stands on the patio, with her hands on her hips. From the position of the sun, I can't see what her expression is, but I can only imagine that she's not happy.

"Hi baby."

"I'm not a baby."

I sigh. Harrison rests his hand on my back and his thumb rubs small circles there. I'm surprised to find that it calms me. "I'm sorry, Peyton."

"I'm hungry."

"It is dinner time," Harrison says quietly. I nod, acknowledging that our little interaction is over. "What do you say we all go out to eat? I just have this small bit to finish. Five minutes tops."

"Are you sure?" I ask, turning slightly.

"Of course, let me finish and I can meet you someplace after I pick up Quinn."

I look back at Peyton who stands defiantly. Maybe it's not me that needs a man in my life, but her. Harrison's very good with Elle maybe he can break down Peyton's wall.

"Okay." I take a last look at Harrison and walk toward Peyton. She doesn't look at me when I get to her. I kneel down and move her hair out of her face. She turns away. Every time she does this it breaks my heart.

"We're going to go out to dinner with Harrison and Quinn."

"I don't want to."

I close my eyes. Tough love, that's what she needs.

"Okay, well I think Jenna is home, so I'll call and see if she can babysit."

I get up and walk away, leaving her outside. I'm not going to cave to her attitude. If she wants to ruin her night, she can. I close my eyes and take a deep breath before seeking out Elle. I know she'll be excited to go.

"What are you doing?" Elle asks, almost laughing.

"I'm trying to calm down." I open my eyes to find my mini-me with her eyes closed. "What are you doing?"

"The same."

"Why, what's wrong?"

"I'm hungry."

I can't help but laugh. "Would you like to go out to dinner with Harrison and Quinn?"

Her eyes flash open with excitement and my heart breaks because I so want Peyton to look at me like this. "Yes!"

"Okay, go change." I wait a few heartbeats before turning around and looking out the sliding door. Harrison and Peyton are talking, and for the first time since we've returned from Disney, she's smiling. And even though I can't tell him, he's just chipped away a little more at my heart.

It may be a year since we lost the man we all love, but if I can give my girls' one moment to smile today, does it matter that the man making them smile is causing ripples in my heart?

CHAPTER 19 - HARRISON

I FLICK ON THE LIGHTS IN THE ROOM THAT HOUSES 4225 West. Liam struck the jackpot with this house. The basement, which is now the studio, is completely decked out and soundproof. I'm not sure how much longer we'll be able to call this home. I can't imagine Josie wants to continue to have us here, especially late at night when she's trying to sleep. Even though she can't hear us jamming, I'm sure she wants her house to herself.

It's been a month since we've worked on anything. We all needed a break after the tour mishaps. But work has to be done. We have songs that need to be written and recorded. We have a CD to release, with or without a tour. We can't let our fans down. That already happened when we had to cancel the rest of the tour. No more. 4225 West refuses to let this shit bring us down. I'm excited to be in the studio; to hold the wood of my drumsticks between my fingers; to pound out my aggressions and create magic. JD and Tyler will be here at any moment to get things moving again, but I'm not so sure about Katelyn.

I stop in front of Katelyn's office and look into the dark

room. We didn't discuss business the other night at dinner two weeks ago. Believe me, it was the last thing on my mind when she was sitting across from me. I was thinking more of how I could get my hands on her. I was imagining all the places that I wanted to kiss her. I wish I could say that I've seen her every night since, but I can't. When I go over to mow her lawn, she's not home. I've deduced that dinner was just a thank you, and not the fucking breakthrough I've been waiting for. It's going to happen. That's my mantra each morning in the shower. Say it one hundred times and it's true, according to Quinn.

What does Quinn know?

More than me, I do know that.

Katelyn wants to quit. She's coming in today to talk to us about her job. Liam, he's upset with her, but is trying to keep the professional side separate from the personal side. I'm not sure how he's going to do that, I can't. I want her around all the time. She excites me, makes me feel like I'm about to skydive. I could live off the adrenaline I feel from her alone. But I don't want to force this job on her if she's not comfortable. I'm just having a hard time buying she could mess up this big. Maybe I should've spoken to her at dinner the other night when the kids ran off to play, instead of discussing a drop off schedule for school.

I sit on my stool and spin around one time. I pick up my sticks, running my finger along the wood to check for damage. They look okay for now, but I'll need to have Katelyn order more if she's going to stay on. If not, I'll be doing some mundane bullshit by myself, which means it'll never get done. God, I need Katelyn in more ways than one. I just need to find a way to tell her this before it's too late.

I feel for the foot pedals with my feet. Closing my eyes, I press down. One thump. Then another, back and forth until my legs are warm. I flex my wrist before setting my sticks down on the drums. One hit, then two. Over and over again until I'm jamming out. I go over the rhythm for the song I wrote about Katelyn. Playing it over and over again. I don't know when we're going to record it, but I can't wait to play it live.

"That'll sound good."

I stop playing when JD and Liam walk in.

"What was that?" JD asks.

"Dude, what the fuck is on your neck?"

JD smirks and covers his neck with his hand. "*That* was Tracy, or Tanya... I can't remember. Something with a T, though, definitely."

"That's just wrong." Liam laughs. I shake my head and throw one of my sticks at both of them. They duck. My mouth drops. Katelyn is standing at the door holding her head. I fucking hit her with my stick. I jump up from my stool, my leg crashing into my set when I stumble by.

"I'm sorry, Katie."

"What'd you call me?"

I stop when I get in front of her. Liam is laughing harder. I look at her and see nothing but pure hatred in her eyes. Her shoulders are heaving and she's breathing heavily and not from the work out I just gave her.

"What?"

"I don't know, Harry, what did you say?"

"Oh ballbags," JD sniggers under his breath with more laughter from Liam. I look back at him. He has tears in his eyes. I rub my hand over my ball cap, pushing it back and forth over my hair.

"My name's Harrison, not Harry," I say as quietly as possible. When I was in school the kids called me Harry and I hated it because they attached other not-so-nice names to it.

Katelyn puts her hands on her hips, but my eyes focus on the large red spot in the middle of her forehead. "My name is Katelyn. That's K-A-T-E-L-Y-N and only one man is allowed to call me Katie and you're not him... ever!" She pokes me in the chest, hard, and walks off. My hand rubs over the spot as I watch her hips sway back and forth.

I lean forward and bang my head on the door jam.

"What the fuck was that?" I ask as I step back into our recording room.

"That, my friend, was Katelyn Cohen Powell giving you the what for."

"Yeah, but why?"

"Clearly she doesn't want to be called Katie," JD adds for good measure. I roll my eyes at him and push him in the shoulder when I pass by.

"You're observant, JD."

"That's not it," Liam says as he tunes his guitar.

I sit down and push my foot pedal to get his attention. He looks at me. I throw my other drumstick at him. "Fill me in, asshole."

"Only one man is allowed to call her Katie."

I roll my eyes and shake my head. I can't freaking compete with a ghost. It's getting to be too much. "Great, so I just made her cry because I brought up Mason? Score one for James." I hit two rim shots and the cymbal – *ba-dum-tsh*. I guess the joke's on me.

"Not even Mason was allowed to call her Katie, just his dad. I don't know how it started, when we were little I think, but he's always called her Katie and she refuses to let anyone else use that name."

"Duly noted."

"Have you met Mr. Powell yet?"

I look at Liam questioningly. Is he serious? "Um yeah, I don't think we're at that stage in our relationship. Ask me in five years when we've graduated to texting."

JD starts laughing. Liam throws my stick back at me. I duck and cringe when it clanks against the wall.

"He's your ticket, moron. She won't date until he tells her it's okay."

"What the fuck, how do you know this?"

Liam shrugs. "I heard her talking to Josie before she left for work this morning."

"Bastard," I mumble as he winks at me.

"All right, let's get this done. We need to figure shit out about Katelyn," Liam says as he shuts the door.

"You know my vote. I think she just needs a little guidance. We threw her to the sharks."

"Bet you can't guess what I heard." JD pipes up.

"No, I can't JD... Well, shit head what did you hear?" Liam rolls his eyes. I can tell this is going to be a productive day in the studio.

"Sam's been sniffing around. I saw her at the *Roxy* the other night. She was after a quick shag, but I don't do leftovers."

Liam's face turns red at the mention of Sam. I know what he's thinking. If she's around and trying to get with JD that means she's trying to cause trouble.

"What else?" Liam asks.

"DeVon was playing that night and they definitely know each other."

"Fucking hell," we both say at the same time.

"Page, are you thinking what I'm thinking?"

Liam nods. "So help me, if she set this shit up I'm going to fucking kill her."

"I wouldn't put it past her. She was trying to convince me to join a new band, but I told her to piss off and take her skanky arse somewhere else." JD has such a way with words. I swear he could be a poet.

"I don't want to talk about Sam. I need to think," Liam says as he flicks the light to let Tyler know we're ready to record. Although I'm not sure what we are working on. "That song you wrote, let's work on it and we'll perform it tonight at Ralph's."

"Ralph's?"

"Yeah you know, the pub where Liam likes to take the missus."

"I know what Ralph's is, JD." Sometimes I think he's still the same nineteen old that asked us if he could jam with us one day. He walked right up to us after a gig and asked. He hasn't left yet.

"We have a gig tonight," Liam says this as if it's an everyday occurrence for us to set up at Ralph's. Whimsicality, yes, but not Ralph's.

"Well great, thanks for letting me know." I grab my headphones and put them on. JD and Liam do the same. I want to hide when Liam starts singing my lyrics, but the song is good, and he makes it sound even better. If we are performing at Ralph's tonight, we better be on our game. The last thing we need is for a local gig to turn out shitty.

FIVE MINUTES.

That's all it took for me to get a hard-on from standing next to her and all I did was touch her fingers. Her fingers for Christ sakes! How does that even compute in my brain? It's also a mistake following her up the stairs, but there is no way I was showing her what was going on in my shorts. She'd be mortified. I'd probably run out of the room like a sissy.

But watching her walk up the stairs is pure hell. The *swoosh* of her skirt, the fabric moving along her ass with each step she takes, makes my issue stronger. There's no way I can have dinner with anyone right now. The worst part, the guys will know, especially Liam. He purposely left me to deal with her. I'm the one who had to break the news that we were having a band meeting in his kitchen and her presence is required. He left me to deal with the sad face she made because he knows I'll do everything I can to make her smile. So what did I do? I touched her. And while that might not have made her smile, it did me because she didn't pull away. She allowed me to hold her hand before she stood up and straightened that tight ass skirt of hers and walked out of her office.

Of course, the guys have set up in the kitchen and not the dining room where there's a nice long table for us to gather around. No, we are in the nook, crammed around some small table, making my current problem even more evident.

Something needs to change, but I'm not sure what. Either my cold showers need to be longer, or I'm really going to have to make a play for her, because I'm not sure I can stand the pressure anymore. It's like a fucking tease show. I'll let you kiss me when I'm drunk. You can hold my hand when you're sober. We can make-out during a scary ride, but everything else is a 'no' when we are in our everyday lives. I hate not being able to touch her. I *really* want to touch her.

Instant dread washes over me when I look at the empty seat. JD is in the corner trying not to laugh and Liam is

From where we're sitting, we won't be able to see them very well. Not that I need to watch them, although this is my opportunity to check out Harrison without him looking. Yes, I admit it, he's starting to get to me, but it's not enough for me to throw in the towel. He's intriguing and I have a feeling there's more to him than a drummer in a rock band. I'm just not sure I'm the right person to figure out who he is exactly. I don't have anything to offer him. I'm afraid I'm not enough for someone like him.

The lights dim and the fans start screaming. There's excitement in the air, I can feel it coursing through me. Today I can be a fan without having to make sure the guys are taken care of, Ralph will do that tonight.

Josie stands on her chair and whistles as Liam takes the stage.

"Hey baby," he says into the microphone, making all the women go nuts. Too bad he's only talking to her. I shake my head and start laughing. It's like those two were never apart.

I decide to stand on my chair too or I won't be able to see. I'm praying no one will bump into me. The last thing I need is to do a table dive. Jimmy comes out next and instantly starts flirting with some of the women in the front row. He holds one of their hands and leans down to their ear. Who knows what he's saying, probably giving her his number. I'm honestly surprised that he's not more of a PR nightmare. Some days he acts like a family man and the next, he's the man-whore of the group.

Harrison comes on stage last. He's switched from a beanie to a baseball cap that he's wearing backward. I remember very clearly the last time I saw his hat like that. I hold my breath when he looks out into the crowd. Is he looking for me? Half of me wants him to, but the other half wills him to find someone that can give him what he wants.

Harrison makes a few adjustments before he spins his sticks in between his fingers, then he claps them together and counts to four. I look over at Josie, who is nodding her head and yelling at Liam.

The song is new, something I've never heard before. Josie seems to know the lyrics because she's singing right along. My heart aches with love for Liam and Josie. He has this talent and is able to write songs about her. I can't even make it a day without thinking about what Mason's voice sounded like and how I'll never hear the words *I love you* said to me again, and here's my best friend, being sung to like it's the last thing he'll ever do for her.

The words of the song are touching, about how his heart trumped his mind and that he should've known better. I move to the beat of the song, swaying back and forth as I watch Harrison pound on the drums. I can't tell if he's looking out to the crowd or not. I wish he would, even just for a moment. Maybe I'd wave and he'd smile. Liam sings about love being a sure thing and I wish things were that simple.

Moving on should be simple. Picking up the pieces and opening a new door to my life should be easy. So why isn't it? Why am I second-guessing everything? I sit down and grab another beer. I need to drown my sorrows or at least keep the voices out of my head. I can't love another man. I just can't.

For each song the guys play, I drink at least two beers. Too much talk about broken hearts, love, sex and life. Ralph refills the bucket and Josie eyes me. I shouldn't have come. Listening to them sing is far different from being backstage and working for them. I should be working – that's what I should be doing – not sitting here feeling sorry for myself.

The guys play a few more songs before taking a break.

I shrug and look down. I don't want him to see my tear streaked face. "I'm a sloppy drunk."

Harrison chuckles. "Oh, I don't know about that. I happen to enjoy drunk Katelyn."

"She's stupid."

"She's honest and lets her feelings show."

"I'm confused."

"That's makes two of us," he says as he lifts my face again and looks at me, his eyes going back and forth.

"You have beautiful eyes."

"Everything about you is beautiful."

I step forward and rest my forehead on his chest. He sets his arm around my neck, holding me to him.

"Why did you say I didn't want you here?" he asks. I was hoping he'd forget, but apparently I haven't been missing from the table that long.

"I don't know. Josie told me you wrote that song —"

"Yeah, so?"

"So I thought you'd want to spend time with her," I whisper. I pull back so I can make a quick escape when he tells he plans to start seeing his crush.

"I am spending time with her."

I look up immediately to find him smiling down at me.

"Come on, I'll take you home."

Harrison leads me into the parking lot. He doesn't say anything to make me uncomfortable with the situation. I'm not sure how to take what he said, but I do know I'm listening loud and clear. The song that Liam sang tonight is about me, and Harrison wrote it.

I've never had a song written about me before and that alone makes me feel loved and nervous all in one. I don't know what my response *should* be, but I know what's it's *going* to be. I can't continue to fight my feelings. It's taking far too much effort on my part to deny what my body and heart are telling me. This man... the one with his arm around me protectively has dealt with my bullshit, my hot and cold reactions to him and most importantly, treats my children with the utmost respect. I'd be a fool to walk away from something that could be an eye-opening experience.

I just need to find the words to tell him.

CHAPTER 21 - HARRISON

The hot water beats down my neck and back. I roll my head from side to side hoping to loosen the muscles. I think I'm going to start paying someone to mow my own lawn because mowing two twice a week, plus band practice is starting to take its toll. Either that, or my age is finally catching up with me. I can't give up mowing Katelyn's yard. It's worth it just to see her bend over her flowerbed. I have to say she has the finest roses in Beaumont. Not that I'm looking at any other roses, but the preening she's been doing is starting to show.

I turn the water on hotter and work my muscles. Maybe I need to workout or play the drums more. I definitely need to bring my other set back from Los Angeles when we go. I want to ask Katelyn if she'd like to drive back with me, but I haven't found the right moment. That would be a huge step in any direction, and while I know I'm ready, I'm not sure she is. But she's getting there. I can feel it.

Last night was interesting. I've never run after a woman before, but seeing Katelyn about to cry and question whether I wanted her there not only confused me, but almost had me standing on the stage proclaiming my undying affection for her. Josie told me that she spilled on the song we played, but did so in an offhanded way because she didn't want to come right out and say it.

When I found Katelyn outside, I wanted to hold her in my arms and show her how much she means to me. Last night, I saw something in her eyes, in the way she looked at me. I can only hope my instinct is right because if it is, I think I'll be seeing her a bit more, especially away from the studio.

I'm going to follow my intuition on this one and the next time I see her, I'm going to tell her... I don't know what, but I'll say something to her. Maybe that will open her eyes. I'll let her into my world if she'll give me one little glimpse of hers. That's all I ask for.

The water turns cold, effectively shutting off my massage technique. I should make an appointment with a chiropractor or a masseuse. Hell, maybe I can convince Katelyn to put her hands all over my body. That would be enough for me to relax most of my muscles.

I turn off the water and pull the shower curtain back. I step out onto Quinn's white mat that turns red when it's wet. It makes it look like you're bleeding. He likes it. Thinks it's funny to scare people with. I put my towel over my head and rub my hands back and forth to dry my hair.

When the door swings open, I peek through the small opening of my towel. Katelyn is staring back at me, her mouth dropping open as her eyes travel down my very wet and naked body.

"Oh crap," she says, covering her mouth, but not her eyes. She's totally checking me out and I'd be an idiot to say it's not turning me on. I take my time as I step into my

it, but I think about you all the time, and even though I tell myself no, I'm finding it harder and harder to stay away from you."

I capture her lips with mine. I cup her face and hold her to me. If that's all I'm getting for now, I'll take it. My tongue moves against hers in slow movements. Her hands drop to my sides, gripping the waistband of my sweats. If I stand, guaranteed they won't fall down, they're tented by the freaking boner I have for her now. I try to move her away from the offender, but she's not budging. She can feel how much I want her.

I'm not in any hurry to end this kiss. I want to savor every moment so I can dream about her later. I pull away first, reluctantly. I rest my forehead against hers and kiss her nose.

"Want to go grab some lunch after you clean up that coffee mess?"

She looks down at her shirt without making me let her go. Her white shirt has a nice brown stain now.

"I have a shirt you can wear," I offer excitedly. Seeing her in one of my shirts will no doubt send me over the edge and back into the shower.

"Can we go back to my house so I can change?"

"Of course."

Now that she's let me kiss her and hasn't pulled away and changed her mind, I want to do it more. I take a chance and lean in. She smiles. I smile.

"Mommy?" her smile fades all too quickly for my liking, but I get it.

I move away from her, picking up my t-shirt and putting it on. She watches me dress. I want to tell her that she's seen me naked and it's only fair that I see her too, but have a feeling that wall would go right up and I'd be shut out again.

So I'll bite my tongue and wait for drunken Katelyn to return.

She turns the lock and opens the door to a very angry Peyton. She's standing there in a dark blue football jersey with her hands on her hips.

"What're you doing?"

"Talking."

With our lips, I want to add, but bite back my childish comment. The kids don't need to know what we were doing in the bathroom.

"About what?"

"Adult stuff."

Peyton raises her eyebrow and all I can think is that Katelyn has got a tough road ahead of her. Peyton is definitely calling the shots right now, and that's not good.

"We were talking about what you, Elle and Quinn need for Christmas so when we meet with Santa, we can give him the appropriate list."

Peyton's mouth drops open and her eyes light up. Katelyn looks at me. I shrug. It used to work with Quinn when he'd get moody.

"Elle, mommy is making the Christmas list," Peyton yells as she stalks back down the hall.

"Nice save."

"Whatever works. I'm going to get changed." I cup her cheek and let my hand linger there for a heartbeat or two. She's going to have to give me some guidelines because I don't want to overstep the boundaries that are in place. I know I won't touch her in front of the kids, but now that I've had uninterrupted minutes and feel pretty confident that she's not running anytime soon, I'm not sure if I'll be able to keep my hands to myself when she's near.

I need to find a resolve.

I KEEP my hands buried deep in my pockets as I walk side-by-side next to Katelyn. We stay back while the kids run up ahead of us. Her arm brushes mine, making me wonder if she wants to hold my hand. And as much as I want that, I don't want to put her in a position of being questioned. She has to know there isn't a woman alive that can hold a candle to her. She has every ounce of my attention and more.

The kids are jumping up and down when we enter the Fun Palace. This place is a mecca for noise and a money sucking machine. I know Quinn likes this place, he likes to play the games and collect tickets to buy some ridiculous toy that only lasts a few days. Both girls look excited, and I imagine this is some type of relief for them – to be in a kid environment with no stress.

The cashier smiles brightly when we step forward. I feel Katelyn step back into me. I want to wrap my arms around her and rest my head on hers, but I don't. If she needs to be close to me, if she needs to assert herself, she's more than welcome. I stand behind her and read the menu board.

"What kind of pizza do you want?"

She turns slightly and looks at me over her shoulder. I wink at her, loving this change. God how bad do I want to kiss her right now? The ache is building, more so now that I know she's willing to try.

"I like mostly everything, but no onions."

"Oh yeah, are you planning on kissing someone later?" Please say yes and that his name is Harrison James. She rolls her eyes and smiles. "Pepperoni?"

"That's fine. The girls like cheese."

I nod. "I figured as much."

"Can I help you?" the cashier asks loudly, in her sugary-pitched teenage voice, when I step forward. I suppose she has to speak loudly over the noise in this place.

"We'll have one large cheese, one large pepperoni and five sodas."

"And what you would you like for tokens?" she hands me a list. My eyes just about bug out of my head when I see the prices. If my life as a drummer ever ends, I'm opening up one of these places. I look over the list and decide to get the most expensive package. All I can think is that this will afford me a little more privacy with Katelyn while the kids are playing. Or she and I can play and for some reason, the thought of playing a video game with her suddenly sounds extremely sexy.

"I'll take three of these," I say as I point the package with three thousand tokens.

"Harrison," Katelyn sets her hand on my back when she steps forward. "That's too much." I look at her and then at the three sets of eyes peering up at me. They all smile at the same time, each of them missing teeth. It'll never been too much.

I look at Katelyn and hand the cashier my card without breaking eye contact. "It's worth seeing them smile."

Her face lights up. She closes her eyes and shakes her head. Her hands cover her eyes briefly before looking back at me. "Thank you," she whispers.

It's in that moment that I know I'll do whatever I can to make this family smile, because it's so going to be worth it.

CHAPTER 22 - KATELYN

I PULL MY COMFORTER UP TO MY CHIN AND ROLL OVER, facing Mason's side of the bed. The alarm is going to go off in about thirty minutes, but I've been awake for over an hour, tossing and turning, trying desperately to find some way to shut my mind off. Every time I close my eyes, yesterday morning replays in slow motion, all scenes that I'm having a hard time forgetting.

Yesterday marks the first time I've seen a man naked, aside from Mason, and I couldn't look away. I didn't even try. I think I knew deep down he was in there. Subconsciously, my mind heard the water running and shut off when my hand reached for the doorknob and opened it. I don't know if I was meant to find him like that, but I certainly wasn't going to leave, not this time.

The night of the show, the song, those words; they tore through me. I was so jealous of Josie while I sat there listening to Liam sing words that I was sure were meant for her. I wanted them, even though I don't deserve them. The only thing I deserve is to see Harrison on the arm of some bimbo groupie because I can't make up my mind. I'm so hot and cold with him, yet he sticks around, patiently waiting for me.

I told Harrison I'm going to try, and I am. Each day that I wake up will be a new day with a new adventure. I'm not trying to forget Mason or replace him, but make room in my life for something different, some*one* different. Dr. Brooks told me that it's okay to date, and that's what I'm going to do, not that I know a thing about dating.

Yet, I have fear in my heart. I don't want the girls to get attached. They already like Harrison and expect him to be around because he lives in Beaumont and is in the band, but what if we stay together for a while only to break up, what then? I know I'm getting ahead of myself. He may not want me after a month or two and I'll be back to square one.

Today will be an obstacle and one I haven't really considered or thought would be necessary, but it is. I need to tell Mr. Powell my decision to start dating. I don't know how he's going to take it, with it only being a year after Mason's death, and for him that might not be enough time. I'm not sure if it is for me, but I need to take a chance that these feelings I have for Harrison are real and not just because he shows me attention. He's bringing out sensations that I didn't know existed.

I close my eyes in a last-ditch effort to get some sleep. Harrison's there right before my eyes. His body is dripping with water. The droplets pebble and roll down his torso. My mouth falls open as I take in almost everything I've been wondering about. Quinn is etched across his heart. There are others, but this one stands out because I know how much he means to Harrison. I don't know where to put my eyes. If I look down, I see him, more than I ever thought I would, but looking at his chest isn't much of a difference. The silver ring hanging from his nipple sends a shiver down my spine. I've never seen one up close. I clench my fist to keep myself from reaching out and touching it.

Everything is moving in slow motion. My body temperature is rising steadily. I know I should leave, but I can't. Even if I wanted to, my body is being a traitor. I'm cemented to the floor. I feel antsy, excited. I need to do something, anything. He looks at me, his eyes hooded. He knows I'm staring, taking him all in.

Words are exchanged. I'm mortified. I don't turn away, but watch him as he steps into a pair of worn out gray sweatpants. He comes toward me. He looks dangerous. Sexy. He reaches behind me and shuts the door. The telltale click of the lock turning into place doesn't scare me.

Harrison rests against the counter, pulling me to him. It's now or never. I want to touch him. I need to feel him under my fingertips to know if this is real or not. I stand between his legs. My knees are pressed against the cabinets below. I give in and let my hands roam up his chest. I purposely avoid his nipple ring. I want to savor the moment when I can pull it in my mouth. I finally push the offending towel off his head. He closes his eyes as my fingers delve into his hair. I've been aching to see him without a hat, and now that I have, I'm not sure I'll be able to get enough. His dark hair is soft to the touch and showing a hint of curl. Each pass-through rewards me with a new thought. What does he look like with longer hair? Shorter? Does he ever shave it off, or does he keep it this length? Most importantly, will he allow me to touch him freely whenever I feel the need because right now, I can't get enough. The wait has been too long to only touch once. He keeps his hair covered for security, why? Who's he protecting himself from? I want him to let me in and teach me how to be the security we both need. Everything about his man is turning me on when I thought that wouldn't be possi-

ble, but standing here, pressed against him, I know that I have to try, that I owe it to myself to see if we're capable of being together.

I startle awake. Looking at the clock, it's time to get up. My body is on edge, racked with nerves and anxious to see him again. I don't know if I should call him or maybe show up at his house. We don't have plans to see each other and I'm afraid to admit that it scares me that we don't. I refuse to allow myself to think he has plans with someone else, but the truth is, I don't know. I can't help but second-guess everything and I know I need to stop.

When I enter the living room, the twins are sitting on the couch together sharing a bowl of dry cheerios and watching cartoons. This was Mason's way of making them wait until I woke up before we had breakfast. Breakfast together on the weekends – that's how things are in the Powell household. Knowing that they're content, I sneak off to the bathroom. I rest against the closed door and think about Harrison and everything that happened yesterday comes flashing back. If men can get away with a cold shower, what can women do?

"PAPA, PAPA," both girls yell as soon as they are out of the car. My father-in-law, Michael Powell, steps out onto his wrap-around porch. He bends down and embraces both of them, rocking them back and forth. They are all he has left of Mason and his wife, Susan. I don't really count. I was just his daughter-in-law, but those girls... they are his link to the two most important people in his life. I know he loves me, though. We've shared a bond from the first day I stepped into his house.

"Dad," Mason yells through his house. He drops his football bag on the living room floor and strides down the hall. I stand at the door with my back pressed against the wall. I straighten out my skirt. It's long, just below my knees and flowing. I feel stupid wearing this today, but my mother insisted. She said a young girl doesn't meet parents in shorts or jeans. I'm surprised she let me ride in Mason's truck and let me come over. I've seen her watching us from the window when we're swimming and he's sneaking kisses. I tell him not to kiss me in the swimming pool, but he doesn't listen.

"Katelyn?" I look up from the floor and grin at Mason. He's so cute and hot, definitely one of the cutest boys in school. I like that he's my age, but it scares me that I'm not his first girlfriend. I try not to think about what will happen when school starts. I know he's going to dump me for someone else. I'm just his summer fling because we have a pool, that's what my mom says.

But right now, I'm enjoying it when he's kissing me, encouraging me to touch him when we do. I felt his chest yesterday and I liked it. I don't know if he liked it though, and that worries me. What if I'm not doing things right?

"Katelyn," Mason steps forward and pulls my hand into his. His fingers interlock with mine and swallow my hand. "This is my dad, Michael Powell. Dad," Mason looks at me, he smiles so big that I can count his teeth if I wanted. "This is my Katelyn." Mason squeezes my hand. I try not to let my body react, but my heart is beating so fast that I think it's going to jump out of my chest. He said 'my Katelyn'.

Mr. Powell steps forward and offers his hand for me to shake. I let go of Mason's hand and place it in his. I know Mason's parents. I've told him this, but Mason said it's different when you introduce the girl you're seeing to your parents.

"It's good to meet you, Katie." I hate that name. My mother uses it and I purposely ignore her when she does. It's not my name, but Mr. Powell has always called me 'Katie' and I'm too polite to correct him now.

"Hello, Mr. Powell. This feels funny, don't you think?"

"A little, but Mason says it's necessary."

"Yes he does." I poke him in the ribs only for him to take my hand back into his.

"Well if you'll excuse me, I'm cooking dinner." Mr. Powell excuses himself from the living room, leaving us standing there. It feels a bit awkward and I don't really know what to do. I swing our arms back and forth and look around the room, anywhere but at Mason.

"Want a tour?"

I nod, unable to find my voice. He leads me through the house, stopping and talking again with his dad. When we reach his room, the jitters are in full-force. I know I'm not allowed in a boy's room, but curiosity gets the best of me. I step over the threshold and look around. His room is a little messy, not spic and span like mine, but it looks comfortable. I walk around, touching his trophies that sit on his shelf and the ribbons that hang along the wall. I pick up a picture of him and Liam Westbury and study it. It's of them in their football uniforms from the fall. Josie and I went to a few of their games this past fall. I'd like to think I'll be going to more as Mason's girl, but I'm not getting my hopes up.

The creak of the bed gets my attention. I turn and see Mason sitting on the edge, watching me. He's quiet, reserved. Does he not want me here? I've heard so many things about him from other girls that I know he's experienced. He's probably brought me here for sex. I'm not ready for that at all.

"Come here," he says. He doesn't pat the bed and offer me a place the sit. Do I sit next to him anyway? I smile softly *and walk toward him. He places his hands on my hips when I'm close enough for him to touch. Even when he's sitting, he's taller than me. His hands move up and down, over my hips. "I wish you weren't wearing a skirt."*

"Why?"

"Because I like the way your legs feel against my hands."

My throat feels tight. Would he really want to have sex with his dad downstairs?

"My mom says a lady wears a dress when meeting parents for the first time." I close my eyes and wish I could crawl in a hole and die. Did I really just say that?

"You've met my dad before, Katelyn."

I shrug. "I guess this was different."

"Why, because you're my girlfriend?"

My heart stops beating when he says the word 'girlfriend'. I want to smile, but my mom warned me that boys say things to get into girls' panties.

"Girlfriend?" I squeak out.

"Yeah, I mean unless you want to date around or something. I just thought..."

"Okay," I blurt out.

"Okay," he says. He kisses me softly. Small, sweet pecks. "Can I try something?"

"I guess."

He doesn't tell me what he's going to try, but he kisses me again. This time, I feel his tongue on my lips. I pull back and look at him.

"You'll like it, I promise."

I shake my head. "I don't know, Mason. I'm not like those other girl's you've been with."

"What girls?" he asks as his hands start roaming again.

"I've heard the rumors."

Mason sits back a little. He looks at me and shakes his

head. "*Katelyn, I promise you, I've done nothing but kiss a few girls.*"

"*You're not having sex?*"

"*No,*" *he laughs and leans forward placing his hands back on my hips.* "*Now let me kiss you good and proper.*"

"What are you thinking about?" Mr. Powell shakes me from my daydream. I have to shake my head to clear out the cobwebs. So much has happened in this house, so many memories.

"Thinking about the day I met you, officially."

"That was such a long time ago." He pulls me into a hug. I want to remind him that it wasn't really that long, that our connection was just taken from us far too soon.

We walk up the steps, his arm around me as he ushers the twins inside. Nothing has changed since the first time I was here, except for minor cosmetic things.

The girls run up the stairs and put their stuff in Mason's old room. I haven't been up there since before Mason died and have no intention on going up there now. There are far too many memories of the two of us in that room.

"Can we talk?" I motion for us to sit down. He follows, taking the cushion next to me. He's my second father. I could tell him everything and not worry about him judging me, but now? Now I'm not so sure he won't judge.

"What's going on, Katie?"

I take a deep breath and close my eyes. When I open them, he's not looking at me. His face is pensive. I know he's missing Susan and Mason. "I've met someone."

He bites his lip and looks even farther away from me. "Are you taking the girls away from me?"

"What? No! Why would you ask that?" I pull on his arm so he'll look at me. When he does, my heart breaks for him. His eyes are glistening. I shake my head and fight back the tears. "I'd never take them from you, ever."

"Who is it?"

I swallow hard. "Harrison James."

"Liam's friend?"

I nod, biting my finger. The pain it causes me is nothing compared to the pain in my heart.

"Are you ready?"

"I don't know, but I'm willing to try."

"It's only been a year."

I nod. "I know. Believe me, I know. But I'm not sure there's a pre-determined time frame. We've been seeing Dr. Brooks and he thinks it's okay to date and that's all I'm doing, dating. Nothing more."

"Do the girls like him?"

"They do, especially Elle. He's very good with them. Peyton doesn't like many people right now, except Noah and Liam, but she's nice to Harrison and his son, Quinn."

"He has a boy?"

"Yes, he's just a few years older than the girls."

"And they get along?"

"They do. They're all in school together."

"Can I meet him and his son?"

"Of course you can." This elates me. If things were to work out between us, I'd want Mr. Powell to accept Harrison and Quinn.

"Can you do me a favor?"

"Whatever you want?"

"Can you please stop calling me Mr. Powell?"

"Never," I say as I lean forward to kiss him on the cheek. He laughs, but knows I'll never stop calling him Mr. Powell. I like it, and secretly, he does too. "I'll see you tomorrow. Have fun with the girls." I get up off the couch and start toward the stairs.

"I will and Katelyn?" I stop and look at him. "Thank you," he says. I smile at him and nod. I don't know what he's thanking me for, but I'm going to assume it's because I'm here and so are the girls and that we aren't going anywhere.

MY HOUSE IS QUIET. Too quiet for me, but the break is a relief. Everything in me is telling me to call Harrison, but I don't want to interrupt his time with Quinn or make it seem like I need to see him, even though I do. It's just hard to admit and take the step of picking up the phone.

I'm not there yet. I hope to be, someday. I'm just not sure how to get to that point, but I'm hoping Harrison is persistent and shows me the way to make it happen.

I walk around the house, picking up the girls' toys and backpacks. We're a month into school and so far so good. I'm concerned about Peyton, though and think that extra sessions with Dr. Brooks will be required. I feel like a failure of a parent. Both girls should've been the same. Once they gravitated toward one of us we allowed it to continue. Elle is too much like me and Peyton, she's all Mason. Of course, neither of us thought we wouldn't be here to watch the girls grow up. We were naïve, and now Peyton is struggling and I feel powerless to help her. I can't keep pawning her off on Liam.

I'm pleasantly surprised when I walk into their room and find it clean. Yes, I'm that bored that I'd actually clean their room. I decide to call Josie or maybe Jenna. Wedding plans need to be discussed and I could use a bottle of wine.

The roar of an engine catches my attention. I walk

faster than normal to get back to the living room. There's a knock at my door before I can look out to see who it is. I swing the door open and am taken aback by the man standing at my door. The one I've been fighting my affections for, for so long. I smile as he opens the screen door and steps in. He's dressed in his normal Harrison attire of cargo shorts and combat boots.

I want to reach up and kiss him, but I hold myself back. I'm not sure what I should be doing around him right now.

"Hi." The way he says hi makes my knees weak. I can admit that now. "I was in the neighborhood," he adds. I want to say thank God for that. Instead, I bite the inside of my cheek to keep from embarrassing myself.

"Come on in," I say, stupidly. He's already in the house. It's not like I can kick him out now.

He sets his helmet down and takes off his sweatshirt. It doesn't escape my notice that his hair is covered again. I want to rip the doo rag off his head and run my fingers through his hair.

"Where's Quinn?"

"He's at Liam's for the night."

I pretend like that doesn't faze me, but it does. Not that I'm looking to spend the night with Harrison, but I wouldn't mind a little more kissing.

"Where are the girls?"

"At their grandpa's."

Harrison steps toward me, placing his hands on my hips. His hand slides under my shirt. His fingers press into my skin as his lips come down on mine. There's no urgency in his kiss, he's taking his time.

"Can I take you somewhere?"

I can't think enough to form a coherent thought, so I nod and realize I have no idea what I've just agreed to.

WHEN SHE TELLS ME THAT SHE'S ALONE, IT TAKES every fiber of my being to control the urge to pick her up and take her to her room. I can't do that, not here. Not in the home she shared with her husband. I wouldn't want to put her in a situation like that. If and when we are together in that way, it'll be at my house where she'll be comfortable.

I know one thing for sure, I can't keep my hands off of her now that I know she's willing to try. She'll probably get sick of me with my need to touch her, but I have to feel her skin against mine, even if it's just my hands. And my lips – they burn with desire to kiss her.

She nods when I ask if I can take her somewhere. I've been out riding all day and many times I wanted to just stop by and show up unannounced, but couldn't bring myself to do it. Mowing her lawn is an excuse, but that's not due until tomorrow.

I reluctantly remove my lips from hers and pull her hand into mine. I'm thankful that I have Quinn's helmet with me and that it will fit her. Otherwise, my romantic side might not be able to shine. I lead her out of the front door,

"Are you comfortable?" I ask, praying she says yes.

"I am," she says. Her hand comes up and pulls off my doo rag. I run my hand through my hair, which I have no doubt is standing on end. She drops it on the ground and threads her fingers through my hair. I lean forward and close my eyes, relishing in the attention she's giving me.

"I wish you wouldn't wear a hat all the time."

"Hmm, you don't like hats?"

Katelyn shakes her head. "It's not that, I just like seeing your hair. You've kept it hidden for so long and it's beautiful."

"Beautiful, huh?" I ask teasingly.

"What?" she asks. "Men can have beautiful hair."

"All right, if you say so. I'll try and not wear a hat so much, just for you."

"Thank you."

Being this close to her is something I've wanted for a long time. I can't screw it up, and right now that's my biggest fear. What if she decides this isn't what she wants? There's no way I can convince her otherwise, it wouldn't be fair.

My eyes flash open briefly when I feel her lips on mine. I'm going to let her lead us because it will give me the reassurance I need right now. Her kiss is slow, tentative. She traces my lower lip with her tongue. My lips part giving her access to what she's asking for. A feeling of calmness washes over me the moment her tongue touches mine. It doesn't last before heat is surging through my body. I'm fighting the urge to pull her against me, to rock her body against mine. I can't hold back any longer. I need to touch her. I slide my hand under her shirt and press my fingers into her back pulling her the tiniest bit closer.

Her hands fist at my shirt, pulling herself up higher onto

my cock. "Oh, fuck," I say, breaking away from her mouth. She's grinding against me and I'm about to lose my mind. Her hand clutches at the back of my neck. She takes my earlobe into her mouth, biting softly. Katelyn moves to my neck, biting and licking her way back to my mouth. I can't take it anymore.

My hand roams up her thigh, massaging as I go. It's just my luck that she's wearing a long skirt. I didn't even suggest she change. I want her like this. I know I'm testing my resolve, but I'm going to test hers too. Does she want me the way I want her? My fingers linger at the hem of her panties.

My knuckle brushes against her. She jumps slightly and pulls away from me. I refuse to let go and continue to skim my knuckle against her again. Her eyes drop, she licks her lips and when she looks up, the wanton look in her eyes tells me enough. I keep my hand splayed against her back holding her to me. My fingers inch into her panties, my gaze never leaving hers. I'll stop the second she tells me to. The moment I see fear in her eyes, I'll pull away, but I won't want to.

"Tell me to stop and I will," I say the words to reassure myself that this is what she wants. She licks her lips, urging me on. I brush against her pussy. Her breathing hitches, her fingers grabbing onto my hair. I do it again, this time with more pressure. She pushes toward my hand as the pad of my thumb finds her clit. I capture her lips with mine, wanting to increase the sensation. I add more pressure the harder she pulls.

I moan loudly when I slip my finger in. "Oh, fuck," I say, breaking away. I've wanted this for so long and now I'm here. I want to go slow and savor every fucking moment that I can, but she has other ideas. She rocks forward, setting a rhythm and creating the friction she needs. She knows what she wants and isn't afraid to show me.

Her hands travel under my shirt and roam over my chest. When her fingers pull gently on my nipple ring, I hiss and rub harder on her swollen clit. Heat soars through my body, igniting fervency that I didn't know existed. I add another and move with the motion she's set. This is more than I've imagined and I want more. Katelyn keeps pace, rocking back and forth with her legs wrapped around me. The grinding is almost too much to bear. I want to rip her skirt off, drop my shorts and feel her wrapped around my shaft.

"Harrison," her voice is raspy, out of breath.

"Yeah, baby?" I take her lips with mine, silencing her. She can't tell me to stop now, there's no way.

She bites down on my lip, her hand pulling on my nipple ring. I hiss and move faster, increasing the pressure. I've been waiting for this moment, the moment to feel her like this in the most sensual way. My lips move to her neck, biting gently as she clenches around my fingers. If this is any indication of what's to come, I'm going to be a man on his knees begging her to let me worship her every chance that I can.

Katelyn slows as she comes down from her natural high. Her head rests on my chest, but she continues to caress my ring. I want to show her what that does to me. I know she can feel it, but the exhilaration I feel... the sensation it sends – it's something I can't describe.

I kiss the top of her head and adjust so I can place my lips along her face, her eyes, cheeks, nose, and finally her lips. She closes her eyes and leans her head back, accepting the attention I'm giving her. I remove my hand gently. She sighs and that makes me feel fucking great. I gave her something that every woman needs.

"Harrison," she whispers in between kisses. The way my name rolls off her lips sends chills down my spine. I've waited for this for such a long time. I don't want the night to end.

"Yeah?" My voice is ragged. I kiss her full on the lips before pulling back so she can talk to me.

She threads her fingers though my hair. Had I known she liked to do this, I probably would've let her do it sooner.

"Do you need me to take care of you?" she asks in such a soft voice, I get the feeling that our little exhibitionist act is not up her alley. Not that it's up mine, but there was no way I'd take back what we just did. She opened up to me in a very intimate way and shared something that I know she's only let one other man do before.

I smile at her and kiss her forehead, letting my lips linger there as I hold her to me. "I'm good," I tell her. "It's nothing another cold shower won't take care of later."

"A cold shower, huh? Do you do that often?"

I shrug and look away. Do I admit that it's an everyday occurrence for me?

"You can tell me," she says as she places whispering kisses along my jaw. Fucking hell, this woman is going to be the death of me. How did we go from barely talking to this? I'm not complaining by any means, but I want her to be so god damn sure of herself because I'm not ready for any heartbreak.

"Something tells me that I'll tell you whatever you want to know."

Katelyn pulls back. Her finger tugs again at my nipple ring. I have to bite the inside of my cheek to keep from

have their eyebrows raised with stupid little smiles on their faces.

"Where are you?" Josie asks as she sips her coffee.

We're finally sitting down to go over wedding stuff. Josie and Liam have set a date, right after Christmas to allow them to celebrate their first holiday as a family together. Me? I think they just want more presents. I process her question and realize I need to craft my answer carefully. I'm not willing to divulge what Harrison and I did last night.

"You're off in la la land. Does it have to anything to do with that hunk of a man you've been hanging out with?" Jenna asks. I eye her up and wonder if she's attracted to him? I can't lie and say I've never been attracted to him. He's very good looking. He's confident in knowing he's capable of loving me the way I need to be loved. When I finally pulled my blinders off, I saw the man who oozed sex appeal. I knew it would only be a matter of time before I'd hold him in my arms. Before I'd thread my fingers through his dark, beautiful hair. Before I'd feel him... all of him as he brought me to my peak over and over again as if it would be our last time together. The man who is so confident when he's in the room with me that I can't help but know his eyes are trained solely on me, regardless of how bitchy I am.

"I'm fine," I say, trying to erase the image of Harrison and I on the motorcycle last night. Not that I plan to forget it any time soon, but this isn't the time to let my reaction to one of the most incredibly sexy moments in my life show through. "Did you decide on colors?" I ask, hoping that I didn't miss it.

"No, not yet," Josie says as she opens one of the many magazines sitting on the table. I swear she has every subscription available. "I like red and Liam likes black, but I don't know."

"I think you should wear a red cape over your gown. It goes with your winter theme and will keep you warm." Jenna says.

"Oh I like that idea," I add. Josie's gown is gorgeous and just perfect for her. Liam won't know what hit him when she walks down the aisle.

Josie claps her hands together and writes something down. I don't envy her. Okay, maybe I do. Mason and I had a small wedding. My parents thought I was too young to get married and wouldn't pay for much of it, and his parents paid for what they could. It wasn't much, but it was ours, and that's all that mattered. Honestly, I can't see myself walking down the aisle again.

His caress his soft. He cradles me like a fragile doll, even though I'm not. I'm not going to break suddenly; at least I don't think I will. He slides his hand from my back to my ass and pulls me forward. I rock against him. His mouth moves along my neck to my chest; placing lingering kisses as he keeps rhythm with our bodies.

My hand moves into his shorts. There's not much room between our bodies. This would be easier on the ground or in a bed, but here... on his bike... the need to be with him is so great that I can't stop. I won't. I need this moment with him.

I pull his zipper down carefully, never breaking eye contact with him. His adam's apple bobs up and down each time he swallows. He stands and the bike wobbles, making me wonder if this is a smart idea after all. Harrison smiles and kisses me briefly, before pulling out his wallet. My heart skips a beat when I see the classic foil package in his hand.

"This not how I expected our first time to be," he says. He pulls his shorts down a bit, enough to free himself. I gasp. Something in the back of my mind tells me to run, but my

heart is screaming at me to stay and to give myself to the man in front of me.

"You're prepared."

He sits down and cups my face. "After the other day, I've been hopeful, but I won't pressure you. I want you to be absolutely sure."

"I'm positive. I want this with you."

"Katelyn?" A hand slams down on the table making me jump.

"What?"

"I asked you a question," Josie says.

"Sorry, what?"

"What is wrong with you?" she says. I look from her to Jenna and shake my head.

"Nothing, I'm just tired."

"Late night?" Jenna asks.

"No, not really." My night wasn't long, just over stimulating. I was exhausted when I left Harrison's house this morning. Yesterday, when he showed up at mine, I had no idea we would take our relationship to that level. Hell, I don't even know if we have a relationship, because neither of us discussed it. All I know is if he doesn't want me, I'm going to become a nun and lock myself away.

"Well you seem really tired," Josie says with concern in her voice. If she only knew that sleep wasn't something I did much last night, she'd be giddy and beside herself planning my wedding. I know she's waiting for me to tell her that Harrison and I are together, but honestly, if we are, I want to leave it a secret for a little while longer until I can tell the girls. I'm not sure how Peyton is going to handle me dating. Hell, I'm not even sure if I'm going to handle me dating.

"Sorry, I just didn't sleep well." I add hoping she'll leave it alone. "What was your question?"

"What?" she asks. Jenna starts laughing and I quickly follow. Josie has wedding on the brain and is sidetracked so easily.

"She wants to know if you're ready for Los Angeles," Jenna says, covering for Josie.

"Yeah, it'll be fun," I say. I'm hoping this trip gives Harrison and I some definition on our relationship. We have a few band things to do – if they decide I'm still going to be their manager – and we'll be away from the prying eyes and gossip hounds of Beaumont. Something I desperately need.

"I'm so excited."

"Only because you'll be on that hunk of man's arm when he walks the red carpet," Jenna says, rolling her eyes.

"You need a man," Josie says.

I punch her lightly in the arm. "What's with you? First me and now Jenna? Maybe we like being single."

Josie starts laughing. "I know for a fact you're not single, no matter what you tell yourself, and Jenna... my dear sweet Jenna, it's been four years. Let me find you someone."

Jenna and I roll our eyes. Jenna hasn't dated since she moved to Beaumont and after what she went through, I don't think I'd date either, although someone would be hard pressed to lay a finger on her now. Liam and Harrison treat her like a sister, and that has to mean something to her.

"I don't need a guy, Josie. I have you guys, you're my family."

"But what about sex?" Josie squeals. Jenna turns red and I look the other way. If we were in public, I'd be so embarrassed.

"Sex isn't everything," Jenna answers back and every part of me wants to yell that yes it is, but I keep quiet.

"Okay," he says as he tears open the wrapper and sheaths himself. I scoot forward as he grabs my hips, bringing me on

"My son and I are hoping to have dinner with three very beautiful women that we know."

The room is suddenly quiet as all eyes are on me. I can feel ten sets staring me down, waiting for my answer.

I sit up straight and meet Harrison's questioning eyes. "We'd be honored to have dinner with you and Quinn," I say proudly. The gasps are enough to confirm that whatever Harrison and I are, the group here says we're dating, and I'm very okay with that.

CHAPTER 25 - HARRISON

FAMILY. THAT IS WHAT SURROUNDS ME NOW. SITTING to my left is Katelyn. On my right is Josie. Nestled in my arms is Elle, who just fell and hit her head on the bleachers. Quinn stands next to Liam and Peyton while they stand along the fence cheering for Noah. I'm not a football fan, never have been. Honestly, if I had known Liam in school, I wouldn't be his friend, but here I sit, watching a game I don't understand and yelling as loudly as the next person because that is what family does.

It's been just over a month since I asked Katelyn and the girls to dinner and almost every night since, we've eaten as a family. She's yet to spend the night again, but we've found plenty of time to be a couple. At least that's what I'm calling us. The kids haven't said anything, even though I have a feeling Quinn knows. He's started coming home with Peyton and Elle after school and that all but forces me to pick him up at Katelyn's.

I've been told not to knock and to enter through the side door. Each time I'm greeted with a hug from Elle, half a smile from Peyton, a nod from my son and from Katelyn, I get the look that tells me she wants to rush up and kiss the shit out of me if the kids were in another room.

Every day I learn something new, and with each revelation I fear that I may be falling in love with her. It's definitely a feeling like no other that I've experienced, and I'm not exactly sure how to handle it, except continue to do what I'm doing and let her lead our relationship. If that means I'm going to freeze my ass off on Saturday mornings so we can watch Noah play football, then so be it.

"Hey baby," Katelyn says beside me. Oh how I wish she was talking to me, but since I'm holding half of her precious cargo in my arms, I know otherwise. Elle rubs her face along my sweatshirt. Her fingers are digging into the back of my neck. She fell pretty hard and even though my heart hurt for her, it soared when she opted for me instead of Katelyn to hold her. I shouldn't gloat, but every man needs a little beauty in his life, and Elle is my princess.

"How does she look?" I ask over the top of her head. Katelyn looks worried and that concerns me. I haven't had to deal with Quinn being hurt before, as he's had a pretty sheltered life. Homeschooling and hanging out with my mom don't exactly offer an abundance of mishaps. I know they went to the park often, but aside from a skinned knee, nothing too bad.

"It's a goose-egg and black and blue. She needs ice."

"I'll go get some," I offer. I put my hands on Elle's side only for her to moan and cling onto me even tighter. "Elle, sweetie, I'm going to get you some ice for your bump."

She shakes her head. "Mommy go."

"Don't you want mommy to hold you?" I ask, hoping to change the sad look on Katelyn's face. It's one that I don't think even my kissing can change. Elle pulls herself tighter against my chest.

"I'll go," Katelyn says softly. She rubs her hand down Elle's back before she gets up and steps down the bleachers with ease. I follow her as she walks over to Noah's bench and asks for a bag of ice. I suppose if you're going to have an accident like this, this is the place to do it.

"How are things going?" Josie asks as soon as Katelyn's out of earshot.

"Things are good."

"I heard you've been having dinner together."

I laugh. "It's just dinner. Quinn and the girls get along well and Katelyn is good company." I don't need Josie to be let in on what's really going on. I know Katelyn has been talking to her, but we've been keeping things from the kids for a reason. It's been at my encouragement that we ease the girls into what's going on. I don't want them to think I'm trying to replace their dad, because I'm not. I want to be someone that they can count on and be there for them when they need me. Quinn – I know how he feels – it's just a matter of time before I tell him everything.

"I like Quinn," Elle adds for good measure.

I smile down at her and return to watching Katelyn. She's talking to Noah's coach.

"Shouldn't he be coaching?" I ask just as Liam yells from his spot by the fence. The coach looks at Liam and yells something out to the players.

"Noah doesn't like the coach."

"I don't think I do either." Josie laughs. I look at Liam, who's having an animated conversation with Peyton. She's holding her football under her arm and waving her other one dramatically in the air.

"You're really good with the girls, Harrison. Katelyn sees that."

"Peyton..." I look down at Elle and shut my mouth. The

last thing I want to do is talk about her sister in a way that she could take as demeaning. I want Peyton to like me, not because of her mother, but because I think she's an amazing little girl and want to get to know her. If she's anything like her sister, even though they're opposites, she's going to steal my heart too. I just have to find a way to get past the wall she's put up.

"She'll come around. She was so close to Mason. Everywhere he went, she was with him and for her to wake-up and have her daddy gone... she doesn't know how to cope. Katelyn says things are getting better with Dr. Brooks."

"Someday," I say confidently.

Katelyn returns with the bag of ice. It took that coach long enough to give it her and I'm about to say something completely stupid, until she smiles at me as she walks up the bleachers, making me forget whatever it was. I take the bag from her as she sits down. She slips her hand up under my sweatshirt. My body stiffens as I yell out.

"Sorry," she whispers in my ear, placing a kiss there. "My hand was cold." My tongue is tied, so I nod and wink at her. I'll make her pay for it when we're in Los Angeles.

"It's cold," Elle says turning away from me. I have to pull her away from my body against my will, but we need to put ice on her head to keep the swelling down.

"Just for a little bit." Katelyn sets it back down on her bump and holds it there. I want to put my hand on her thigh to let her know that I think she's amazing and to not let Elle's actions get to her. I can see it in her face, the way it falls each time Elle tells her no or moves away from her. She's trying so hard with both girls. I know she's just looking for a tiny bit of happiness where they're concerned.

Elle snuggles into my chest with Katelyn holding the icepack against her forehead. Josie starts cheering, causing

Elle to turn sharply and almost fall out of my arms. Her sudden movements also send the icepack flying into the man sitting in front of us. I stifle a laugh and scramble to pick it up without dropping Elle. I hand it back to Katelyn, who looks mortified.

"Sorry, sir, it slipped out of our hands," I say, hoping he won't freak out. I sometimes forget that the people of Beaumont aren't like some of the people in L.A. At least here you'll just get a glare.

"I think we should go," she whispers into my ear. Chills spread across my body with all the innuendos that could mean. The simple statement of *we should go* is what's really turning me on. Just to be with her and the kids as a family is all I need right now. Everything else with her is just gravy.

I nod, pick up Elle and wait for Katelyn to gather her purse.

"We're going to take off," she says to Josie, who is so enthralled in the game, she just nods. I jump off the side, holding Elle tightly in my arms, and turn to see Katelyn about to jump too. I reach for her and am rewarded with her hand slipping into mine, before she hops down. I don't let go and neither does she. We walk hand-in-hand to Liam. His eyebrow rises when he sees us. I shake my head slightly. I don't want a scene or any wise cracks coming from him.

"Peyton, we're going to go."

I see the anger in her eyes immediately. I'm prepared for the outburst. She bites her lower lip and clutches her football tighter.

"Peyton?" Katelyn says her name again.

Liam is watching all of this as it's about to explode.

"Uncle Liam, can you give me a ride home after the game?"

Liam looks from Peyton to Katelyn, who nods quickly.

"As long as your mom doesn't have a problem with it, but you'll have to ask her."

Peyton sighs and looks at her mom. "Mommy, can I stay with Uncle Liam?"

Katelyn covers her mouth and I'm oblivious to what just happened. "Yes, you can stay." She steps forward and kisses Peyton on the forehead before turning and walking toward her car, leaving Elle and I standing there.

"What the...?"

Liam shrugs and goes back to yelling at Noah on the field. "Hey man, Quinn can stay too if he wants."

"I want," he says quickly.

"All right. I'll come pick you up later."

"Okay, dad. Thanks."

"You're welcome."

I walk away, still confused about what just happened with Katelyn and Peyton. I was ready for the all out battle that was going to ensue, because we all know how Peyton feels about football, but that didn't happen.

Katelyn is waiting by her car when I walk up with Elle. The back door is open, allowing me to set Elle in her booster. She starts strapping herself in as soon as I move away. Sure funny how she's feeling better now that we aren't at the football game. Katelyn shuts the door and leans against it. I want to pull her into my arms and taste her lips for hours.

"Do you want to come over?"

"Would you think of me as a desperate man if I said yes?"

"No, I'd think of you as a man who wants to spend time with me, and I'd think of me as a woman who wants to spend time with you."

"You need to pack."

Katelyn shrugs. "Maybe you can help while Elle is watching a movie."

"Hmm, maybe." I place my hand on the back of her neck and pull her forward. As much as I want to kiss her full on the lips, I kiss her forehead.

"I'll follow you," I say, not wanting to leave my car at the field.

"Kay," she replies with a nod. I stand there like lovesick puppy while she gets in her car. I can't see her when she gets to the driver's side because she's too short. I try not to laugh, but just thinking about spending the next hour or so with her makes me happy.

I look out just in time to see Quinn running toward me. He's in a full sprint, yelling my name.

"What's up, bud?" I catch him in my arms. He's breathing hard.

"I forgot you're leaving tonight."

"Yeah?"

"I wanted to ask you something."

I set him down on the ground and move his hair out of his eyes. He needs a haircut. Something I'll have to get done when I get back.

"What do you want to know?"

"Do you love Katelyn?"

I bend down so that I'm just a bit shorter than him and set my hand on his shoulder. "I don't know, maybe. I'm not sure what it means to be in love. I love you, I know that, but I think with Katelyn the love is different."

"Do you love Elle and Peyton?"

"I do. Is that okay?"

"Yeah it is, and it's okay for you to love Katelyn too. I won't be mad."

I kneel down on the cold, wet ground and pull my son

into my arms. I'm not sure how I got so lucky, but I did and I'll never take him for granted.

"I love you, Quinn. Do you want to come with me to Katelyn's?"

He looks back at Liam and Peyton and nods. "Yeah, I do. I like it there."

"Me too, bud," I say as I stand and ruffle his hair.

This may not be what Katelyn expects when I pull in, but I know she won't be mad. We're a family of five and neither of us can be complete without our children. We'll just have to spend a lot of time in my bedroom in Los Angeles. One I don't plan to leave until I'm scheduled to be on the red carpet.

CHAPTER 26 - KATELYN

HE HOLDS MY HAND AS WE RUSH THROUGH LAX. DARK glasses cover both our eyes, and even though he said he wouldn't wear a hat, he is today, but I get it. Now I understand why he suggested we take the red-eye flight. Not only were we alone and not bothered, but everyone is in a rush to exit the airport and get to their early morning appointments. That means no one is stopping and asking for an autograph.

The car I arranged for us is waiting by the curb, as planned. I sigh heavily, thanking whoever is listening. The last thing I need is to screw this up. I've been doing a lot of thinking, and I'm not sure I'm cut out to be their manager, especially since things with Harrison and me have developed into what they are now. I don't want him to give me special treatment, nor would I expect it. Liam already does that to an extent, and I'm afraid there will be too much strain if I was to screw up again. I don't want the band to be in a position where they have to fire me, yet I'll still be hanging around. Maybe I'll become their fanclub President or something equally as demeaning. I don't know what I'll do, but I'll manage. 4225 West is far too important to me to do them wrong.

The driver opens the door when Harrison nods at him. I slide in first, with Harrison's hand on the small of my back, guiding me. He sits next to me and reaches for my hand. He hasn't stopped touching me since we boarded our plane late last night. I'm happy, even though I'd never admit this to Josie, that they took a different flight. Harrison and I got to be a couple without those two making faces or gawking at us.

The way he holds me, the way his fingers dance along my cheek, he makes me feel like I'm the only one he's ever seen. Many stolen kisses and falling asleep in the most awkward position made our flight very memorable, at least for me. I don't know how many women he's flown with and honestly, I'm afraid to know, but I promised myself I'd ask the questions that have been plaguing my mind for a while now. Harrison knows more about me than I do him and that needs to change. If we are going to make this work, we need to be open and honest with each other about everything.

The car lurches through traffic. Harrison points out different landmarks and promises to take me on a hike to show me the famous Hollywood sign.

"You don't live in Hollywood?" I ask. I knew Liam did and assumed Harrison does as well.

"I live in Beaumont," he says, catching me off guard. "I have an apartment here. My sister has been living in it, but she's in New York right now."

Sister? This is exactly what I'm talking about. I don't know him and I want to. What's his favorite color or food? Does he like to sleep in on Saturdays or does he get up with Quinn and watch cartoons?

"But you don't live in Hollywood?"

Harrison shakes his head. He cups my face and presses his lips to mine. "I live in Beaumont," he says again. I understand the meaning behind his words. "But I have a place in Hermosa Beach. There's something about living in the city that doesn't appeal to me."

"How far are you from the ocean?" It's been years since I've seen the ocean and played in the sand.

Harrison pushes his ball cap back and forth and lets out a sigh. "Ms. Powell, are you using me for my beach access?"

I punch him lightly and fall into him. He holds me as the car travels down the highway to his place. A slight sense of dread washes over me. I hope he knows I'm not using him. He's not a rebound or anything like that. I truly enjoy being with him and value what we're building. "I'm not using you."

"I know," he says quietly with his lips pressed to top of my head. "If you walk out the sliding glass door and off the deck, you'll be in the sand. Not sure how many steps it is until you reach the water, but I could text Quinn and ask him."

"That's okay," I say. I play with the ties from his hoodie and think about having him partially naked and wet in the ocean. "We can count our own steps."

"Yeah, I'd like that, Katelyn."

Harrison starts humming the melody from the song he wrote for me. It lulls me into a blissful state. We're existing in this cocoon, neither of us willing to punch through and discuss where we're heading. I'm not sure I can say I'm in this for the long haul, it's far too soon for me to even think about where I'll be next year, but I don't want a fling and I don't want to introduce him as someone special, only for him to bail days or weeks later. Not that I think he would, but there's a lingering fear that I'm not what he wants out of life. I'm a widow with two children and he can have his pick of any woman he wants, why would he want me and my baggage?

"Hey," he says. "We're here." He points, but all I see is a tall apartment complex looming in front of me. I know I'm tired, but I swear he said sand and ocean.

"Um..."

"It's out back. Come on." He takes my hand in his and we slide out of the car. Harrison gives the driver a tip and takes our bags from him. "Follow me," he says as he winks. I have no problem walking behind him, I like to stare at his backside more than I care to admit. I like to stare at him in general. I never thought I'd find him attractive with all this tattoos, but I do. They excite me, and each time we're together, I learn something about one of them. He's a story waiting to be told.

Harrison leads us down cobblestone walkways and through palm trees and shade created by stockade fencing. Most have flower arrangements hanging off of them, creating a nice oasis of tranquility. I try to picture myself walking down this path with a bag of groceries and coming home to Harrison. I can see myself here, but I can't leave Mason. I know he's gone, but in my heart, he's still my Beaumont and I'm not ready to give that up yet.

Before I can catch myself, I'm stumbling into Harrison's back as he's trying to open the door. He turns and shakes his head.

"Here, let me." I take the key from his hand and unlock the door. I push down on the lever and open it. My gasp is loud and unexpected. Harrison chuckles behind me. I don't know what I was expecting, but this isn't it. Everything is white with black and red furniture and fixtures. I take tentative steps in and survey my surroundings. Everyday this man does something to wow me, but I think this really sets him apart. On his back wall – with white curtains billowing in the wind – are large doors that are open to the ocean. The sound of waves crashing onto the beach is so soothing that I could crawl up on his black sofa and sleep for days.

Harrison stands behind me with his hands on my waist. "Would you like a tour?" I nod, unable to find the right words. To think there's more of this beauty wrapped up in an apartment is unthinkable.

He pulls my hand into his and kisses my palm, my wrist. The look he's giving me tells me that he wants to do so much more, and I'm powerless to stop him. We step farther into his place and he shows me the kitchen and small bathroom. Down the hall is Quinn's room, which is decorated in primary colors with a drum set sitting in the corner.

"Does he play?"

"Yeah, and the guitar," Harrison says proudly as he shuts the door.

He shows me another bathroom that he claims is Quinn's and never goes in there. The next is his sister's, he doesn't open her door, and I respect that he's keeping her privacy when she's not home. The last door is his. I know this before he even says anything.

He opens the door wide and steps aside, giving me all the access I need to see another side of him. His bedroom in Beaumont is really no different from what Josie had. He hasn't painted the walls or rearranged the furniture she kept there. But this room, it's all Harrison.

Three of the walls are painted in a mural much like you'd see on his arms. The other wall opens up to the beach. His bed is large and done in white and blue patterns that you'd find yourself staring at for hours to try and figure out. I close my eyes and imagine myself on this bed, nestled deep in the comforter with Harrison's arms wrapped around me. The windows are open with the wind blowing, bringing in the smell of sea salt.

I step in and trail my fingers along the large oak dresser that is stained perfectly. The mirror that sits on top shows my tired reflection, but also shows the bed. My imagination runs wild with Harrison standing before me, getting dressed for practice. I can watch myself trace his tattoos, burning each one into memory.

"This is beautiful," I say, clearly stating my thoughts.

"It's empty." He steps behind me, but doesn't touch me. My skin awaits his caress, yearns for it. Demands it.

"Why?"

"I haven't found someone to fill it until now."

"Yeah?" My voice breaks. If I was curious about where his head is, I'm not now. I turn, brushing against him. I take a deep breath before peering into his smoldering green eyes. He's taken his hat off, much to my enjoyment.

He pulls his lower lip into his mouth and places his hands on my hips. "I've had this whole speech planned for when we got here and were alone, but I've forgotten it all. Seeing you in my room, my house where Quinn and I have lived until we moved to Beaumont, you have no idea what it means to me, or what it does to me."

I push against him and smile. "I know what it does."

He shakes his head and picks up my hand, placing it over his heart. "I want to share this with you and the girls. I know you're thinking it's too soon and maybe it is, but I don't want lines crossed here, Katelyn. I want you to know how I feel. How Quinn feels."

"I can't move." The words break my heart, but if he's expecting me to leave Beaumont, I can't.

"I'm not asking you to move. We could come here for

the summer. Let the girls run on the beach until they're so tired we have to carry them in. You can sit on the deck and read a book. I'll cook our dinner on the grill. Life here is quiet with no expectations."

"And Quinn, what will he do?"

"He'll show the girls how to make the biggest sand castle and teach them to body surf. Everything that we have here, we want to share with you and the girls."

"What about your sister? The one I didn't know you had?"

Harrison moves my hair behind my ear and kisses my nose. "There's a lot we don't know about each other, but can learn. Yvie is a ballet dancer in New York City. She stays here when she's home because I'm not here, but wouldn't be here when we come back."

The James family is beyond talented, and here they are mixing with my mundane family. The only talent I have is for screwing up something as simple as a tour. I know I'm not cut out for the showbiz life, but I'd like to fit into his.

"Can I think about it? I'd like to properly introduce you to the girls if we're going to be serious —" Harrison interrupts me with a deep searing kiss.

"You don't know what those words do to me, baby," he whispers as he grinds into me.

"Yeah, well I think you should show me."

"My pleasure."

Harrison picks me up and sets me down gently on his bed. He hovers over me and just when I think this is going to be wild and unadulterated, he surprises me by taking his time.

CHAPTER 27 - HARRISON

I startle awake and reach for Katelyn. The spot where she laid is empty and the sheets are cool to the touch. The moment I feel the wind tickle my face, I know where I'll find her. I sit up and look out the open door. The sun has already set. I quickly look at the clock on my bedside table and realize we've slept the day away. This isn't how I had planned to spend the day, but I wouldn't trade it for anything.

I sit up and watch her, well the back of her. I wonder how long she's been sitting in the sand, staring at the ocean. I contemplate whether I should bother her or figure out what we're going to eat for dinner. I chide myself for getting carried away earlier. I wanted to show her around, give her a tour, but having her in my room was a dream come true, and there was no way I could pass up the moment of having her in my arms. Having her in my bed is definitely something I plan to do again, repeatedly.

Slipping on my boxers and shorts, I make my way into the kitchen and hope my mom stocked up well. I suppose I could grow up and really start doing everything for myself, but it would be moments like this where I have to call for some type of food delivery and I really want to be alone with Katelyn before band business gets in the way.

The refrigerator is exactly as I expected it. "Thanks, mom," I say out loud, because not only did she fix me up right, but she's given me an idea. I take out what I need and start preparing. I move around the kitchen quickly for fear that Katelyn will come looking for me. Or is it hope? All I know I want to take this to her because she's not expecting it. Just like I didn't expect her to make such an impact on my life.

The sand is warm on my bare feet as I walk toward her. As I get closer, I notice that she's wearing one of my dress shirts. It doesn't even bother me that I know she went into my closet to get it. It's sexy as fuck seeing her in my clothes.

I set down the plate of food I made and sit behind her. She leans against me, her head resting on my shoulder. I could live like this and be happy for the rest of my life. The only thing missing are the kids running around in front of us. They complete us.

I pull the wrap off the plate and pick up a piece of cheese and apple wedge. "I have something for you," I say as I reach around her and place the offering at her lips. She doesn't say anything. She just takes a bite and nuzzles into my neck. I get the feeling that something is wrong, but I'm afraid to ask her what. I'm not sure I'd like the answer if she told me that she doesn't want to spend the summer here or if she's starting to second guess us because of what I said earlier.

I take a few grapes off the vine and feed both of us, alternating between her and me. There are a few surfers out in the water, but for the most part, the beach is deserted right now, which is shocking. I'm not complaining. It gives us more privacy.

"You're not what I thought you'd be," she says as her lips graze my neck. What I am is losing my resolve not to spin her around and watch her come undone from my touch. Her body is the one drumbeat I can't master, but I'll never give up trying. I try not to overthink her statement. I'm not sure I want to know what it means, but leaving it unquestioned will only burn me later.

"Meaning?" I ask as I feed her a strawberry.

Katelyn shrugs. "Everything I thought about you was wrong. I had a list a mile long of reasons why we wouldn't work. First with your tattoos, I assumed the worst. Then there was the woman at the bar when we were in Florida. When I saw that happen, I thought there was no way I'd be able to trust someone like you and wondered how Josie was doing it. I was so standoffish, and yet you come over twice a week to mow my lawn, even though I never asked you to. I kept saying we couldn't be together and now that we are, I can't find a reason for us not to be. If anything, you should hate me for being a bitch to you.

"Here we are, at your gorgeous place that you left to live in Beaumont, and I can't understand why. You're feeding me, and that is definitely something I never expected from you. Hell, it's never even happened to me before. And this afternoon, the way you made love to me..." Katelyn sighs and shakes her head. She leans forward and covers her eyes, hiding from me. I'm not sure what I'm supposed to do here. Everything I've been doing so far, I've done because it felt natural, but right now, I don't know if I'm supposed to reach out and touch her or leave her to sort through her thoughts. Right now, I'm lost and confused. Earlier, things seemed fine, but that's definitely not the case at this moment.

My throat is tight. I clear it a few times, but am unable to find my voice. I'm afraid to move. What if this is not what she wants? I sit like a statue and fight the pressure in my chest. I can't take anymore.

"I don't..." I have to clear my throat again. "I don't know what I'm supposed to say here, Katelyn."

She shakes her head again and stands. My shirt is long enough to over her ass, but I know she's not wearing anything underneath. She turns and takes two steps forward before falling to her knees in front of me. I'm afraid to touch her, even though I'm burning to pull her to me.

"Why do you hide from me?"

I look at her questioningly. "What're you talking about?"

"Is this the real Harrison James sitting in front of me?"

Well, isn't that a loaded question with many possible answers? "What do you want to know?"

"Where are your parents?"

I run my hand through my hair and sigh. I look down the beach and smile. "My mom lives about ten minutes away. I told you earlier that my sister is in New York and my dad – he died when I was four. He was a police officer and was shot in the line of duty by a gang member."

"Harrison," she says my name so quietly, but full of sorrow. Katelyn cups my face, her fingers dancing along my jaw, playing with my scruff.

"It was a long time ago, Katelyn."

"But you were so young." This I was, and I suffered dearly for not having a father figure around and a mom that had to work two jobs to make ends meet. I love my mom more than anything. She had to be not only a mother, but a father, and she tried so hard to make mine and Yve's life the best she could. I need to change the subject before I tell her the horrors of my childhood that will surely send her running for the hills.

"What about you? How was life as an only child?"

Katelyn shrugs and plays with the hair at the nape of my neck. "I had Josie, so it was like having a sister."

"When did you and Mason start dating?"

Katelyn pulls back a little and looks at me. Her head moves from side to side. She pulls her lip in between her teeth. I reach out and pull it out with my thumb and place a kiss where she was biting it.

"You don't have to answer."

"It's not that. Do you really want to know?"

I take this opportunity to pull her into my arms. "He's a part of your life and he's part of the girls' life. I'll never ask you not to talk about him when I'm around. I'll never ask you to stop loving him. If he was here, I'd hate him." I shake my head because that's not true. "No, I probably wouldn't know you if he was here, and for that I'm both thankful and remorseful because his girls are the best, most beautiful girls that I've ever encountered, and I want to do right by not only them, but him too."

Tears begin to roll down her face. I wipe them away before she has a chance to. She stares at me with wet eyes that are breaking my heart. I didn't mean to make her cry, but it's the only way I can get across with how I feel.

"We started dating the summer after freshman year. He was so popular and cute. My mother said he only wanted me for my swimming pool, but that wasn't the case. We all grew up that summer."

"Liam told me a lot about him. Sometimes I feel like I know him, especially when I'm with you and the girls."

Katelyn smiles and curls up in my arms. "Everyone loved him. He was the high school football star who returned to coach the team. He was supposed to go to school with Liam, but changed his mind and gave up a scholarship to the University of Texas to go to the state school with me. I wonder now, had he gone with Liam, if things would be different."

"Like how?"

"I don't know. Would they be in the NFL doing what they loved? Would I be one of those wives you see on television, bitching about her husband or involved in some marital scandal? Nothing went according to plan once we graduated high school."

"And now, you're involved with someone who doesn't fit your norm, sitting on the beach in my dress shirt and about to attend your first red carpet event."

"You wrote me a song."

I can't help but smile. "I did and we are performing it tomorrow night at the awards show."

"I'm your date."

"You are, and from what I've heard, you have a pretty smoking dress that I'm going to want to rip off of you."

She rolls her eyes. "Can I ask you about my job?"

I sigh. I've been hoping to avoid this topic. "Sure," I say.

"I've done a bad job. I let the band down."

I wrap my arms around her and rest my chin on the top of her head. Liam and I haven't sat down and discussed what to do. We were going to wait until after this week was over before we made plans to move forward.

"I think we threw you to the wolves without proper training. It's our fault."

"I think I should quit."

"Why?" I'm caught off-guard by her statement.

"Because if we're together, I need to be away from you."

CHAPTER 28 - KATELYN

"ARE YOU NERVOUS?" HE ASKS AS HIS LIPS FIND MY NOW bare shoulder. The dress I chose for tonight is champagne in color with barely off the shoulder straps. I fell in love with the sweetheart neckline, but it was the back – cut low and swooping – that sold me.

We stand in front of his bedroom mirror. I'm trying to put in my earring and he's trying to take off my dress. If we don't hurry, we'll be late. I know it's expected to be fashionably late for Hollywood events, but the long drive into L.A., together with the traffic will make things worse. I had suggested we leave earlier and get ready at the hotel, but he had other plans for us. I conceded once he showed me what he was talking about.

"Harrison," I say, quietly. I want to look good for him, but he's making it difficult. I don't think he understands the magnitude that tonight holds. The red carpet is something he's accustomed to. For me, it's a night of firsts, and with those firsts come the jitters and extreme anxiety. What if I fall or trip for all of national TV to see?

Harrison sighs heavily and replaces my strap. He takes a step back. I watch him candidly through the mirror, as he looks me up and down. I want to shake my head, but rather like the idea that I turn him on.

"My hand is staying right here all night," he says as he places it on my back, his fingers inching themselves under the fabric. "Yeah, I do believe this dress was made for me."

"Incorrigible," I murmur, adding a wink. He kisses the top of my head before disappearing into the closet. I watch his backside as long as I can, secretly hoping that he'll come back out and hypnotize me once more. It seems that I can't get enough of him and part of me dreads returning to Beaumont and to our lives. In one short day, I learned so much about him and us, maybe this is what we needed from the get-go.

When Harrison steps out, he's dressed in a black and white pin-striped suit. I honestly didn't know what he'd wear. I've never seen him out of his shorts and classic t-shirts and felt incredibly awkward asking him, but figured it wouldn't matter, because he's beautiful enough to pull anything off. I am pleasantly surprised, however, to find out he isn't wearing a tux. I know he'll be wearing one for Liam and Josie's wedding; and as stupid as it may sound, I want that to be the first time I see him in one.

He comes over and stands next to me. I watch him do up his tie, and can't help but think of Mason and the countless times I tied his. He never could grasp how to make the knot look just right. I didn't mind and I'm hoping that Harrison has some trouble so I can help him. Sadly for me, he masters it perfectly on the first try.

I slide in front of Harrison and brush some imaginary lint off his shoulders, anything to touch him to straighten out his already straight tie. I'm being sentimental, I know. I can't help myself. I miss this part of Mason. Harrison stands there, I can feel him staring as I pinch the silk. I sweep my hands over his chest and shoulders, clasping his hands with mine.

"There, now you're perfect," I whisper for my own benefit.

He leans down and crushes his lips to mine, pushing me hard against the dresser. His hands slide down my sides and over to my ass as he picks me up. He sets me down on the dresser, urgently. My dress pushes up as he pulls me the edge where he stands. My legs are spread, welcoming him. He moves against me, rubbing up and down.

Teasing me.

Testing me.

He knows the decision is up to me. He doesn't care if he walks the red carpet, but I care enough for him and the band. I won't be the Yoko Ono of 4425 West.

"The car... shortly." I can barely speak, let alone string together a complete sentence. Harrison smiles against my mouth, enjoying the torment he's bestowed upon me. I try to push him away, but my fingers have a different idea and find themselves entwined in his hair. It's already been styled with wax, so I can't do any damage.

He grinds against me, making it impossible for me to say no. My fingers seek out the buttons on his vest, then his shirt. I start at the bottom and work my way up. I throw his tie over his shoulder and unbutton the rest of his shirt. My lips are blazing a trail down his chest. I pull hard on his nipple ring just as he pushes up my dress and rips my panties off, the ones I bought especially for tonight.

"I'll go fast," he says, dropping his pants. He slams into

me once before pulling out. His green eyes are blazing, a fiery pit of lust. I hitch my knees over his hips, holding onto him as he thrusts again. I moan as he fills me instantly. He grips my ass as his knees bang into the drawers. The dresser has become our own earthquake as we shake the contents onto the floor. The mirror bangs, loudly, against the wall.

"Harrison," I say breathlessly, as he moves with such fluidity. He pulls away from my neck, his hand coming up under my knee. His other hand pushes my dress up more. I watch his eyes as they bear down on us. He watches himself as he rocks, working to reach his peak.

"Fuck, baby," he grits out. His head falls back. His movements are faster, harder. I lean back, my head rubbing against the wall and let out a sound I didn't know I had in me. He looks at me and smiles, pulling me up to his chest. I meet his thrusts eagerly as we ride out our orgasms together.

He kisses me deeply, cupping my face. I love that he holds me to him when he kisses me, afraid that I'll disappear if I'm not in his hands. The doorbell sounds, causing me to pull back. I'm afraid of what I look like now. Ripped panties, a bunched up dress and hair that is surely messed up. I don't want to look, but know I'll need a few minutes to get ready.

He kisses me again before stepping away. He pulls up his pants, but doesn't bother with the buttons on his shirt as he leaves the room. I slide off the dresser, tentatively. My legs are shaky, my knees locked. I take a deep breath and turn around. My mouth drops as I lean forward and observe my red swollen lips. My mascara is smudged from the light sheen of sweat on my face. My hair – I want to cry – but thankfully it's fixable. I stand up and look at myself, shaking my head.

"I guess I know what it means to be thoroughly fucked."

"I say we stay home and do it again."

I follow his voice and realize I want to cry out in agony. He stands there with his hand in his pocket, leaning against the door jam. His shirt is still unbuttoned and now his tie is undone as well. He looks delicious, edible.

I have to tear my eyes away, demand that I focus on anything but him. He's a temptation. A risk.

He's my reward.

I bypass him without a second glance. He chuckles and even though I smile, it frustrates me that he has that much power over me. When did I let this happen? I shouldn't question myself. I'm done doing that. I'm where I want to be.

THE CAR DOOR FINALLY OPENS. The screams are deafening. We are in between Liam and Jimmy's cars. I understand why we couldn't ride together, something about making an entrance. Harrison kisses me quickly before he steps out. He stands by the door and extends his hand, waiting for me to grab hold of it. His name, along with Liam and Jimmy's are yelled loudly. The guys stand together and chat, pointing at some of the fans. When they do that, they erupt. Josie and I stand behind them, both of us mocking Jimmy's date. She looks bored and only half dressed, and leaves no doubt in my mind that what Harrison I did before we left, they did in the car on the way here.

The guys walk over to the fans that are barricaded by a steel fence, each one of them starting in a different location and moving down the line as phones and pens are shoved in their faces. They sign everything and pose in the most awkward ways, but do so with a permanent grin.

"You know, I'm surprised you're not at the hotel with us." Josie moves closer, away from Jimmy's date so we can talk. Even in my four-inch heels I have to look up to see her.

"Harrison has a place on the beach. I'm staying there."

Josie nods and tries to hide her grin. She looks at the guys, then back at me. "Are things good?"

"Things are great." I never thought I'd be in a position to say that about my life, but I can, especially with how I feel about Harrison. If having a little bit of bliss can make me feel good about things, then so be it. I'm going to embrace it. Soak it in and hopefully share it with my children.

"Harrison looks really happy, Katelyn. That's because of you." I give him a once over and smile when he leans in for a picture with a fan. If things hadn't changed with us, I'd be wondering which one he'd want to take back to his place tonight. But I know after everything that has happened since we arrived in Los Angeles, that he only has eyes for me.

"We'll see," I say. "I'm trying not to get my hopes up. Everything, right now, seems too good to be true."

Josie nods. "I felt the same way about Liam, but you have to let your heart lead you. No one is saying that you need to run off to Vegas and get married, just be happy and have fun."

"Speaking of... What's our plan?"

Josie's eyes light up. We're now going to talk about her favorite subject. "Tonight we have a music industry party to go to, and tomorrow we're going to just hang out and sight-see, but tomorrow night is when the fun will begin."

"What kind of fun?" I ask, but Josie's not paying attention to me. She's watching the guys as they walk across the road to where the red carpet starts. Liam veers toward us, but Harrison doesn't. I try not to let it hurt my feelings. It's not like we can hold hands or anything, the kids are watching.

Harrison turns just as I step forward to follow Josie and Liam. His expression is unreadable. I can't really tell if he's happy or not right now, even though he's grinning from ear to ear. I surmise that it's an act and that he really wants to be someplace else right now and I'm going to agree with my assumption, because I'd give anything to have his hand in mine.

The moment the guys reach the media section, they are ushered to a radio station. Microphones are pushed into their faces and questions are fired off.

"How was your tour, Liam?" A sense of dread washes over me. Josie grabs my hand and gives me a squeeze. I lean a little closer to hear his answer.

"The tour was great. We took the kids and made it a vacation." I exhale heavily, thankful that he didn't tell the disc jockey what a colossal fuck up the tour was.

"How's the new album?"

"It's coming together nicely. It should be out by Christmas."

"I hear you're debuting a new song tonight?"

"We are, Harrison wrote it."

"What's it about, Harrison?"

He looks around everywhere except at me. I wait with bated breath for his answer. He runs his hand through his hair twice before he opens his mouth to answer. "I met someone and she's very special to me. I wrote it for her."

"Well, we're looking forward to hearing it. Thanks, guys."

Just like that, they're dismissed. The guys step away and maneuver through the crowd. The flashes are instant. Their names are yelled. It's very disorientating. I don't even know how they know where to start. I have a feeling this was supposed to be my job. Yet, another reason why I can't be their manager. I don't know what I'm doing.

Josie and I stand in the middle of the red carpet, watching the guys as they go from photographer to photographer. They pose for individual pictures and group photos. We follow behind, content with being observers.

Harrison brushes by me and gives me a look. I'm not sure if I should follow or stay where I am. He steps up to a reporter and kisses her on the cheek. I instinctively step toward them and try to hear what they're saying. I know I shouldn't, but I can't help myself.

"Harrison, you're looking good," she says this in a tone that I don't like. She's too sugary for me when she should be professional.

"Thanks, Emily, so are you."

They're on a first name basis and it makes me wonder how well they know each other. I know I have no right to be jealous, but I am. All these people know this Harrison better than I do. She's not asking him any questions and whatever he just said to her made her laugh. I roll my eyes when she throws her head back and her hand lands on his chest.

"Who finally captured your heart?"

Harrison looks at me. I try to smile, but I don't succeed. He looks down at ground as he puts his hands in his pocket. I want to know what he's thinking, but don't dare step forward and ask him. "She's someone special."

I step away as quickly as I can. I don't want to hear what else he has to say. This was a mistake. I should've stayed back at the hotel and let him do his thing tonight. This scene is not for me and I don't know how Josie can handle it.

Easily, I decide when I see her. She's standing with Liam and giving an interview while I stand in the middle of this big production with Jimmy's one-night stand.

CHAPTER 29 - HARRISON

THE MOMENT I LOOK OVER EXPECTING HER TO BE
there, she's not. In fact, she looks like she doesn't want to be
here or with me. I know it's my fault because I'm an idiot. I
panicked after I got out of the car and couldn't recover fast
enough. I forgot how to act around her. Putting my feelings
aside, she's my friend and I failed to treat her as such.

"I gotta go," I say to Emily, skipping out on her guaranteed interview. Emily and Yvie have been friends for years
and I've always interviewed with her, tonight being the
exception. My head hangs in shame when I step away from
the media line and stalk toward the retreating Katelyn.
She's far enough down the line, standing with Josie that she
doesn't know I'm coming.

"Come with me," I say close to her ear. I don't give her
an opportunity to say no. I place my hand on her back; the
same spot I deemed mine earlier and lead her through
the crowd.

Members of the media and fans yell my name, trying to
get my attention. I hate ignoring my name being called.
This is my job and I love it, but right now, she's far more

WE DIDN'T TELL the girls that we've been nominated for best single with *Painkillers*. Once it was known that Liam was off the market, the song shot up the charts. When we were told, we decided to keep it a secret.

I pull Katelyn's hand into mine as soon as the presenters step onto the stage. Clips are shown of the nominees and when 4225 West is shown, the girls gasp loudly. Katelyn turns to me, her eyes full of excitement. I wink and fight the urge to lean over and kiss her.

"And the award for Best Single goes to... 4225 West!"

This is not our first award, but right now, it feels like it. Everyone is cheering, but I tune them all out and focus on Katelyn. I lean over and kiss her not once, but twice. I know I just told her that I wanted to be able to tell the kids, but this moment called for it and I don't want any lingering questions about how I feel dancing around in her mind.

We stand and man-hug each other before walking to the podium. Liam is handed the trophy as he steps to the microphone. He looks at it and shakes his head.

"Who knew that being such a fuck up would win us best single," Liam says earning him a solid round of clapping. "There are really only two people I have to thank for inspiring *Painkillers*. The first being my buddy, Mason; had he not left us so early, I wouldn't be standing here; and the other is Josie. I needed to find a way to show you what I was feeling when we weren't together. I have to thank Harrison and JD for helping make it the hit that it's been."

The warning music comes on, causing us all to laugh. Liam holds the trophy up and says, "this is for our kids; Noah, Quinn, Elle and Peyton, we love you and we'll be home soon."

We walk off stage and are ushered to the green room to get ready for our performance. The room is busy, but relaxing. Liam is being interviewed and that's fine by me. It gives me a chance to take off my jacket and loosen my tie. I'm tempted to change, but failed to bring extra clothes with me. My mind was definitely someplace else earlier.

Loud clapping catches my attention. I turn and instant dread washes over me as Sam stalks toward us. I turn away from her, determined to ignore her, but she steps in front of me, brushing her breasts against my chest.

"What are you doing here?" Liam asks from behind me. I roll my eyes and move away from her. I have no history with her other than the fact that I can't stand her.

"This is an industry event, is it not?"

Sam steps closer to Liam. He moves back a step, keeping space between them.

"What, no kiss hello?"

"Why the fuck would I kiss you?" Liam asks. I have a feeling this is going to get ugly very quickly.

"Because you know you need me."

Liam shakes his head. "I don't need shit from you."

"Well we both know that's not true." She runs her long, red dagger of a fingernail along his jacket. He bats her hand away, but that doesn't stop her from moving closer. Liam sidesteps and comes to stand by me. I hope he doesn't think I'll protect him from her. On second thought, I wouldn't mind slapping the bitch a few times.

"4225 West's contract with Moreno Entertainment has been severed, Sam. You no longer work for us."

"We can fix that easily enough. The band needs me, as evidenced by your failed tour. Besides, you and I have unfinished business."

Liam runs his hands over his face in frustration. I look at JD, who is shaking his head.

"How do you know about our tour?" I ask.

Sam shrugs. "I have my sources."

"Called DeVon," JD adds sourly.

I watch her face for any sign that she was behind the double booking, but she's stoic, mechanical even.

Liam's face turns red. He steps toward her with his finger directed at her face. "I'm going to find out if it was you, and so help me, I'll sue the shit out of your company."

"Is that going to be before or after you tell your little wifey that you knocked me up? Or should I tell her?"

Liam screams, his hands curling into fists in frustration. "You fucking bitch, I'll —"

"4225 West you're needed on stage."

Our name is called before Liam can finish his sentence, which I'm very thankful for. I have a feeling the ending would be a threat that Sam would make sure he paid for. JD pushes Liam away from a laughing Sam and out the door toward the stage.

Liam is worked up, agitated. I set my hands on his shoulders to try and calm him down. "You gotta block it out. We have to perform."

"I'm going to kill her."

I know, I want to say, but I don't. "She's grasping at anything to hang onto you. You can either tell Josie or wait Sam out. My suggestion is to tell Josie, because hearing it from you is going to be a lot easier than hearing it from Sam."

"She'll hate me."

"For what? You weren't together. It's not like she wasn't planning on marrying someone else."

"Besides, you gave her Noah, so, happy days, it's a win-win for her," JD adds. I look at him and shake my head.

"Jesus, JD, where do you come up with this shit?"

He shrugs and downs a bottle of water just as we're told we can go on stage now because it's a commercial break.

"You good?"

Liam nods, but I know he's not. He walks on stage slowly and picks up his guitar. He's going through the motions, but something's missing. He's back to being the Liam Page of old.

"Hey, Page," I yell from my stool. He turns and looks at me.

"Do you have this or what, because my girl is out there and we're about to show the world this song and if you fuck it up, I'm going to be pissed."

He looks at me for a minute before answering. "Yeah, I got this."

He fucking better or I'm going to be pissed.

We get the cue that we're back on TV and that the presenter has just announced us. I bang my sticks together four times, one for each kid watching from home, and bring my sticks down on the drums to start us off. As soon as the spotlight is on us, Liam Page is wooing the crowd like he's been known to do. I wish I could see Katelyn and watch her face as Liam sings about her, but it's impossible to see anything with all these lights.

JD plays out the last riff much to the crowds delight. When the lights go down, I can finally see again. I have to blink through the black spots, but it's nice not to be blinded. We go back to the green room to get something to drink and freshen up. We have to look somewhat decent when the camera pans over us.

"You okay?" I ask Liam as he sits down.

"Yeah, I'm just stressing and Josie is going to know something's wrong."

I sit down next to him and polish off a couple of bottles

an unlimited tab and nowhere to be for two days. The only thing missing, at least for me, is Harrison. After skipping the planned after party and being in his arms all night, the last thing I wanted to do was leave.

I was shocked when Liam and Harrison presented us with a spa package. At first, I was hurt because I wanted to spend time with Harrison, but when he said they were heading back to have some "dad" time with our kids, I conceded. It was when he said *our*, I realized I wanted to give him a chance to bond with the girls.

Josie and I said good-bye to the guys at the hotel and were promptly whisked away in a black stretch limousine that was stocked with fresh fruit, cheese and champagne. If this is Liam's idea of a bachelorette party, we need to have a few more of these.

The woman bends and starts rifling through her bag. The lifeguard bends too, but clearly for other purposes. He rubs his chin with his forefinger and thumb while he openly gawks at her ass. I swear she shakes it for him, but can't be certain.

"What are you doing?" Josie asks. I look at her briefly before turning my full attention back to the cougar and her prey.

"I can't help it, it's like a train wreck waiting to happen."

Josie lets out a bellowing laugh and throws a pillow at me. She almost hits my drink, earning her a nice glare. No kids, no responsibility; I'm going to relax and have fun.

"I bet it's common around here."

"What's that?" I ask.

"Women like that." Josie nods to the cougar. "She's probably married to some B-list actor or some Hollywood exec and she's lonely. She won't cheat with the pool boy at her house, but will definitely come to the spa and hook-up."

"Did you just make that up in your head, or is it something you've read in one of your novels?"

Josie shrugs. "I've thought about it a lot actually. Wondering what I would be like if Liam took me with him when he left?"

"Shit happens for a reason, Josie."

"I know, but I wonder about things all the time and even more so since he dropped a colossal bomb last night."

I sit up and face her. Her eyes drop and her finger spins her engagement ring back and forth. I look down at my hand, now bare, but still harboring a faint tan line. I took my rings off after Harrison kissed me the first time. I didn't want to, but felt that I was cheating on my love for Mason, or close to it with the feelings I was having toward him. It saddens me to be without my rings, but Harrison deserves my finger to be free of something he didn't place there.

"What did Liam say to you?"

Josie fiddles with the tie on her swimsuit. I look over my shoulder at the cougar, apparently my subconscious doesn't want to miss anything. It's like a bad soap opera playing out on a live stage. I turn back, raising my eyebrow to let her know I'm waiting.

"I can't be mad at him, but I can be hurt."

"Josephine Preston, what in the blue hell are you talking about?"

"Liam and Sam."

I shake my head, not understanding where she's going with this.

"When they were together, she got pregnant."

My mouth drops open, slowly. Josie doesn't look at me, but her eyes gaze over the pool before dropping her hands back to her lap.

"Liam told me he doesn't have any children other than Noah."

"He doesn't, she miscarried."

"Wow! I'm... I don't know what to say," I reply. I sit back and resume my position. My daiquiri sits half full. I pick it up and take a long pull through the straw.

"He was using her for sex. He said he never wanted to have kids with anyone but me. When she told him, he freaked out. She wanted to get married and already had a nanny picked out. He left her and then she called him to say she had miscarried."

"I'm calling bullshit. Look how shady Sam is. I bet she wasn't even pregnant, just trying to trap him."

"Doesn't matter," Josie says solemnly.

"You're right, it doesn't because in a month, you're going to marry him and as petty as this sounds, you had his baby before she did, so you win."

Josie looks up and smiles. "I win."

"Yeah, Josie, you win." I signal to the waiter as he passes by. He takes our empty glasses with promises of his imminent return with more fruity drinks. "She's on the move." I nod toward the cougar. She's picked up her bag and is walking in the opposite direction of the lifeguard.

"He's probably on lunch."

"Or he needs to check in with his mom," I say biting back laughter.

"That could be Noah someday, can you imagine? He's acting more and more like Liam and it scares me."

"He's just testing you, I'm sure."

"I hope you're right."

Am I? Who am I to give parenting advice? I know there's something bothering Peyton, but I'm not sure if it's still Mason or something else. Since school has started she's been more withdrawn and not willing to engage in anything. Aside from watching Noah play football, she sits in her room facing her wall and it's like I have to force her to be social. Dr. Brooks says it will pass, but I'm not sure how long I'm supposed to wait until I can comfortably start freaking out that my kid is walking around like a zombie.

I lose sight of the cougar when the waiter arrives with our drinks. I hold the ice-cold glass in my hand, using it to cool down while I search for her. I don't know what my fascination is with her, but she intrigues me. How does one decide to flirt with a lifeguard, or anyone else for that matter? I failed miserably at it with Harrison, and if it wasn't for his persistent pursuit, I'd be alone right now.

"Hello?"

I choke on my drink when the cougar speaks to us. I hit my chest, trying to clear my airway. I can hear Josie next to me trying to stifle a laugh.

"Hi," Josie says for the both of us. I set my drink down and covertly wipe my mouth with my towel. I must look like a complete fool.

"Mind if I join you?" Josie and I share a glance, both of us conveying 'what the hell'. Really? We are in a private cabana and she wants to join us. What about all the general population of chaise lounges that are poolside?

"Sure," Josie says. I want to whack her upside her head.

The cougar sits down on my chaise, setting her over-sized bag down on the ground. Now that I can see her more clearly, my earlier assumption of her age is far off. The woman sitting on the edge of my chaise is young, mid-twenties I'm guessing, but she's been weathered, as my mother would say, one too many trips in the tanning bed. "So, I'm Alicia." She extends her hand to Josie and then to me. We shake, and I offer up the fakest smile

We aren't given an opportunity to respond before she steps out of the cabana and disappears. Josie comes over to me and wraps her arms around me. I sob into her shoulder. I knew everything with him was going to fall apart. Everything seemed to fit into place far too easily for us. It was too good to be true. I was right to second-guess my feelings for him. I should've listened to my head when it was screaming at me to stay away from him, but he assured me that we were solid.

He lied.

CHAPTER 31 - HARRISON

I'm bored.

I spin on my stool like I used to do with Quinn when he was little, waiting for inspiration to strike. Liam is at 'work'. He forgot, in all his infinite wisdom, that it takes at least two people to run Josie's store, so he's working with Jenna for the next couple of days.

And I sit here, bored. The kids are in school. JD stayed in L.A. I came to work to get my mind off Katelyn and her not being here, but it's not working. All I can think about after waking up next to her, is that being alone only solidifies my desire to be a part of her life. I'm not sure what step is next, except for telling the kids. But after that, what happens next? I know that I need to see her every day to feel alive. I just don't know what she wants or needs. I plan to find out, though.

I pull my ringing phone out of my pocket. My heart starts beating faster thinking its Katelyn. I look at the unfamiliar number and hope soars.

"Hello?"

"Mr. James?"

I feel as if my heart suddenly stops beating. The voice on the other end is not Katelyn. I should've known better. We may be sharing ourselves intimately, but we have yet to talk on the phone, and I was hoping that would be rectified.

"Yes?"

"This is Mr. Lumsden, Principal at Beaumont Elementary —"

"Is Quinn okay?" I blurt out before he has a chance to tell me why he's calling.

"Yes and no. I need you to come down and meet with me. When can you be here?"

"I'm on my way." I press end and pocket my phone. I bump into my drums as I move out from behind them. I knew public school was a bad choice, but my mom assured me Quinn would do well.

I take the stairs two at time and run to my car. I take a deep breath before starting it. My phone goes off again. I hit answer without even looking at it.

"What are you doing right now?" Liam asks.

I pull out of his driveway and head toward the school. "I'm heading to school. Something's wrong with Quinn."

"Oh boy," Liam says. "Listen, the Principal just called and said that Peyton needs to come home. Josie and I are her standby when Mr. Powell can't get the girls, and he's not home. I'll let them know you're picking her up. I believe Katelyn added you to the list."

My heartbeat picks up again. "We should call Katelyn."

"No, we shouldn't. She needs this vacation and he didn't say what was wrong, so it might be nothing. Just go get her and take her back to the house."

He hangs up before I have a chance to say anything. I try not to think about what both of them could've done for the principal to call, but I'm about to find out. I pull into the parking lot and take the closest spot I can find. I'm not sure my feet even hit the pavement as I run into the school and into the office.

"Dad!"

I spin around and find Quinn and Peyton sitting in chairs along the wall. Both of them have their backpacks sitting on the floor. I give Quinn a good hard look. He stands and shakes his head.

"It doesn't hurt," he says, stepping closer.

"You have a black eye."

"It's my fault," Peyton says quietly.

"No it's not, Peyton, stop saying that." Quinn says through gritted teeth. Peyton looks like she's about to cry, which spurs my desire to be there for her. She crosses her arms and looks away from me.

I put my hand on Quinn's shoulder and give it a light squeeze. "Go sit down, I'll find out what's going on, okay?"

"You'll be mad."

I sigh and nod. "Thanks for the warning, buddy."

I walk back to the counter and announce myself to the woman behind the counter.

"You can go in and see Mr. Lumsden now."

I remember the days I would spend in the principal's office, waiting for my mom to come and get me. The first few times I would get into trouble, grounded. But those quickly stopped and all she would do is cry. I couldn't stop her tears, no matter how hard I tried.

I knock once and open the door. I'm anxious and want to get the kids out of here. The principal stands and shakes my hand. We both sit. He makes a teepee with this fingers and acts like he's thinking about what he needs to tell me.

"Mr. James, there is never an easy way to say this, but your son has been in a fight."

"How'd you know it was her?" he asks, his face full of shock.

"Good guess," I say, trying to bite back the smile forming.

"She doesn't want anyone to know."

I nod. "Okay," I say respecting their bond. "I want to talk to her though, so can you go get her for me?"

Quinn reluctantly gets down from the stool and walks to the door. "I'm sorry, dad."

"I know, buddy." He exits, leaving the door open. I take these few moments to think about what I can do to help Peyton. Probably not much, but we are more alike than she'll want to accept. I don't even know what I can tell Katelyn without her freaking out and coming home early. She needs this vacation, but if her daughter is being bullied at school, she needs to know so she can deal with it.

Peyton appears out of thin air. I didn't even hear her come down the stairs. She stands in the doorway with her arms crossed over her chest. Now that I know what's going on, this stance makes sense. She's protecting herself and that breaks my heart.

"Want to come in?"

She shakes her head no.

"Okay," I say. I move my stool closer to her and sit down. "We can talk right here."

She drops her eyes to the floor. Either she really hates me, or she's embarrassed. I'm going to go with a bit of both just to cushion my ego.

"Do you want to tell me what happened today?"

"You're not my dad."

"No, I'm not and I'm not trying to be, but I want to be your friend, Peyton, if you'll let me."

"I have Noah and Quinn."

"You do," I agree. "They're some pretty great friends, aren't they?"

"Yes."

"Can I tell you a story?"

Peyton shrugs and still avoids making eye contact with me. So I start my story in hopes that she'll understand that I've been through the same things she's going through now.

"When I was four, I lost my dad. On the day he died, he kissed me goodnight and went to work. When I woke up, my mom was crying and she told me that he was gone. I didn't know what that meant until we had his funeral. I was too young to understand that my life had just changed, that everything I knew was going to go away. I had to move from my big house with all my toys and friends that I played with every day, to a very small apartment and was only allowed to bring a few things. A year later when I started school, I was scared because I didn't know anyone. My friends were all going to a different school. I was alone and some of the other kids picked up on that. They would pull my hair or make fun of my clothes. They would say hurtful things about my dad and laugh at me when I would cry. This didn't stop until I graduated high school and no longer had to see those people.

"If you're being bullied, I can help you. I don't want to know who is doing it because there's no use in talking to his parents. Besides, you're more important to me than some idiot kid who thinks it's funny to make fun of people. People like him will get nowhere in life."

Peyton finally looks at me. I don't know what I said, but whatever it was I'm thankful. I reach forward and wipe away her tears.

"Do you want to know what I used to do when I was younger to get rid of all my anger?"

"What?" her tiny, broken voice asks.

"Come here, I'll show you." I get up and move JD's stool back to where it was and walk over to my drums. Peyton stands next to me. I pull her closer, lifting her up on to my lap. I thought for sure she'd balk and run away, but she doesn't. I place a drumstick in each hand. She looks at me questioningly.

"Do you know what the mean kid looks like?"

"Uh-huh."

"Good. Now picture his face on the drum and hit it."

Peyton does, but only taps the drum.

"No, Peyton. I want you to hit it hard. Let it all out on my drums. You can't hurt them, so don't even worry about that right now."

Peyton hits the drum again, but barely.

"Is that all you got?" I ask. I pull another set of sticks out and hit the drum hard. I do this over and over again, saying things that make me angry. Peyton tries again, this time much harder. We take turns hitting the drums until she has both sticks pounding down. I sit there, holding her steady in my lap so she doesn't fall forward.

When she's done, she drops the sticks and turns in my lap. Her face is red and puffy from tears and it breaks my heart to see her going through so much pain.

"I'm so sorry, Peyton, no one deserves this much pain."

"Your daddy went to heaven too?"

"He did."

"Did you cry?"

"I did. He was my best friend."

"So was my daddy."

"I know." I pull her into a hug and she squeezes me as hard as she can. I don't know if this is a turning point for us or not, but right now, I'm willing to accept whatever she needs to dish out, whether it's good or bad. "You can come down here anytime you want."

"You won't be mad?"

I shake my head. "No, not at all."

She turns and picks up the sticks and taps them down a few times. She touches the cymbal and laughs at the different noises it makes.

"Harrison?"

"Yeah, sweetie?"

"Will you teach me to play?"

My heart soars with relief. I try not to think too much into what she's asking, but if this is a way for us to connect, I'm running with it.

"Anything for you, Peyton."

me. He's a lying bastard, a cheater, and I don't have time for him in my life."

"Katelyn, just listen to me for a minute." She stands and places her glass and the wine bottle on the nightstand. She kneels, taking my empty hand in hers. "I'm not saying anything to defend anyone, but I think you need to look at this with clear eyes."

"I am," I bark out.

"You're not. Something isn't adding up. Liam wouldn't lie to me, and he's told me many times that Quinn's mom is out of the picture —"

"Well, obviously Harrison is lying to Liam."

"Oh Katelyn," she says shaking her head. She stands and takes my wine glass from me. "I'll call the airline and have our flight switched." She's closed my door before I can respond.

I never thought in a million years that my best friend would take the side of a man who just ripped my heart out.

NOTHING about my trip to California will ever make sense. The way Harrison treated me, the way he made love to me like I was the most precious person to him, and the way he told me that he wanted the world to know I had stolen his heart – all lies. He played me like he plays his drums, with perfection.

We're a day early, and I know there will be questions. I'm neither ready nor willing to answer them. Josie drops me off in my driveway. I stand there while she pulls away. I stare at Mason's truck, then my car. The girls' toys have been picked up and the lawn mowed, probably for the last time this fall.

I drag my suitcase behind me and slide my key into the lock. Twisting the knob, I push the door open. I hate coming home to a dark house, but no one knows we're back yet. I asked Josie not to say anything to Liam. I don't want Harrison anywhere near me. It's not that I need time to think. I just need time to compose what I'm going to say to him.

I flip on the switch. My lower lip quivers as my hand covers my mouth. Hot tears stream down my face. A *Welcome Home Mommy* banner hangs in my living room. There are flowers everywhere and a wrapped present on the table. I wipe my face angrily. Why did he do this? I touch the hand painted letters one by one. The girls have painted their names in the corner. I'm so tempted to take it down, but I can't. It will break their hearts not to see it up tomorrow when we come home.

The slamming of a car door alerts me to his presence. Of course he'd be at Liam's house. It was stupid to come home early. I should've stayed in Los Angeles by myself to figure this shit out.

The door is open and he's there before I have a chance to lock it.

"What's wrong?" he asks. I want to scream at the top of my lungs that he's what's wrong, but I don't. I shrug and look away.

"Katelyn?"

I can smell his cologne the closer he gets. He's tentative, moving with caution. Maybe Alicia called and told him about our little run-in. Sure funny how she knew where to find us.

"I met your girlfriend at the spa."

"I don't have a girlfriend," he says, stopping his assent toward me. "I mean other than you."

"I'm not your girlfriend."

"What's going on, Katelyn?" he asks again. This time he steps behind me, placing his hands on my shoulders.

"Don't touch me," I roar as I spin around. I place my hands on his chest and push. He stumbles briefly before catching himself.

Harrison looks at me with confusion. God, he should get a fucking Oscar for this performance. I want to rip his hat off and throw it away, but I don't want to touch him. I don't even want to look at him right now.

He looks at me, his eyes glistening. I can't look at him. I shake my head and turn away. "You need to leave."

"Why?" he asks. His tone is uncertain, questioning.

"Because I said so, I don't want you here anymore."

"Please, Katelyn, I'm freaking out here. You're home early and something is clearly wrong."

"Like you don't already know. Did you have this planned from the beginning? Seduce the poor, single mom who just lost her husband? Was that your plan? Why don't you tell me how it's supposed to end, so I know what I should expect?"

Harrison rubs his hands over his face. He takes off his hat and throws it on the couch. He crouches and fingers the ribbon on the present sitting on the table. He's too calm for me right now. Why isn't he fighting for me?

"Baby —"

"I'm not your baby," I reply, grinding my teeth together.

Harrison stands and comes over to me, backing me against the wall. "I don't know what the hell has changed your mind, but you need to tell me what the fuck is going on here, Katelyn. Josie showed up bawling her fucking eyes out and you're not with her. In fact, you're supposed to be at the fucking spa getting pampered and shit, but you're here and

something is wrong. So tell me, God damn it, so I can fix it."
His voice is soft and caring, but I know he's doing this on
purpose. This is the way he got me into this bed.

"I met Alicia."

Harrison's face turns pale and to stone. He straightens
and backs away from me. Now that he knows I know, he has
nothing to say. He stands there, not staring at me, but the
wall behind me.

"How would you even know who she is?"

I shrug, "I didn't, she found me," I reply sarcastically.

"How?"

"I don't know, Harrison, I'm assuming you paid for her
day at the spa too."

Harrison shakes his head. His finger starts playing with
his lip. He looks at me, his eyebrows squished together. "I
haven't spoken to Alicia since she walked out of my apartment, you know that."

"No," I yell as I step forward with my finger pointing at
his chest. "I know the lie. I know the stories you told me to
get me into bed, to get me to trust you. The sad-single-dad
whose girlfriend walked out on him and their baby."

"She wasn't my girlfriend, Katelyn. I've told you this."

"You lied!"

"About what?" he roars. He throws his arms up in the
air in exasperation. "Why the hell do I need to lie about that
shit? Do you think it makes me proud that I was fucking
drugged and raped by a groupie and produced a son that I
didn't fucking want? What purpose does that serve me?"

"I saw pictures," I yell louder. "You kissed her on the
red carpet." I lift my chin higher in defiance. "You played
me for a fool and I won't allow it anymore."

"I'm so fucking confused right now, Katelyn. I sent you
to the spa to get pampered and you think I sent Alicia there

too? That I'm having some torrid affair with the mother of my child, whom I haven't seen since he was born? And what... am I keeping Quinn from her too?"

"Oh, I'm sure Quinn sees his mother all the time. It just proves to me why you won't kiss me in front of him."

Harrison rakes his hands over his face and lets out a groan. He shakes his head and wipes wildly at his eyes. For some reason, it breaks my heart that he's crying and it shouldn't.

"Katelyn, I don't know what happened at that spa, but I can tell you there are no pictures of me and Alicia, unless they are from the night Quinn was conceived —"

"I have them," I say as I go over to my bag. I pull them out, disgusted that I'm even touching them. I drop them at his feet. I don't want him to touch me, to pull me into his arms. I don't think I can handle that.

He bends and picks them up. He flips through each one before throwing them down on the table.

"You know..." he shakes his head before putting his hands in his pockets. "I'm in love with you, but I see now that it's not going to matter." He bites the inside of his cheek and lets a tear drop. "You believe the lies over me, and that's fine. I told you I thought you were naive when it came to the industry, and this just proves me right. If you can't trust me, this will never work. I just wish I found out sooner."

He picks up the pictures again and hands them back to me. "I want you to really look at those and tell me why she's wearing the same fucking dress you were. And tell me how someone that is about five foot seven without heels doesn't even come up to my shoulder."

I don't take the photos from him. He lets them drop to the floor. My eyes follow them as they scatter all over. Of course he'd buy her the same dress I wore so he could use it as an excuse.

"I don't know how she found you, but I'm so fucking sorry that she did. You don't deserve this and frankly, neither do I. I haven't been with another woman since the night I met you at Liam's. I'm not going to stand here and try to fight for something you don't believe in. I have a feeling I'll be wasting my breath."

I take a chance to look at him and wish I hadn't. He doesn't bother to wipe away his tears. I hate that he's crying, but he deserves it for what he's done to me.

When he moves toward the door, I don't try to stop him. I won't. I need to close this chapter and move on. The door opens, letting in a gust of wind.

"If you don't believe me, ask Quinn. He's never met his mother, he'll tell you that."

I scoff. "I can't believe you would drag your son into this."

Harrison stalks over to me. "I wouldn't, but you're leaving me no choice, Katelyn. You'd rather believe her fucking lies than me. The man you've given yourself to. The man you said you'd try with. This isn't fucking trying. This is bailing. You're looking for any damn excuse to shut me out, and you've done it. You want to trust someone you don't fucking know, good luck with that. You need to open your eyes and look at those pictures and tell me what you see."

"You need to leave."

Harrison shakes his head as he moves away from me, toward the door. "Last chance," he says. I don't know what that means and I don't care.

"Go," I say loudly.

He turns and steps out, slamming the door hard. It

bounces back open from the force. The window rattles and the girls' pictures fall from the wall. I jump when the glass shatters and hits the ground.

I slide to the floor clutching my knees to my chest and sob. Everything is ruined.

CHAPTER 33 - HARRISON

I made the mistake of stopping at the store before heading home. The thought of sitting in my empty house, alone, did not sit well with me. Except now I sit in my empty house, alone, hurt and drunk. And I think I've broken my hand, but that's neither here nor there.

I flex my fingers into a fist and back out again. The pain is a dull ache now, but that's likely to be from the amount of beer I've consumed. The bottles are lining up nice and perfect on my coffee table.

I don't know how long I've been sitting here, but the sun is up. That can't be a good sign. I tip my newest bottle back and take in the contents in one swig. I set the bottle down next to the others and lean back. Each bottle mocks me. From the first to the last, each one is laughing at me.

Her words replay over and over in my head.

I met your girlfriend.

I met your girlfriend.

I met your girlfriend.

If I knew how to get hold of Alicia, I would. Not that I'd know what to say. It's not like we have history. I know nothing about her, except that she's an evil, conniving bitch hell-bent on making my life hell. We weren't a couple. We weren't in love. We didn't have a falling out and decide to go our separate ways. That's what Katelyn doesn't understand. I haven't seen her since the day she left Quinn with me. My last image of her is her retreating backside as she hightailed it out of my apartment.

She believes the lies. Every single one of them, and for the life of me, I can't understand why Alicia would say those things or take the time to doctor the photos to show us together. This would all make sense if Alicia and I had broken up recently. I can see a woman scorned making up some shit, but this doesn't make sense.

I pop the top off another beer and realize I'm almost out, which is very unlucky for me. It's not like I can go down to the store to get some more. I don't think I can even make it to the bathroom without falling over.

I down the contents, as my heart kindly reminds me that I cried in front of her. I fucking cried like a god damn baby. Worse yet, it didn't even faze her. She didn't care. She just wanted me out of her house.

And I left.

I left because I can only take so much rejection.

I lay back and close my eyes. She flashes before me. She's smiling one minute and the next, she's kicking me out of her house and out of her life. Tears seep down my face. I hate it. I hate myself for crying over her. I should know better.

THE CLANKING of bottles wakes me. I roll over, suddenly.

Mistake.

I groan and hold my head as I try to sit up. My eyes are blurry, laden with sleep. It's dark out, which means I've slept the day away.

Liam comes into view. He's carrying a garbage can and picking up my bottles.

"I'll do that," I croak out.

"I got it," he says shortly.

I stand, weary that I consumed an abundance of alcohol. I make my way to the bathroom. I shut the door and lean against it, exhausted. My hand throbs and is black and blue. I have to lean my head against the wall while I relieve myself. I can barely stand on my own, clearly I'm still drunk or extremely hung over.

I drag myself back into the living room, which is now clean. I sit down next to Liam, who's flipping through my newest DRUM! Magazine. I don't know why he's here; maybe Katelyn went and told him that I walked out on her.

"Quinn wants to know when he can come home," he says nonchalantly. I look at him like he has three heads.

"What are you talking about?"

"Quinn's been at my house for two days now. I guess he's a bit anxious and wondering what happened to his dad."

"Fuck," I yell. I rake my hand over my face, pulling at my hair. I've never left him, at least not unintentionally. I've always made him a priority and now look at me. Some chick breaks up with me and I forget about my son. Guess I'm not making dad of the year any time soon. "I'll go get him."

"Not yet," he says. He sets the magazine down and stands. "We need to go to the hospital first and have your hand looked at it."

I look down and shake my head. "It's fine. I'll go after. I

she's laughing. If circumstances were different, I'd probably date her.

"And I don't know who took this one, but I'm willing to bet Sam didn't expect me to have it." Liam hands me a photo. He doesn't need to stay anything. The picture speaks for itself.

"Is that money?" I ask.

"Looks like it."

"Why would Sam give Alicia money?"

Liam shrugs. "To drug you."

"Son of a bitch."

I get up and pace. Every part of me hurts right now, and there isn't shit I can do about it. It seems ever since I met Sam Moreno, my life has been nothing but turmoil. If it wasn't band business, she was up in my personal life like she owned me. And maybe she did, and I was just too dumb to understand my contract. I don't know, but drugging someone and having it result in a pregnancy is the lowest someone can go. Seems like it wasn't just Liam's life she was hell-bent on ruining.

"This doesn't help me."

"I know," Liam sighs. "But at least we know why Alicia did what she did."

"Do we? I don't know shit, except that Alicia somehow knew where to find Katelyn and gave her a bunch of phony photos."

"That's not all."

I stop in my tracks and look out the window. Liam clears his throat. "What else?"

"Josie says that Alicia told Katelyn that you guys are still together."

I nod. "I figured as much, with some of the things Katelyn was saying to me. Thing is, Liam, Quinn doesn't know Alicia, so if I'm in some type of relationship with his mom, don't you think she'd be around?" I push off the counter and walk back over to photos. "Show me the years of pictures of us together as a couple. Wouldn't we ever venture out of the house as a family?" I lean over the table, careful not to put any pressure on my hand. "She believes this, not me."

"So what, you're going to leave? You're going to take Quinn out of school and go back to L.A.?"

"I came here for her and she doesn't want me. It would be one thing if we hadn't been together, but I'm in love with her and I can't... I won't sit by and watch her be with someone else."

"You love her?"

"You know I do."

"I know, but this is the first time you've admitted it." Liam sighs and I know he's thinking about what the future is going to hold for the band. "Can you at least do me a favor?"

"Sure," I agree.

"Wait until after the wedding. It's just a few weeks away and I could use my best friend here, especially after Josie dropped a bomb the other night."

I nod. Staying until the wedding is the least I can do. "What'd she say?"

"Nick's back and we're having dinner tonight with him and his new wife."

Liam doesn't wait for my reaction. He starts packing up the photos. He leaves a few of the ones of Alicia and me on the table. I don't know whether I should thank him or not, but I suppose it will be nice when Quinn asks about her. I can at least show him a picture of the both of us before the night turned into a haze.

"Anyway, he's back and Josie wants to be friendly. I want to hate the guy, but can't because my son likes him, and bitched all throughout football on how bad it sucked that Nick wasn't his coach."

"So what are you going to do?"

"I'm going to go to dinner and play nice in the sandbox."

"Lucky you," I say, ducking before Liam can hit me with the box of photos.

———

I ARRIVE at Liam and Josie's with my hand wrapped in a nice black cast. Liam is going to love it. I'll have to find a way to either play with one hand or figure out how to hold my drumstick. Somehow I think taking a break isn't an option.

Quinn jumps into my arms as soon as I'm through the door. He holds me tight. His head is pushing into the crook of my neck. I've never done this to him. He's always known where I am and when I'll be home.

"I'm sorry, Quinn. I should've called."

"It's okay, dad, I was scared though."

"I know, buddy. I won't do it again. I promise."

He looks at me, his eyes puffy. I can tell he's been crying. He may look tough on the outside with his black eye, but deep down, he's still just a little boy. He leans in and whispers, "Peyton is downstairs waiting for you."

"Do you mind if I go down there?"

He shakes his head. I set him down and ruffle his hair.

"What happened?" he asks as he looks at my cast.

"Very stupid adult stuff," I say with a shrug. He'll see the damage at home and ask why. I won't lie to him, but there's not much to tell. It's not like he knew Katelyn and I were together. I never got the chance to tell him. "I'll be back in a bit, or just come downstairs when you're ready."

I walk into the studio and find Peyton banging on my drums. She's wearing headphones that are too big for her, but she's having fun. She smiles at me. I have to paste on a smile because it's killing me that I'm not going to be a part of her life anymore.

"Whatcha doin'?" I ask, pulling up a stool next to her.

"I'm practicing."

"Well, you sound wonderful." I'm rewarded with yet another smile, something I've rarely seen from her.

"Harrison?" I look up to find Noah and Quinn standing in the doorway.

"What's up?"

"We have an idea and we need your help."

Noah and Quinn step into the studio and shut the door. Noah tells me their idea and I ask Quinn and Peyton if the both of them, as well as Elle are all in on this. They nod. I can't help but smile at how enthusiastic they are and agree to help them.

"We're really pregnant!"

"Very," I say showing him the picture.

"Why does the baby have two heads?" I shake my head. Sometimes he's the poster child for dumb football players, I swear.

"Twins," I say quietly. We can't afford one baby, let alone two.

"I made two babies?"

I roll my eyes. "Yes, Mason, your super human sperm created not one, but two babies that have taken over space in my body."

Mason fist pumps. I don't think he understands the magnitude of what's happening here.

"You know two babies means double everything."

"I know, I can count."

"Of course you can." I sit down on the couch and cradle my head. I don't know how we're going to make it. We live in a two-bedroom apartment with Josie and Noah, there's no way we can add two more of everything there. "We have to move."

Mason sits down next to me and pulls me to him. "I talked to my dad the other day. He and mom suggested we move into the house until we can save for a down payment on our own place. He says that we can take what we'd spend in rent and put it away."

"Is that what you want to do?" The thought of living with the Powells doesn't exactly appeal to me, but living with them is better than living with my parents.

Mason shrugs. "I don't know, think about it. Mom would be there to help with the babies and you know she wants to."

I nestle into the side of his neck. His thumb is moving back and forth along my abdomen. "We'll never have alone time."

Mason adjusts and pulls me into his lap. "Seriously? I'm fairly sure you and I have had a lot of alone time in that house. For all we know, these guys were created there." He pulls up my shirt and kisses my stomach.

"If you think we should move to your parent's home, then I'm okay with it."

"I do. Just think about how much fun Mason Junior and Mason Junior Junior will have there."

"Oh my god, Mason, we are not naming our children that." I punch him lightly in the shoulder.

He pulls me into a hug. I cling to him as if it's last time I'll hug him like this.

"You know the girls spent their first Christmas here."

"And others," he adds.

"After Mason died, I realized I wasn't going to be able to make the house payments by myself and Liam helped. He told me that I can't lose the house that holds all of their memories of Mason, but this is where we brought them home too."

"You'll move in?"

I smile widely. "We'd be honored."

I SIT in my car and stare at his house. It's dark and his car isn't in the driveway. I suppose I'm thankful he's not home, because getting caught lurking in the shadows is something I definitely don't want to happen. I don't know what I'm doing out here. What I thought I'd find.

I feel as if I've deceived Mr. Powell. I should've told him that Harrison and I are no longer together, but I couldn't bring myself to say the words. They sound easy in my head, but I'm not capable of saying them out loud because that would make this all too real and I'm not sure I can handle that right now.

My thoughts run away as I ponder all the things he could be doing now. Is he at the bar dancing with some woman that he doesn't plan on knowing the name of? Does he hate me for leading him on? That's how I feel right now. I was just waiting for the other shoe to drop. Looking for any excuse to kick him out of my life and that's what I've done.

"Mommy, what are we doing?" I look in my rear view mirror at Elle and close my eyes to erase the thoughts of Harrison.

"Nothing, mommy just had to stop and think for a minute," I say as I put the car in drive and make my way over to Liam and Josie's to pick up Peyton.

I open the door to Liam and Josie's house and am met with just the sound of the television. Usually this house is loud and boisterous, especially when the kids are all here. Elle runs past me into the living room and shrieks.

"What are you doing?"

"Coloring," I hear Peyton respond. My heart stops and my stomach falls. I close my eyes and pray that she hasn't done too much damage to Josie's living room wall.

My steps are tentative. I'm afraid of what I'm going to find when I walk into the room. Both girls are laughing as I enter. Harrison catches my eye briefly before he turns away. My mouth drops in shock. Peyton is sitting on Harrison's lap with a marker in her hand and Elle is sitting next to him.

I walk around the front of them to get a better look. Both my girls are coloring on Harrison, filling in his tattoos, bringing them more to life than they already are. "What are you doing?" I ask in shock, repeating Elle's earlier question.

Peyton sighs. "Coloring."

"I see that, but why?"

"Because Harrison is a real life coloring book." Harrison laughs along with Peyton. Her laughter is music to my ears. He's found a way to make her laugh, and I can't even thank him.

I look at Harrison, who isn't looking at me. I just want to see his green orbs so I know that this is okay, but he's focusing on the girls. He's ignoring me, and rightly so after what I've done.

I stand back and watch Peyton interact with Harrison. He moves when she asks him to and even holds the markers for her. I don't know what happened while I was gone, but something changed for them. I'm not sure how I feel about it now that he's not going to be around, but I know I like that she's responding to someone other than just Liam.

Harrison looks relaxed and he's clearly enjoying himself, pointing out places that have been missed. I try not to stare, but can't help it. He has both my girls wrapped around his finger like he was meant to be in their lives.

"What did you do to your hand?"

For the first time since I've been here, he looks at me. His lips are in a thin line. I recoil and shrink back into myself. I have to look away for fear I'd start crying under his gaze. He doesn't answer, but goes back to paying attention to the girls.

"Are you going to answer me?" I ask again. I know my tone is demanding, but I can't help it.

"Don't do this in front of the girls," he says quietly. Both of them look at me, confused. I don't know if he's trying to placate me or what, but it's not working. Peyton glares at me before she goes back to coloring. "I'll be right back," he says to them. They groan and huff, but let him get up. I watch as he leaves the room, knowing I should follow, but I can't make my legs and feet cooperate.

Both girls are staring at me, wondering what just happened. I have no idea how I'm going to tell them that Harrison won't be around anymore. I finally relent and go look for him. I square my shoulders when I find him at the kitchen sink. He stands with his back toward me. I want to reach out and touch him. Trace my fingers over the newest ink placed on his arms by my daughters, but I can't. I have to let go and move on. We aren't right for each other.

"Harrison," I say, alerting him to my presence. I see his back visibly stiffen and wonder how he went from being comfortable to this awkward stance so quickly. Is it that easy to just shut off emotions?

He sets his glass down hard. I jump at the sound of it hitting the counter top. He leans forward, even farther away from me. "What do you want, Katelyn?"

I want to yell out that he's the one I want, but I can't. I won't be something he keeps on the side. I need to be everything to him. I need to matter.

"What happened to your hand?" I ask again, more for curiosity than anything. He holds up his casted hand, one that has been colored with gold and silver markers and twists it in the air. He doesn't turn around to address me and that bothers me.

"I hit a wall and broke it in two places. Anything else you want to know about me?"

"N... no," my voice is quiet as the word gets stuck. He pushes away from the counter and walks to me, stopping when we are shoulder to shoulder. There's no eye contact. There's no touching.

"All you had to do was trust me."

He walks away without looking back, without waiting

for me to catch up. He talks about trust, but I can't, not with what I've been told. Not with what I've seen. Photos don't lie, do they?

I walk back into the living room, but stop at the entry and watch Harrison interact with the twins. They're being their usual selves by acting like monkeys and he doesn't even care. He's not fazed by them in the least. He tickles them and their laughter is music to my ears. He's bringing it out of them in droves.

Why can't life be as simple as laughter?

CHAPTER 35 - HARRISON

IT'S BEEN THREE WEEKS SINCE SHIT HIT THE FAN AND my life imploded. Twenty-one days since a malicious lie ripped out my heart out and destroyed my chance at happiness. I can't even count the hours, because there are too many. All I know is that I hate the emptiness I feel each day when I wake up, and the loneliness that threatens to consume me at night. There hasn't been a moment that I haven't thought about revenge. I've waited for Alicia to call or show up, but she hasn't, and today I'll see her in court. I really want to ask her why. Why go through the trouble of destroying my life if she wasn't planning on showing up like she told Katelyn and Josie she was?

Liam is determined to beat Sam at her own game. He wants her far away from him before the wedding. I don't blame him. She's dangerous. We should've seen the signs a long time ago, but we were young and stupid, and she made being in a band easy. Liam hired a private investigator and turned over all the evidence he uncovered himself. Within a week, we had enough to go to a judge and ask for help. So now we're sitting here, waiting.

Waiting is the hard part. It makes me anxious. I stare down each woman that walks into the courthouse, wondering if it's Alicia. Aside from the doctored images she produced with her face, I haven't seen her in eight years. The way Josie described her doesn't fit the picture I have of her from that fateful night. I've hidden the photos of us in my room for when Quinn asks about her. I want to be able to show him that yes, we were smiling at one time in our lives. I'm not sure how, or even if I'll ever tell him about that night. I'd like him to make his own decisions about his mother, and not be forced by what she did to me. I wouldn't be able to tell him anyway, other than what she told me. Remembering that night is like staring off into space – nothing's there.

I'll be asking a family judge to issue a no contact order against Alicia. She hasn't done any physical harm to Quinn or me, so a restraining order is out of the question, but as his primary legal guardian, I can ask that she's not allowed to contact him until he turns eighteen. My lawyer seems to think that we shouldn't have any problems obtaining this. She's hasn't shown any interest in Quinn, just me as of late, so there's no need for her to be near him until he's old enough to make that decision on his own.

Liam is next to me, his leg bouncing up and down. He's nervous, I know. We've underestimated Sam and it's done a lot of damage to the band and our personal lives. We've filed a restraining order against Sam and Moreno Entertainment. It's a long shot, we know, but our private investigator uncovered a lot that we didn't know, and this is our only recourse. We talked about filing a lawsuit, but our attorney advised us to try this avenue first in the hope that Mr. Moreno would put a leash on his daughter.

My name gets called, as does Alicia's. I look around, but

don't see anyone walking toward the clerk standing at the door.

"I'll be waiting here," Liam says before I step away. How we ended up with hearing times an hour apart is mind blowing. I thought for sure it would be months before I'd get in front of a judge, not weeks.

I walk into the judge's chamber, followed by my lawyer. He hasn't changed much over the years; he's still pudgy and just as bald. We sit on one side of the table and wait.

"Is she going to show up?"

"She was served and if she doesn't, he'll sign the order."

"I want to see her," I say abruptly. I have no idea why I said that, but it's true. I want to look at her and try to figure out what makes her tick.

We stand when the judge comes into his chamber. The bailiff tells us that we can sit.

"Where's Ms. Tucker?"

"Not here, Your Honor," my lawyer says.

The judge looks at his watch and writes something down.

"Are you the father of Quinn James?"

"I am," I say proudly.

"It says here, Mr. James, that you're seeking a no contact order against Ms. Tucker."

"That's correct."

"And Ms. Tucker isn't here to dispute this?"

"No, Your Honor, she was served and awarded a public defender, according to my records," my lawyer adds.

"Very well," he says as he scribbles on his paper. "Motion granted. Ms. Tucker is to have no contact with the child in question until he reaches the age of eighteen." The judge gets up and leaves; and like that, we're done.

I walk out of the office with my lawyer and shake his hand. I tell him that I hope I never see him again and he laughs. I can't imagine ever needing him, unless Alicia requests the order be lifted. I would hope that if that was to ever happen, the judge would see through her bullshit.

I nod at Liam from across the room and he motions for me to look to my left. There stands Sam with her dad and their lawyer. Her father is prattling on about something, but she's not interested, she's glaring at Liam. I shake my head and walk into her line of sight and stand so she can't see him anymore.

"Alicia didn't show. One ho down another to go."

Liam laughs, but tries to hide it. I know the bitch is standing behind me throwing daggers, but I don't give a shit. Honestly, I'm surprised she even showed up, considering her clone didn't.

"Are you happy?" Liam asks. I nod. I am, even though I wanted to see her, to speak to her, I'm happy that for the next ten years, she can't do anything to Quinn. She can come after me all she wants, but not my boy.

JD walks in just as our lawyer tells us we can enter the courtroom. We pass by Mr. Moreno, who doesn't smile at us. Not that I'd expect him to, but it would be nice for him to show some recognition. We made him a lot of money, and he thought he'd reward us by pawning us off on his daughter because she had a serious hard-on for Liam. Sam was the beginning of what could've been a huge downfall for us.

The three of us sit down, with our lawyer on the edge. We don't watch as the Morenos enter and take their seats. We can hear Sam and her exaggerated huffing and puffing to know enough.

We stand as instructed by the bailiff and wait for the judge to sit. We have a woman judge, and I wonder if this will play into our favor.

"Good afternoon," she starts. "I've been over the files that were submitted at my request." She folds her hands and looks at us. "I've asked for special consideration with this case because of the complexity. I've never seen a file so thick for something like a restraining order." The judge shuffles a few papers around.

"Mr. Page, do you feel that you and your family are in danger from Ms. Moreno?"

"Yes, Your Honor."

"Mr. James, I ask the same question to you."

"Yes, Your Honor."

"Mr. Davis, and you?"

"Yes, Your Honor."

"Mr. Moreno, are you aware of what your daughter has been doing for the past ten years?"

I think we hold our breath waiting for his answer. All three of us lean forward and watch him as he settles in front of the microphone. "No. Surely, if I knew I would've put a stop to it."

The judge doesn't respond, but moves more papers around. "It says here in an email from yourself to Sam Moreno and I quote *"it's best to keep the clingy girlfriend away from Liam. What he doesn't know won't hurt him"* end quote. Do you remember writing this?"

"No, Your Honor."

"Messrs. Page, James and Davis, you've instructed your lawyer to ask for a restraining order, but he took it one step further and attached what you'd call a civil suit. It says here that you're looking for restitution from lost wages from your tour, is that correct?"

"Yes, Your Honor," our lawyer answers. I wasn't aware we were asking for money, and by the look of it, neither was Liam.

"Ms. Moreno, it saddens me that you would keep a child from his parent. That, to me, is probably the lowest thing you can do. The years of abuse these men have suffered at your hands, ending with their recent tour, is deplorable. You should be ashamed of yourself, but I have a feeling you're not. I hereby grant a full restraining order, which means Ms. Moreno, you and your heirs are not allowed to communicate in any way, shape or form with the members of the band and their families and employees. You are also not allowed within one thousand feet of them. You are also ordered to pay two hundred thousand dollars in lost earnings."

The judge slams down her gavel as we sit there stunned. We just wanted the restraining order so we can move on with our lives peacefully. We didn't expect this at all. We stand as the judge exits. Liam shakes our lawyer's hand, as do JD and I. We follow him out of the courtroom, elated with our victory.

"I've got to head off," JD says. "See you guys in a couple of days." I don't bother telling him that Quinn and I will be moving back to L.A.

"What the fuck just happened?" Liam asks.

"That, my friend, was a judge who can't stand the Morenos. When I found out we drew her, I modified my request. I took a gamble."

"That was crazy," I say, running my hand through my hair.

"Let's get out here," Liam says as he motions for the door. I couldn't agree more. I want to get back to Beaumont and finalize everything. The movers are coming the day after the wedding, and I need to start packing. Quinn will go back to being homeschooled by my mom. There will be no more calls from the principal telling me he's gotten into a fight.

There's a commotion behind us. We turn in time to see the courtroom doors fly open and Sam storm out. She looks like Elvira on a rainy day. Her make-up is running down her face. She points at Liam and storms toward him. I grab his arm and pull him outside. We don't need to listen to what she has to say.

"YOU!"

We both stop.

"Liam, why would you do this?"

"You don't need to answer her," I say.

She moves in front of us. Tears run down her face. If I had an ounce of respect for her, I'd care, but I don't.

"You loved me once, Liam, why did you do this? I just lost everything in there."

Liam sighs and moves away from her. "I never loved you, Sam. You were a plaything, something to pass my time. You were a mistake, and something that I regret every day of my life. You took my son away from me. You took Josie away from me, and for that, I hate you. I lost ten years with my family because of you and your father."

I tap Liam on the shoulder and point to the car waiting for us. Sam grabs Liam's arm and pulls him to her. He stumbles. I reach for his hand, keeping him upright.

"You're mine, Liam."

Liam rips his arm from her. "Go home Sam, you're not wanted here."

"You can't leave me, Liam. You love me."

"No I don't," he says through gritted teeth. "I never loved you, Sam. Listen to me. You're nothing to me."

"Take that back," she says quietly.

"Hey, can we get a little help over here," I holler for the police officer standing a few feet away from us. He comes over and Sam lets go of Liam. "We have a restraining order against her," I add. We watch as he pulls out his handcuffs. Sam steps away, shaking her head. The officer steps forward, but isn't fast enough for Sam. She runs down the steps and he chases her, yelling at her to stop.

Sam heads to our car and slips into the driver's seat and pulls away from the curb. The driver is shouting, waving his arms back and forth. The police officer is screaming for back up. In a matter of minutes police cars are flying down the road, chasing Sam.

"I think this will make the evening news." I laugh, although I don't mean to, but it seems fitting that this would end up making the front pages.

Liam shakes his head. "What's her problem?"

I put my arm around his shoulders. "I hate to tell you this, but she's nuts and you just made it worse."

"Gee, thanks."

"Anytime." We don't get very far before we have to give a statement. The officer who chased after Sam keeps scratching his head. It baffles me that he couldn't detain her. Barney Fife could've done a better job.

"Come on, let's go home." Liam says, as he signals for a taxi.

He steps away and heads for the yellow and black-checkered car. The word *home* hits hard, but I know my decision is the right one. I can't stand by and watch her fall in love with someone that isn't me. It hurts that we aren't together over something that was a lie.

We have a flight back to Beaumont tonight. When we land, the ball will start rolling. I have to finish up my project with the kids and help Liam find Josie a present. My Christmas shopping is done. All that's left are goodbyes.

CHAPTER 36 - KATELYN

JOSIE AND I ARE FINISHING LAST MINUTE SHOPPING FOR everything that we need for the wedding, Christmas and her New Year's party – it all has to be done today. I know I'll be back here tomorrow with the girls though. They've begged me to take them shopping so they can buy something for Harrison and Quinn. Christmas will be the first time he and I will spend any time together since we split. I've been able to avoid him at all costs, and that hasn't been easy.

I never realized how much our lives were intertwined and they continue to stay that way. Quinn still comes to my house after school, but Harrison no longer comes inside to pick him up. I know Elle misses Harrison and is always asking to go to Liam's to see him and now he's connected with Peyton – albeit after we split - and she's spending time more and more with him. I want to tell him that he needs to stop seeing them, but he's making them laugh and right now, that's the best thing for them.

My days since I've come back from Los Angeles have been spent helping Josie. I'm either working at her shop or it's not because she's right or that I miss Harrison. That's just not possible.

I SWIPE AWAY the fallen leaves from Mason's headstone. My fingers find the grooves of his name and trace them. The Christmas tree the girls brought last week is still standing, despite the windy days we've been having. I straighten a few of the bulbs before setting my blanket down.

"It's hard to come here, but I think you know that. I know your dad finds it harder and harder to visit, but the girls make him come. They don't ask me though, and I'm not sure how I should feel about that. They miss you so much, Mason and I do too. Our lives are so different than they were a year and half ago."

I sit down and look at his name. His mom is buried next to him, and his dad, when his time comes, will be buried next to her. Mason and I never bought plots or even made a will because we never thought anything would happen to us. Yet, here I am about to ask my dead husband what I should do.

"I met someone. Everyone tells me that you'd want me to move on, but it's so hard to believe that you would. I remember how jealous you would get if someone would talk to me, so it's hard to imagine you'd be okay with me loving someone else.

"I tried to be with Harrison. That's his name. He's a friend of Liam's; they're in the band together. The girls love him and he treats them really well, but I can't help but think you wouldn't be okay with this. How am I supposed to know that you're okay with me bringing another man into my life? Into the girls' lives?

"I need a sign, Mason. I need something to show me that you want me to move on. That it's okay to love someone else, because right now, I'm set to be all myself if that's what would make you happy."

I lie down on my blanket and look at the clouds. The day is gray and overcast. I turn on my side and run my hands over the grass that covers his casket. "Tell me what to do Mason and I'll do it. You hold my heart, and I'm so afraid to give it to someone else without your approval."

No sooner do I speak the words does it start snowing. I roll onto my back and close my eyes, letting the snow fall slowly down to me. The snowflakes dance along my skin, landing on my eyelashes. *Snow kisses* Mason used to call them. Is this my sign? Is this enough for me to open my heart to someone else with his approval?

I'M crazy for planning this party. I'm not sure what I was thinking except I needed to get my mind off of things and what better way to do it than to have my girlfriends over for a mini party. The music is on and drinks are flowing. The girls are with my parents and we're having a slumber party. I know it seems childish, but it's better than driving home drunk.

I carry a tray of nachos into the living room. Josie, Jenna and Aubrey are on the floor, pillows surrounding them. We'll all in our pajamas; it's high school all over again. The only thing missing are the boys looming outside, ready to climb up the trestle. I wouldn't put it past Liam to do that tonight.

"Okay, we should play a game," Aubrey says with a

smile. I'm glad she decided to come and hang out with us tonight.

"Oh, games are fun," Jenna replies as she reaches for the nachos.

"Josie, these margaritas are good." I don't know how many I've had, but each one tastes better than the last.

"What game are we playing?" Josie asks.

"How about a slight variation of twenty questions," Jenna suggests. "Obviously, we know a lot about each other and we're getting to know Aubrey, but it's girls night so let's get down to the nitty gritty."

"I'm game," Aubrey says.

"Katelyn, remember when Mason had that party and we played spin the bottle?"

"Oh God," I choke on my drink when Josie brings that up. "He got so pissed that we never made it into the closet, which I didn't understand, since we were already... you know."

"No, I don't know, tell us." Aubrey winks and Jenna starts laughing.

I roll my eyes. "You know..." I say nodding my head, but Aubrey just shakes hers. "Fine, we were having sex, so I didn't see why it was so important to go into the closet. Only later did he tell me that it's a rite of passage that all boys need to experience. Our next date, he took me to the freaking closet!"

They all start laughing. I can't contain my laughter and snort so loudly that they all stop, only to start up again.

"Okay, okay, okay," I say holding my hands up. "Seriously, my husband wasn't always the most romantic, but..." I lose my thoughts. "Shots," I call out to diffuse the tension I just created in the room.

Josie lines up the shots of tequila on my coffee table. "Lick, suck and slam, ladies, I'm almost a married woman."

"Oh shit, that burns," Aubrey says after she knocks hers back. I agree, but keep that to myself. "One more time," she suggests, and none of us disagree.

Josie pours and lines them up. We count to three and repeat the process. We break out in a fit of uncontrollable laughter.

"Katelyn, do you think Liam will try and sneak in here tonight?"

"Yes, I do. And probably Nick too, although not at the same time."

"Were they ever friends?" Aubrey asks.

"Not really. Nick had a crush on Josie and Liam is possessive," I say. "Nick moved here and just tried to fit in, but Mason and Liam had a solid friendship and it was hard for him."

"They get along now," Josie adds.

"Nick really loves Noah, you know," Aubrey adds with a smile. I know she means well, but this isn't the time to discuss their odd family relationship.

"I know he does. We're trying, Aubrey."

"I know and he appreciates it. Can I ask a question?"

I stop mid-bite and crunch on the chip I just picked up, slowly. I want to hear what Aubrey has to ask. I need a little bit of excitement in my life, even if it's at the expense of my best friend.

"Sure," Josie says.

"When Nick asked you about the wedding, you told him that you hadn't set a date, why?"

Josie shakes her head slightly before looking at Aubrey. She smiles, genuinely and I know she likes her and is glad that Nick found someone.

"It was awkward to talk about getting married less than a year after he and I broke up. I froze and blurted out the first thing that came to me. I meant no disrespect and I'm happy that you're here tonight."

The room grows quiet except for the sounds of chips crunching and the music playing in the background.

"Most public place you've ever had sex?" Josie blurts out.

I'm going to need more to drink if we are playing sex games.

"Bleachers," Jenna replies.

"I've never had sex in a public place, Nick was my first and it's very cold here." We try not to laugh, but we can't help it. Aubrey starts laughing too. "I'll tell him we need to try."

"Oh yeah, Nick will love that," Josie adds. "Fifty-yard line... last night," she says. We look at her. Our mouths drop open. She shrugs and takes a drink of her margarita.

"I can't believe you."

"What, why not? Liam's hot and yesterday he was Liam Page and I couldn't resist. What about you Powell?"

I feel the blood rush to my head. I've only had sex outside one time, and that was with Harrison. "I, um... at this place called The Point, on a motorcycle."

"What? Mason never had a... oh my God." Josie covers her mouth. I feel my cheeks start to burn. I try to get up, but she pulls me back down. "On his motorcycle?"

I nod and am rewarded with squeals.

"Katelyn, that is seriously hot and with Harrison too. I'd do him." I look up at Jenna and wonder why she'd say that. "Oh let's play Kiss, Marry, Screw." Jenna continues, "I'll go first. I'd totally kiss Matt Dillon, but only when he was in the Outsiders. I'd marry Harrison and screw Jimmy."

"What? Ewe Jenna. Jimmy is a such a dirty dog," Josie says, but I'm still trying to process what she said about Harrison.

"Why Harrison?" I ask.

"Why not Harrison? A man that's good with his son? Heaven."

"Okay, my turn. I'd kiss Vampire Erik, marry Will Smith and screw Ryan Gosling," Aubrey adds.

"Hey girllll," Jenna throws out there. I look at her with confusion. "It's his thing," she says.

"I guess it's my turn," I say. "I'd kiss McDreamy, marry Prince Harry and screw Ryan Stevenson."

"Ryan Stevenson?" Josie asks. I realize I've made a mistake.

"He's a drummer."

"You know other drummers?"

I sigh and cover my face. "Harrison showed me a picture of him one night." I pour myself another shot and down it.

"Why would you want another drummer when you have that fine man waiting for you," I look at Jenna questioningly. She shrugs. "Harrison's a catch."

"What?" I choke out.

"Nothing. My go," Jenna says enthusiastically.

"Josie didn't get a turn," Aubrey adds.

Josie waves her hand. "Liam, Liam and Liam for all my answers."

I roll my eyes. "Figures."

"I have a good one. I'd kiss Nicholas Hoult, marry Henry Cavill and screw David Beckham," Jenna says with a bit of flair.

"What's with all the Brits?" I ask.

"It's the British accent. It does things to me."

"Ah, so that's why you want to play with Jimmy," Josie teases.

"He's sweet," she says.

"But he'll never settle down. He likes the ladies too much." Josie knows this from Liam, I'm sure. Harrison and I never really talked about Jimmy. "But Harrison on the other hand, I can see him settling down."

I raise my eyebrow at Josie. I don't know what she's playing at but I don't like it. I take another shot. I need to erase him from my mind.

"Maybe I should ask him out," Jenna responds.

"Um, no, maybe you shouldn't."

"Why not?" she asks. Josie moves closer, holding a pillow in her lap.

"Because you can't."

"But you broke up," Josie throws out there. I lean over and cover my face.

"You guys, I think you're embarrassing her." If I could lean over and kiss Aubrey I would.

"I'm going to text Liam and tell him to come over." Josie suddenly changes the subject.

"Oh, have him bring Harrison too," Jenna says excitedly.

"No, don't," I hastily reply. The last thing I need is for Harrison to turn up and make things even more uncomfortable than they already are.

Jenna looks over at Josie and Aubrey before continuing, "Well, if the boys aren't coming over here, maybe we should go and see them. Josie, you can give Liam a booty call and I can get to know Harrison." I don't know whether it's the amount of drinks I've had or the fact that Jenna seems to have a fixation on Harrison, but I do know that the idea of her getting to know him better is not okay with me.

"I don't think that's a good idea." I say quietly.

"Why not?"

"Because... I don't."

"But why? He's single, I'm single, I think it's a great idea."

"Because I think I'm in love with him," I blurt out. The room goes quiet and I notice Josie and Jenna exchange looks. Aubrey scoots next to me and puts her arm around me.

"What are you going to do about it?" Josie asks.

I shake my head. "I don't know. I can't..." I stand up and try to pace, but I'm too dizzy. I sit back down and pull my legs to my chest. "I can't take anymore hurt."

Josie kneels in front of me and takes my hands into hers. "Harrison won't hurt you, Katelyn, he's in love with you and he loves Peyton and Elle. Just give him a chance."

"I did."

"And he didn't do anything to break that trust. You were duped, just like I was last year by that wretched woman. He's taken care of her. If he didn't love you, he wouldn't have done that."

I shake my head. "I don't know."

Josie puts my hair behind my ear. "You do know, sweetie, you just have to look in front of you."

I nod and wrap my arms around her. I don't know what I'm going to do, but maybe Harrison and I can sit down and figure things out after the wedding.

CHAPTER 37 - HARRISON

"Merry Christmas!" Quinn bellows out. He runs into the house, excited to spend his last few days with his friends. He hasn't told Noah or the girls, said he didn't want them to be sad around Christmas time or for the wedding. I respect his decision.

The sound of laughter rings throughout the house. Quinn and I carry in our presents for everyone. The girls are dressed in matching outfits. I eye Peyton, who looks like she's going to scream with excitement. I smile at her and am rewarded with one of the sweetest smiles I've ever had from her. Since the day we had our chat, things have been really good between us. Elle is twirling around like a ballerina, giggling. I feel like I'm missing something I never really had, and it hurts.

Katelyn sits in the chair next to the fireplace. Her legs are curled underneath. I miss her, but I can't let that show, especially today. A year ago, I walked into this house and saw the most beautiful woman I had ever seen. When I held her hand, I knew she was going to be someone special. Everything I did, I did because I saw her as my future.

Now, she's my past, and in a few days she'll go from someone I know and see occasionally to someone I see rarely, if at all, and that doesn't make me happy. But it's my choice.

Liam walks in with a Santa hat on and the kids start jumping up and down. I kneel in front of the tree and put the presents that Quinn wrapped underneath it. I hold the one I bought for Katelyn in my hand and wonder if it should be included with the rest, or if I should leave it in her mailbox on my way out of town. It's not meant to be a parting gift, it's something I bought for her before shit went down. I've thought about not giving it to her, but it has meaning and I can't bring myself to return it to the store.

I try not to watch her, but I can feel my body gravitate toward her. Her hair falls in her face as I pass by. I have to pocket my hand to keep me from caressing her cheek. I pinch my leg, reminding me that she quit us. I didn't.

"Present time," Liam announces. The kids yell with excitement and gather around the tree. Liam distributes the presents to each child, leaving the adults for last.

I try to keep my thoughts at bay. I don't know if moving is the right thing to do, but right now, it's what I need. I've put myself out there with her and I wore my heart on my sleeve. I sit back and watch as the kids tear into their presents. Wrapping paper flies all over the room and laughter rings out. Josie brings in breakfast. She hands me a cup of coffee. I know the look on her face. She feels sorry for me, and she shouldn't. She smiles softly and turns to look at Katelyn.

I don't want to look, but I can't help myself, and much like last year, she's staring at her girls, probably remembering her husband. I can't imagine holidays get any easier

The beat of the drums soothes me. This is my escape. I need this, even if my left hand is hampered by a cast. I know I'm a shit for ditching out on Christmas, but I need to be able to clear my head. When she's in my vicinity, my judgment is clouded. All I want to do is pull her into a corner and beg her to give us a fair chance. There's no way I can do that and save face at the same time. She was loud and clear when she kicked me out of her house that night. She wasn't willing to look at the possibility that the photos were lies. She just thought I was a liar and a cheat, something I've never been.

I freeze when the beat of her song starts coming from my drums. What would possess me to play this, I don't know. I put the sticks down and take a deep breath. The door opens and footsteps come near me.

"Are you really leaving after the wedding?"

I look up at Liam and nod. "I can't be in the same room as her and she's always around. I need my space."

"How does Quinn feel?"

"He's fine," I say as I run my finger of the rim of my set. "He knows we'll come back sometimes, and since he'll be homeschooled, he can travel back and forth with me."

Liam sighs and pulls out another stool to sit on. "With you back in L.A., JD won't want to come here. He'll be asking me to come back there to work."

"Don't put this on me, Liam. You want someone to blame; blame Sam or hell, blame Katelyn for the bullshit. If she didn't want me, she should've just stayed away. I was doing fine from a distance, but no, she had to show that she was jealous of other women and act like she cared so that I'd pursue her harder."

"I know you're hurting."

I shake my head. "Nah, man, it's beyond hurt. I can't

look at her without wanting to kiss her and shake her at the same time. I don't get it."

"She's scared."

"Well, that's no way to live your life and we all know how short life can be."

"I believe in second chances," Liam says. I know he does, or he wouldn't be getting married the day after tomorrow, but not all of us can be so lucky. "If you need time, you should take it."

"It's not me needing time. I know what I want. I want those three girls upstairs to be in my life permanently. I want my son to have Katelyn as a mother figure, because that's what he wants. I don't need the time to figure that shit out. I already know it." I rub my hands over my face and groan. "It's not me, Liam. I'm not running or shutting doors. I'm moving because it's too hard to sit back and watch her life go on while mine is teetering on the edge, waiting for a glimmer of hope that she might, someday, want to be with me."

Liam comes over and pats me on the back, squeezing my shoulder. "Josie says brunch is in thirty minutes."

"I'll be up."

No sooner does Liam shut the door than it opens again. This time, my visitor is a short and sweet little girl with a black velvet ribbon in her hair. She comes over and climbs into my lap. Her arms wrap around my neck as she hugs me tightly. I squeeze her back with all that I have, hoping that I leave an impression for her.

"How come you don't come over for dinner anymore?"

I'm not sure how to answer her. What do you say to a child who has lost so much in her life? "I'm busy with writing music. Sometimes it takes a lot of my time."

I adjust Peyton and set her on my knee. "Mommy cries a lot at night again."

"What do you mean, 'again'?"

She shrugs. "I think she stopped for a little while, but now she does it again."

I push her hair behind her shoulder and offer her a smile. I don't know what to say. Part of me hopes she's crying because we aren't together, but I should know better. She misses her simple life and with that, comes the longing she has for her husband. She doesn't shed tears for me.

"Wanna play?" I ask her, holding up the sticks. Her grin spreads from ear to ear as she takes them from my hand. She spins in my lap and is ready for me to give her the signal.

Except this time I don't.

This time I bring out another set of sticks and play with her. We pound on the drums, creating our own music. When we have a decent rhythm going, I hit record on my laptop and we play again and again until it's time to eat. When we're done, we're tired and sweaty. Peyton hugs me again. Her arms are tight around my neck. I hate that it's taken so long for us to be friends and now that we are, I'm leaving her.

"I love you, Harrison."

"I love you too, Peyton." My response is automatic. My heart is beating wildly in my chest, threatening to come out or break at a moment's notice. If loving her, Elle and Katelyn is right, why does everything I do feel so wrong?

CHAPTER 38 - KATELYN

"Are you ready?" I ask as I straighten out Josie's train. It's pinned to the French braids that meet at the back of her head. Her dress is strapless and tight around her waist. The silk is bunched and pinned statically, making her dress poof more. Jenna does a last minute fix on her make-up, as Josie is nervous and keeps touching her face.

"Stop touching," Jenna says, slapping Josie's hand.

"Why are you so nervous?" I ask.

"I don't know. This is a huge step."

Jenna and I start laughing. "Seriously? You have a son and you live together. Usually this step happens first."

Josie closes her eyes and takes a deep breath. "What if he's not there?"

"Oh my God, Josephine, get a grip. It's time to go." I push her toward the door. Jenna opens it and Mr. Preston is standing there, waiting for his daughter. I give him a kiss on the cheek as I pass by him.

Jenna, the twins and I walk into the vestibule. Music is playing softly. We wait for our cue. The girls walk out, dropping rose petals along the path. Their dresses match

Josie's, except with straps. Their beautiful hair is braided to match Josie's, with pieces curled and hanging down. Jenna steps out next. I count to twenty like we practiced in rehearsal, and step out.

The three white roses that make up my bouquet are held tightly in front of me. My dress, crimson red, falls just below my knees, with a bow in front, just off to the side. I love my dress and not many people can say that about their bridesmaid dresses. The strapless, form fitting top and flow of the dress makes me feel sexy.

I avoid looking ahead for fear of what may break my heart even more. I smile at the guests on the sides, all eyes watching me until I pass. Each pew is decorated with white roses and red ribbon. Jenna and Aubrey have done a wonderful job with the flower arrangements.

I make a mistake and look toward the front to see Liam, wondering what expression he's wearing. I don't see him or Jimmy, even though they're both there. All I see is Harrison, dressed sharply in a black and white tuxedo. His hair has been cut and styled nicely. He doesn't look like the man I've declared my love for. He's too covered. He's not the story-book I've become accustomed to seeing.

His eyes connect with mine. I bite my lip to send a sharp reminder to my brain and my heart that I'm here for a reason, and that is Josie and Liam. Anything to do with Harrison will have to wait until my duties are done.

I step forward and take my spot next to Jenna. The girls are sitting on the steps, as are Noah and Quinn, who had the duty of escorting the guests today. They are dressed to match Harrison. I glance at Quinn, who smiles at me. His hair is tousled and in need of a trim. I shouldn't have those thoughts though, but I can't help it. In Noah's lap is the ring pillow. It's fitting that he holds the bands that will tie his family together.

Everyone stands as the music changes. I know I should be watching Josie come down the aisle, but I can't take my eyes away from the man who is staring at me. He's not looking at Liam or Josie, but at me. I don't know if I should smile or look away. I don't know what I'm doing anymore. Josie and Liam step up to the minister and in my line of sight. I'm no longer connected to Harrison. I can no longer see him clearly.

The words from the minister ring out over the church. He talks about love, life and finding someone that makes you happy. I know the words aren't meant for me, but they hit home. In the short time that Harrison and I were together, I was happy. He made me smile and feel loved. He treated my children as his own, and even though we are no longer together, he still does. That should be enough for me.

"Liam, please recite your vows to Josie."

Liam rolls his neck and shakes out his shoulders. The guests laugh.

"You'd think because I'm a musician this would be easy, but let me tell you, finding the words to say to this woman is very difficult."

Liam clears his throat before he looks into her eyes.

"Josie, in your eyes, I have found my only home. In your heart, I have found my only love. In your soul, I have found my only mate.

"Josie, with you, I am whole, full and alive. You make me laugh. You allow me to cry. You're my every breath and every heartbeat. I am nothing, if you're not mine as I am yours."

Josie sniffles. I don't blame her. I have tears pooling in my eyes as well. The minister nods at her, letting her know that she can start. She takes a deep breath and starts speaking to the love of her life.

"Liam, I promise to encourage your individuality, because that's what makes you unique and wonderful. That's what makes you mine.

"I promise to nurture your dreams, because without them, we wouldn't be standing here today.

"I promise to help shoulder our challenges, because we're a team and are stronger than ever.

"I promise to always be your best friend, your lover, your wife and most importantly, your partner.

"I promise to share with you the joys of life, because with you, they'll be that much sweeter.

"Liam, lastly I promise to you perfect love and perfect trust, because tomorrow will never be enough."

Josie never shared her vows with me and I'm thankful for that. When she speaks about a perfect love and trust, she speaks from experience. She's been through more than just losing the love they shared once, she's had to learn to trust the public side of Liam, and she's done it gracefully.

Noah hands his parents their rings. Liam gives him a fist bump, much to the guests delight.

"I now pronounce you husband and wife. Liam, you may kiss your bride."

Whistling and laughter ring out as Liam dips his bride back and kisses her. When he rights her, he raises their hands in the air. I hand Josie her bouquet, and watch as my two best friends rush down the aisle to start the next chapter in their lives.

The kids follow, Noah with Peyton and Quinn with Elle. I step forward and loop my arm into Harrison's. This is the closest we've been in weeks. It doesn't feel forced or uncomfortable. It feels natural. It feels like home.

THE MOMENT the wedding party is announced, Harrison leaves my side. I know I shouldn't have expected him to stay next to me, but a small part of me hoped he would. That small part hoped that the wedding vows and the love in the air would spur him to take a step and demand that I talk to him. No such luck, and there's no one to blame but myself.

Josie and Liam move right into their first dance. They hired a band to play live music tonight. The band plays one of the songs Liam wrote for Josie. Why she chose this, I'll never understand, but it's their song. When they finish, we all sit and enjoy dinner. The atmosphere is so laid back you'd think we're at a party, not a reception. I've been to many and while most have been boring, this has a nightclub vibe going on. I have a feeling this will be an all-nighter for some.

The dancing begins as soon as the dinner plates have been carried away. Liam, Josie and Noah all dance together for one song, uniting them as a family. Jimmy stands next to Harrison. Both of them are without their jackets now. Jimmy's bow tie is undone and his hair is standing on end. It makes me wonder which one of these women is his date for the night as I look around for someone who looks like they just came out of the coat closet. That image is enough for me to be thankful I didn't have to coat check anything.

Time moves too fast. The cake has been cut. The bouquet tossed and Liam performed a very erotic dance to take off Josie's garter. If she wasn't embarrassed, I was enough for the both of us. Harrison caught the garter and spun it around his finger. He smirked when he caught me watching him. He licked his lips before turning away.

That's the rocker side of him showing, reminding me what I gave up.

The singer of the band tells us it's time for our speeches. He helps me step up on the stand and lowers the microphone stand.

"Hello," I say. "It's hard to prepare a speech for your best friends, especially when mine are so special to me. I could thank them for the countless hours they've been by my side or tell you how they've been my rock through my most troubling time, but that doesn't tell you about them. I've known them forever and it was only fitting that they became a couple. Whether we did this years ago or today, it was bound to happen. Today, I watch the union of two people who have triumphed over every obstacle thrown at them. They're truly the epitome of romance and love to me. To Josie and Liam, thank you for showing me the path that I need to take."

They meet me at the side of the stage and we hug. When Harrison takes the stage, my heart stops beating. That's where he's most comfortable. Where he shines.

"Good evening," he says into the microphone. "As the best man, it's my honor to give this speech. I've known Liam for over eleven years now and we've been through just about everything one can imagine. When he invited me into his home just over a year ago, I saw with my own eyes what had been missing from his life. I'm proud to stand up here tonight and congratulate my friend on finding the missing piece to his life, for having the guts to chase it down and for taking the steps he needed to make it his. Liam and Josie, you're an example for us all.

"Before I leave, I have a gift for you. Weeks ago, four very talented people came to me and asked for some help. What they asked for, I thought couldn't be done in weeks, but they practiced every free minute they could. These four persevered, and I'm proud to introduce to you Noah Westbury and Quinn James on guitar, Elle Powell on lyrics and Peyton Powell on drums. And for the record, I didn't pick the song."

My mouth drops open as the kids take the stage. I have to blink to be sure, but Harrison is right, my daughters are there and one is sitting at the drum set. Harrison moves around each child making sure they're all set. When he gets to Peyton, I see it. I see how they connected.

Josie and Liam come over to me and stand. "Did you know about this?" Liam asks. I shake my head. "I'll be damned."

As soon as the music starts, the guests start laughing. The kids are playing their own version of *Call Me Maybe*. The lyrics Elle sings don't really set with me because I'm focusing on Peyton. She's so poised and determined behind the drum set and most importantly, she's smiling. I haven't seen her smile that big in a very long time and she's doing it because of Harrison.

When the song is over, Peyton hugs Harrison before she comes rushing off stage. I pick her up and hug her tightly. "Oh Peyton, I'm so proud of you." I set her down and she beams at me.

"Was I great?"

"You were the best drummer I've ever seen." It's not a lie, at least not for me.

"Harrison taught me after the boy at school started teasing me. He said to take out all my anger on his drums. He didn't care if I broke them."

I replay her words over in my head. I don't remember a boy teasing her. "What are you talking about?"

Liam sets his hand on my shoulder. "When you were in

L.A. there was a mishap at school. I thought Harrison would've told you, but I'm guessing now he was trying to save his relationship and it slipped his mind."

"Is she being bullied?"

Liam shakes his head. "No, Quinn took care of that."

I try to make sense of what they're saying but I can't. I need to hear it from Harrison. I look around for him, but don't see him anywhere.

"Where's Harrison?"

"He went home. He has an early flight to L.A. in the morning."

"Why?"

Liam looks away and down at the ground before meeting my gaze. "He's moving back."

CHAPTER 39 - HARRISON

As soon as I step off the stage, the boys start their riff. We had to modify their song just slightly, but it works. Peyton has the hardest part and has worked really hard to learn her beats. I stand behind her, waiting to lend a hand if she forgets. But she doesn't forget. She nails it each and every time she's supposed to.

I watch the crowd, looking at all the guests lined up to support the kids. I couldn't be more proud of the four of them, and am so happy that they asked me to help them put this together for Liam and Josie.

Peyton looks over her shoulder at me. I step up and guide her hands where they need to be. It only takes her seconds to remember what she's supposed to do. Standing behind her, I have a clear shot at Katelyn, who is standing there in the middle of the dance floor staring, not at her daughter who is singing, but the one playing the drums. Her mouth is open in shock and honestly, if I was standing next to her, I think mine would be too. I can't imagine what these guys look like to the rest of them, but to me, they look perfect.

As soon as they're done, Peyton jumps into my arms. I hold her tightly. She tells me thank you over and over again. Her words make my throat tight. I can't find the words to tell her what she means to me or tell her how much I'm going to miss her and her sister. I'll be back next week, but only to get Quinn and say my good-byes. I can't say them today, not like this. Not on a happy day when everyone is laughing and enjoying themselves.

"You should go see your mom," I say, reluctantly letting her go. She smiles and runs off stage, right into her mother's waiting arms. I can't watch them. It's too much. I wave at Quinn, letting him know that I'm ready to leave.

He comes over and gives me a high five. "I missed a riff."

"It's okay, you did good." I ruffle his hair. "I'm going to go now. I'll be back in a week unless you need me to come back sooner. All the things you need are at Liam's, okay?"

"I love you, dad."

"I love you too, bud. Call me tomorrow."

Quinn waves and goes back to the party. He's getting pats on the back for his performance. I never thought about what I'd want him to be when he gets older. If music's his thing, then so be it and if he wants to be a doctor, that's fine too. I just want him to be happy.

I walk along the back of the room to the exit. I take one last look at the life I'm leaving behind. Katelyn is talking to Liam. Josie is dancing with my son, and the two girls that I wanted to call my own are dancing with Noah. I feel a pang of jealousy that everyone is so happy and content when I could've been that way, if it wasn't for the actions of someone else.

The night air is cold. There is a light snow falling, just enough to leave footprints on the ground when you walk. I don't wait for my car to heat up. After the snow is cleared, I pull out of the parking lot and head for home. The lights from the reception shine in my rear view mirror. Half of me wants to stay, but the other half wants to get the hell out dodge before my heart shatters beyond repair.

By the time I pull into my driveway, the snow has become heavier. If this delays my flight, I'll drive to Los Angeles. Even though there's nothing there waiting for me, staying here has become torture.

I flip on the lights as I enter the house. I only have a few more things to pack before I'm done. The movers will be here tomorrow to drive everything back and if it's not in a box, it doesn't make the trip.

I change quickly into a pair of jeans and t-shirt, hanging my tuxedo up in the closet. Josie and Liam aren't going on a honeymoon until February, and Liam said he'd make sure the tux gets returned, along with Quinn's.

I walk into the kitchen. The linoleum is cold on my bare feet. Boxes are made up in the corner. I pick up one, along with some bubble wrap and get to work. This is a tedious job and I know why I've left it for last. Wrapping dishes and glasses is probably the most mundane thing I've ever done.

I look at the clock when I hear knocking on the door. It's too late for anyone to be paying a visit, and everyone I know is at the reception. Twisting the doorknob, I open the door. I bite the inside of my cheek to avoid having an expression. This is the last thing I want to deal with right now.

"What are you doing here?"

"We need to talk." She steps in without being invited. I slam the door shut behind her, causing her to jump. She stands there without a jacket on, her skin wet from where the snow has landed on her. It takes every ounce of strength that I can muster to keep from touching her. She left me, I remind myself.

"So talk," I say with a bit of a bite. My wall is up. No more emotion from me.

"You're leaving?"

I look around at the boxes and frown. Does she think I'm remodeling?

"Yep," I reply and walk into the kitchen to finish packing. I have a feeling I'll be up all night doing this shit, so might as well make good use of my time.

"Harrison?"

"What, Katelyn?" I slam the glass that's in my hand down on the counter. I feel like a shit when I see her lower lip tremble. I don't want her to cry, but I can't be a doormat for her. "Look, I don't want to fight with you. As you can see, I'm moving back to Los Angeles."

"Why?" she asks as her shoulders drop.

I can answer her one of two ways; truthfully or easily. I lean against the counter and clear my throat. Suddenly the floor has become very interesting. I close my eyes and take a deep breath. "I can't live in this town and watch you fall in love with someone else. I just can't, and that's going to happen someday and frankly, I don't want to see it."

"So you're leaving? What about Quinn?"

"Quinn will be fine. Spending a few months in public school and leaving isn't going to scar him for life. He's used to a different way of living, he'll adjust."

"But he has friends here."

"And he'll see them when I come back to work once a month."

"So that's just it, you're just going to leave us?" Her voice breaks, which causes me to look up. There are tears streaming down her face, ruining her make-up.

I shake my head and push away from the counter. "There is no us," I say as I walk past her. I open a couple of boxes until I find what I'm looking for. Against my better judgment I wrap a quilt around her shoulders. I let my hands linger on her for a beat too long. When I pull away, she looks at me.

I run my hand through my hair and tug at the ends. It's too short now. I don't like it. "I have a lot of packing to do before my flight and the movers come, you should go." I don't wait to see what she says or what her reaction is. I go back to packing and focus on it like it's my professional job.

I hate that she's still standing there, watching me. Every so often, she sniffs and I think she's about to say something, only I'm rewarded more silence. I can't look at her for fear that I'd fall to her feet and ask her for another chance. I won't do that because I didn't do anything wrong. I'm not about to apologize for something that I had no control over, when all she had to do was listen to me.

"Harrison?"

I set the plate in the box and look at her questioningly.

"My daughter was being bullied at school."

I take a step back and realize that I never told her about Peyton. I would've, but she ended us. I nod and lean against the counter. "You were in L.A. and I got a call to pick up Quinn from school. Liam got a call about Peyton because your father-in-law didn't answer or something. Anyway, I went to pick up Quinn and he had a black eye and I knew that Peyton was involved, but I thought she punched him. When we got back to Liam's, Quinn told me a story about a friend that was being bullied and how he asked the boy to stop, but he wouldn't. When the boy touched Quinn's friend, he reacted."

I chance a look at Katelyn and see that her hand is covering her mouth. Tears continue to stream down her face, breaking my heart even more.

"I put two and two together and figured with her outbursts and reluctance to do things, it had to be Peyton. So I called her down to the studio and showed her what I did when kids would bully me."

"What?" she squeaks out.

"When I was a teenager, I found a drum set and brought it home and taught myself to play; but I'd imagine the faces of those kids who made fun of me day in and day out as I beat the drums. Every day, I'd pound and pound until I had nothing left. I gave her some sticks and let her go to work. She hit the drums so hard, I swear I could see the anger leaving her body."

"You helped her."

"Good," I say.

"You taught her to play as well?"

I nod. "They came to me with an idea. They wanted to play a song for Liam and Josie. So we worked very hard on making it just as perfect as possible."

"She smiled."

"What?"

"Peyton... she smiled at me for the first time since Mason died. And it wasn't just any smile, her face lit up because of you, because of what you did for her." Katelyn moves in front of me. I press harder against the counter.

"Look at me, Harrison, I have something to say."

I look up with hesitation. Her watery eyes slice right through my heart. My hands grip the countertop, giving me something to hold on to.

"I've been so stupid these past few weeks. It took a village of people to show me how wrong I was about you and those pictures. I thought I could let you go, that I could move on and just be a friend, but every time I turn around, you're doing something that slaps me in the face to remind me that you're here. You gifted my daughters with the most precious gift and for me... You gave me a bracelet that bears another man's initials. Why?"

"Because I told you I'd never ask you to stop loving him. He's a part of you and I would never ask you to give him up." I answer her against my better judgment.

"Those are things I should've remembered when I saw those pictures. I shouldn't have allowed someone to cloud what my heart knew, but I did, and I'm sorry."

I bite my lip to keep myself from breaking down. I look down and push my thumbs into my eyes. These are words I wanted to hear weeks ago.

"Harrison," she says as her hand pulls mine into hers. My heart soars as heat spreads through my body. I've missed her. Her fingers lock with mine as she brings our hands up between us. When her lips touch my skin, I want to push her away and tell her no. Tell her that I'm done and the damage can't be changed, but I'd be lying to myself.

"Katelyn, please don't do this unless you mean it," I beg her.

"You can't leave us. You can't get on that plane and fly back to Los Angeles and leave us here. I'm sorry I failed us, Harrison, and I know I'm selfish and don't deserve what I'm asking."

"What are you asking?"

She steps closer, bringing her other hand into my hair. I have no willpower to tell her no or to stop. She's going to be the death of me.

"Give me... us a second chance."

I close my eyes and get lost in the feel of her hand in my hair. I want this, I do, but I don't know if I can do it.

"I love you, Harrison."

My eyes flash open, my heart races faster. Those are the

words that I've wanted to hear from her for so long and now that she's said them, I can't, for the life of me, remember what they sound like.

"Say it again."

"I love you and I love Quinn. My girls love you and we want you both to be a part of our lives. I need you by my side, Harrison. I want to walk the path that we lay together."

I pull her close before my mind tells me to second guess everything. She came over here in the dark of night to tell me this. My heart fills with love as I look into her eyes.

I do what I've been longing to do for weeks. I move forward, tentatively and touch my lips to hers. Her reaction shocks me as she claims my mouth instantly. She lets go of my hand and grabs onto my shirt, tugging me closer. I pick her up, her legs wrapping around my waist as I try to lead us upstairs. I stop when her hand slides down my pants and I know we aren't going to make it to the bed.

CHAPTER 40 - KATELYN

I HADN'T REALIZED HOW MUCH I MISSED HIM UNTIL now. The way he makes me feel, the way he kisses me, it's like he's claiming me. This is not the adventurous Harrison opening my world on his motorcycle; this is not the sensitive Harrison who makes every cell in my body dance with his touch. No, this is primal Harrison. Domineering, animalistic. This is the rockstar telling me that I *am* his. I can truly understand what Josie means when she tells us about 'Liam Page'. This version of Harrison is my own personal bad boy rocker.

He excites me.

He satisfies me.

He makes me want to beg for more.

I want him.

I need him.

My body is eager for him.

I want him in every way possible.

I slip my hand into the top of his jeans and flick the top button open. It creates enough space for me to slide my hand in. He growls. My legs rest on his hips. I bunch his shirt in my hand, trying with all my might to rip it away from his body. I palm his hard on, desperate to touch him. He hisses as he slams me against the wall, his casted arm pressing painfully against my back.

"Fuck, I'm sorry," he says heavily, his lips barely leaving mine. He pulls back, much to my dismay. I whimper when we're no longer connected. My chest heaves, pushing my breasts closer to his mouth. He pulls the top of my dress down, freeing them. He takes one in his mouth and kneads the other. His tongue swirls over my taut nipple, biting it gently. I move against him, lifting my dress so I can be closer to him. Pressing against him does nothing to ease the ache that I feel.

I tug again at his shirt. He takes it off with one hand, only breaking contact with me for a brief moment. I squeeze my legs tighter around his hips so I can work to free him from the confines of his jeans. My eager mouth attaches to nipple ring. I pull, knowing that he loves the way it feels. It urges him on. He moves against me, building the friction between our clothed bodies.

His fingers dig into my legs as he holds me against the wall. His mouth sears into my skin, leaving a path of burning kisses on my neck. He bites my earlobe, pulling and sucking it into his mouth.

I free him from his captor, sliding my hand up and down his shaft. He pulls back and looks at me. His green eyes bore into mine, daring me to stop this before it goes too far. What he doesn't know is that I want this. I want him. Now, tomorrow and forever.

He moves my panties aside and guides me to his ready cock. I arch against the wall, as he grips the door casing for leverage. He pulls back and thrusts. I scream out, not in pain, but in pure unadulterated pleasure.

He watches me. He takes stock in knowing that I'm coming undone by his touch. He pushes harder. My body slams against the wall. The way he keeps control, the way he keeps his rhythm, it's like I'm the beat of his drum and he's playing me with every ounce of energy he has.

He bunches my dress in his hand and watches as he pulls out. "Fuck," he hisses as he buries himself into me again and again. I pull him to my mouth, my hands woven in his hair as I reach my peak. I give him everything.

My heart.

My body.

My soul.

My life.

Harrison comes hard, grunting and pushing himself deeper. The clarity of this moment makes me realize that I *am* his, and he *is* mine.

He kisses me softly, his mouth lingering over mine. My breath catches when he moves away from me. He holds me in his hands until my feet are planted on the ground. I look down at myself and shake my head. I move to right myself, but he bats my hands way. He adjusts my dress, placing small kisses along my cleavage. He bends and in one fell swoop has me in his arms.

My arm wraps around his neck. My fingers play with the back of his hair. He walks faster, once we reach the top of the stairs, his feet shuffling. I look at him, confused.

"I forgot to button my jeans," he explains as he tries not to laugh.

My heart sinks when I look around his room. Boxes line the walls, ready to be moved back to Los Angeles. He sits me on his bed. I can't look at him for fear he'll see the heartbreak. Am I enough to keep him here?

Harrison uses his finger and thumb to lift my chin. His

thumb caresses my lower lip. My tongue reaches out to taste him.

"Ask me," he demands.

"Stay," I say quietly. "Stay here and be with me. Stay and be a family." I stand so were body to body. I take his hand in mine and press it to my heart. "Stay and love me, love us."

He captures my lips with his with such urgency I have to grab onto his shoulders for fear I'm going to fall. He picks me up and lays me on the bed gracefully. He hovers over me, his eyes boring into mine.

"I love you."

"I love you, Harrison."

MY SKIN PEBBLES as his fingers map out their destination. I think he's touched every inch of my body, some places more than once. But who's keeping track? I'm not. I lay in his bed, surrounded by him. His naked body is pressed to my side as he writes his name on my stomach.

"When did you know?" he asks.

"Know what?"

"That you loved me?"

"The night I came to pick up the girls, they were coloring on you and it's what Peyton said and the way you were with them. I knew my heart was yours even if I was having a hard time letting it go."

He pulls me closer to him, burying his face in my hair.

"The movers will be here soon," he says in a whisper.

I roll over and face him, my hand cupping his cheek. "Move in with me."

His grin grows as my words sink in. "Your house is too small and so is this one. I'll buy us a new one."

I shake my head. "My father-in-law he..." I take a deep breath. I know Harrison will never ask me to stop loving Mason. I respect him for that. But will he be able to live in a house where my husband grew up? That I don't know. "He wants to travel and can't take care of his house. It's big enough for the five of us. The girls were born there and Mason grew up there. I know it might be difficult for you —"

"Do you want us there?"

"I do, so much and so does my father-in-law."

"He does?"

"Yes, he thought... He knows about us and he thought we could live there as a family."

Harrison pulls me to him and kisses me hard. "You'll be okay with us living there, even though there's a history?"

"I love that house, I always have. Wait until you see it. The basement is finished so you could put your drums down there or have a space to get away. The wrap around porch is perfect for sitting out on a hot summer night and watching the sun go down. There are four bedrooms so each of the kids can have their own space. I think you and Quinn will fit in just perfectly."

"Can we talk about a few things first?"

"Sure," I try to sound confident, but I'm not going to lie, my insides are shaking.

Harrison rests his head on his hand and looks at me. "Moving in is a big step toward a serious commitment and that's something I'm ready and willing to do, but I want us on the same page. I spent so much time trying to woo you that I bypassed a lot of the getting to know you crap that a normal dating couple figures out early on; like do they want kids and what are their views on marriage."

"Do you want more kids?"

Harrison shrugs. "I don't know. I can see myself happy with our three and if another one came along, I'd be happy with that as well."

A part of me feels relief, because having twins is a lot of work and I can't imagine adding another one, but another part of me longs to give him a child. I just don't know which part is stronger right now. "I can live with that."

"Good." He leans forward and brushes his lips against mine. "Now, marriage."

I feel my heart drop.

"I'm in love with you, Katelyn, and if you said you wanted to get married, I'd do it, but I'd like for you to think of something first and that's the girls. I've told you that I respect your love for Mason and I'll never ask you to stop loving him, and that includes changing your name. I don't need some piece of paper to tell me that you're mine, what I need is for you to love me, that's all I ask. What I need is for Peyton and Elle to *know* their father and to know that I'm there for them when he can't be. It's important to me for them to decide how they want me around. If they come to me, years from now and say they want me to adopt them, I'll do it, but it has to be their decision.

"This doesn't mean I won't marry you, I will, you just tell me when you're ready, but I think we both know that you might not ever get there. I have no doubt in my mind that you're a one wedding bride, and I'm more than okay with that. I respect that and love you more for it. I know we can have a long and happy life, standing side-by-side, watching our children grow up.

"I know Liam has been taking care of your bills. I know

he paid off your house, but I want to take care of you now. I don't want you to work, unless you want to. I know you like being home when the kids get out of school and I want that for you. Let me provide for you, Peyton and Elle."

Tears pool in my eyes. How he knows me the way he does is beyond me. I move closer and nuzzle into the crook of his neck. His arms encase me, holding me to his body.

"I think if I was someone different, I'd be kicking you out of bed for saying we're never getting married."

Harrison laughs. "Baby, if you were someone else, I wouldn't be here right now."

"No?"

"No," he says leaning back to look at me. "I only have eyes for Katelyn Powell."

CHAPTER 41 - HARRISON

"Are you sure you want to do this?"

"Yes, I'm sure."

"You know I think it's going to be sexy as hell, right?" I pick up our joined hands and kiss hers.

"No, I didn't know that." I can't tell if she's being coy or not.

I shake my head. "Fuck, baby, I'm hard just thinking about it."

I pull into the parking lot of *Rock City*. I feel her stiffen next to me. I know she's scared, but she knows that she can back out at any time. This is something she wants, something that she suggested.

I get out of the car and run around to her door and open it for her. I take her hand in mine and walk with her by my side.

When she came to me and said she wanted a tattoo, I thought she was joking, but she wasn't. In fact, she had the design all picked out. I asked her how long she had been thinking about getting one, and she said a while.

The chime on the door rings out when we enter. I made

her an appointment as soon as she asked. She fills out her paperwork and hands her drawing to the artist, who starts transforming it into something he can work with.

"Right this way," he says. She grabs my hand. I squeeze hers, letting her know that I'm with her all the way.

"Where do you want it," he asks. She looks at me and smiles. The location has been a secret until now. She lets go of my hand and lifts her shirt.

"Whoa, what are you doing?" I ask, as I try to pull her shirt back down.

"Stop," she says, pushing my hands away. She turns and points to her hip, showing the artist where she wants her flower and how it should fit on her body.

"You'll have to pull your shorts down a bit," he says, watching my reaction. "Lie on your side." He nods toward the table and waits for her. With her shirt lifted and her shorts hanging lower than I'd like them to be in public, he sets her design on her and pulls away the paper.

Her flower will sit just above her hipbone with vines above and below. Small stars will be added as accents.

"What color do you want the flower?"

"Purple," she answers.

I pull a chair closer to her and hold her hand. She looks at me, her eyes showing concern. "You'll be fine. You've given birth to twins, this will seem easy."

She rolls her eyes and scoots her head closer to me. She rests there, waiting. I lean down and kiss her on the nose. She stiffens when the gun turns on. I know she's nervous. I was too when I got my first one, but I know she'll do just fine and will likely want another one soon.

As soon as the needle touches her skin, she squeezes my hand. I watch her for any sign of distress, but see none. She keeps her eyes closed, likely concentrating on her happy place. Where that is, I don't know, she won't tell me. Either way, if it keeps her calm and levelheaded, she can go there whenever she wants.

I was informed of said happy place when we moved into the house. Combining two households was a nightmare. We had a mix match of stuff and it didn't blend. A week after we moved in, I threw my hands up and took her shopping. I told her that for seven days the kids and I had listened about how nothing matches and now she can have whatever she wants. She balked at first, saying she can go to her happy place and make it work. I didn't know what that meant, but each day she was spending more and more time there and I'd had enough. She finally relented and bought a houseful of furniture. Now everything is new and ours – which I think was the problem from the get-go.

I kissed Katelyn for the first time in front of the kids on the day that we told them we were moving in together. I figured it was a good time. It was much easier than I thought it would be – kissing her. She gathered them in her living room and told them we had some news. Elle asked if she was going to be a princess again, referring to her stint as Josie's flower girl. Peyton didn't say anything. But Quinn, he looked at me and smiled. He knew. I cupped Katelyn's face and planted one square on her lips.

I wasn't sure what Quinn would think, but he, along with the girls, said it was going to be cool since they spent most of their time together anyway. Peyton asked if she and I would still practice together, and I told her nothing would change, except I'd be around more. The kids seemed to like that idea.

I look over at the design taking shape on her side. The impure thoughts are rampant. I can't wait to lick, kiss and nip every square inch of her body. When she asked me what I thought about her getting a tattoo, I showed her. Words didn't even come close to describing what I thought. We played a little game that night – it was 'let Harrison find the location of the tattoo' – each time I thought I was close, she'd tell me I wasn't and I had to start all over again. I loved that game.

"How does it look?"

"Sexy."

She pushes me in the shoulder. "It doesn't look sexy. I looked up the procedure online. I'm sure it's red and gross looking."

I lean in and whisper, "Baby, nothing on you is gross looking."

She snuggles into my neck and places small kisses there. I refuse to move, relishing in the attention. There are two sides of Katelyn. I learned this as well after we started living together.

There's the mom side. That Katelyn is on her game. She's making breakfast for five, packing three lunches, checking homework, doing all our laundry and making dinner. She dresses in tight ass yoga pants and has her hair piled on top of her head. Believe it or not, this is my *dirty girl* Katelyn. This is my, come-home-at-lunch–for-a-quickie, Katelyn.

Then there's the shy, reserved Katelyn. That's what I have now. She wants to be held and caressed and will show affection, as long as it's hidden from everyone else. She's not afraid to let it be known that I'm hers though, but it takes some good goading for her to be flashy about our relationship. This is the Katelyn that I get at night when we're all sitting around watching TV. She'll curl up in a chair or I'll come home to find all three kids piled around her.

The first time I saw her and Quinn sitting together, I

thought I was going to lose my shit. I almost broke down and cried like a baby. She treats him as her own and that is more than I could ask for.

"You're done," the artist says.

Katelyn bends to look. She gasps and covers her mouth. "It's beautiful."

"I told you," I say, kissing her temple.

He covers it and gives her the instructions that I have memorized. When she hops down from the table, I pull her to me. I kiss her once and move aside, taking my shirt off as I do.

"What are you doing?" she asks.

"It's my turn." I jump up on the table just as the artist returns with my sketch.

"Where?" he asks.

I point to my chest and he nods.

"What are you getting?"

"You'll see."

I lay back, putting my arms behind my head. I'm grinning from ear to ear when he sets the paper down and peels it back.

"Harrison?" Her voice is soft and wavering.

I pull my hand out from behind my head and reach for her. She comes to me, allowing me to hold her. I watch her the entire time, never flinching or needing to look that he's doing it right, I know he is.

Mine is done quickly. He bandages it up and sends us on our way. I don't ask if she wants to go home or if she has other plans. I need to go home. There are three people waiting for us and I have something to show them.

As soon as we pull into the driveway, Jenna is walking out. She looks tired, run down.

"What's wrong?" Katelyn asks her. Katelyn puts her hands on Jenna's shoulder to hold her still.

"I think I have the flu. I'm sorry if I got the kids sick."

"It's okay," Katelyn says, walking Jenna to her car. I wait for Katelyn at the bottom step and make faces at Peyton who is staring at me through the picture window.

"I hope she's not sick," Katelyn says, meeting me at the step.

"I hope not either. She's been acting so weird since the wedding, though. I don't know, but something's off. Did she meet someone there? You know, maybe had a bad one-night stand?"

Katelyn shakes her head. "I don't think so. Heck, the last time I heard her talk about a guy was when she kept talking about you when I had a sleepover. She kept asking me if she could ask you out."

I can't help but laugh. "Oh yeah, what'd you say?"

Katelyn rolls her eyes and leans into me. She stands on her tippy toes to kiss me. "They were mean to me at that slumber party, Harrison. They teased me until I told them that I was in love with you."

I rub my hands up and down her arms. "Poor baby," I say, kissing her nose. "Come on, we have kids waiting for us." I pull her hand into mine as we walk up the steps and into the house.

Three eager children meet us at the door. Quinn is used to me coming back with new ink all the time, but not Katelyn. We didn't hide that she was getting a tattoo from them and they all seemed excited. Peyton, mostly. I have a feeling that she's going to be the hellion of the trio.

"What'd you get?" Quinn asks.

Katelyn lifts her shirt and I pull down the bandage. The

girls move closer and I tell them not to touch it because it needs to heal.

"What'd you get, Dad?"

"How do you know I got anything?"

Quinn laughs. "Because I know you, you got something. Come on and show us."

I take off my shirt, much to the giggles of the girls. They colored on me last night and I didn't bother scrubbing off their ink. I pull down the bandage and risk a look at Katelyn. She has tears pooling in her eyes. Happy tears.

"Perfect," Quinn says, making me happy that he approves. The transition for us has been seamless. We fit as a family. He treats the girls as if they're his sisters and has the utmost respect for Katelyn. In the nine weeks we've lived together, I've heard him call her mom a few times and she didn't miss a beat when she answered him. I think the moment I knew she was in this for the long haul was when she introduced Quinn as her son.

The twins step forward, both of them looking at me with awe in their eyes. I kneel down so that we're eye level. "What do you think, guys?"

"You put our names on your body," Elle says.

"I did."

"We're with Quinn on your heart," Peyton adds.

"That's because I love you both."

Both girls tackle me, knocking me to the ground. I wrap my arms around them and I hold them to me. Quinn finds a spot and wraps his arms around my neck.

"Hey guys, I think we're missing someone," I say above their laughter.

"Come on, mom, there's room," Quinn says, letting Katelyn know that she's needed.

She sits in between my legs and the girls hold her in

their arms. It's in this moment that I realize my life can't get any better than this. Anything that happens to us will just be an added bonus. I have my son, the woman I'm madly in love with, and two beautiful little girls that make my heart sing each time they smile.

What more could a guy like me ask for?

Six months later...

CHAPTER 42 - KATELYN

I STAND ON THE PORCH, ACCEPTING THE SUN AS I BASK in its warmth while watching the kids. The kids... I still find it odd to say that, but at the same time, love it. I love everything about my life right now and have Harrison and Quinn to thank for that. Once I let go of my fear of losing Harrison and being alone with another broken heart, I started living again. The grass suddenly became greener. The sun was brighter, warmer. The biggest change was laughter. The happy sounds that echoed through our house were because of Harrison and Quinn. They made me and my girls' smile, all while never forgetting that another man has been a huge part of our lives.

Pictures of Mason hang in our family room. Harrison hung them while I was out shopping. I came home and once I saw them, I cried. I cried for hours in his arms, telling him that I didn't deserve him. He should've agreed with me, but he didn't. He's the creator of this blended family that looks whole to anyone who sees us. And we're almost whole. I still miss Mason, I always will. Harrison makes sure that he's talked about, that the girls say their prayers to their daddy, and that we visit the cemetery at least once a week to place fresh flowers on his grave.

If it weren't for Harrison, I'd be a walking zombie. Because of him, I sleep peacefully at night. Because of Harrison, my girls are loved and have a father figure to look up to. Because of Harrison, I have a son who treats me not only like his mom, but also his best friend and he loves my girls like they're his sisters. Because of Harrison, I have my life back and a family that my girls and I can love and feel secure in.

The kids are playing in the backyard. The heat is rising fast today and they wanted to get out before it became unbearable. I agreed and couldn't pass up the opportunity to watch them. Today is backwards day. What that means is that Quinn and I will go off and do something together while Harrison takes the twins for the day. We've been trying to do this at least once a month because I felt like I needed to spend some time with Quinn, getting to know him. Before we moved in together, he'd come to my house after school with the twins, but I was afraid to know him. Afraid that his father would break my heart and take his son with him, but that fear is gone.

"Mommy, look at me!"

Elle screams my name as she flies through the air on the trampoline. That thing scares the living daylights out of me, but my partner, who is supposed to side with me on everything, thinks it's best thing ever and loves jumping with the kids. Last night the four of them camped out on it, under the stars. I stayed inside, away from bugs and in the comfort of my bed, missing Harrison.

"Did you see me?" Elle asks, as she comes running over to me. Her hair is all over the place, half in a ponytail and half out. She wants to be more independent and I'm trying to allow that. It's hard, I admit; she's my baby and I want her and Peyton to not grow up, but there's no stopping it.

"You were so high, it scares me."

Elle rolls her eyes, a trait that I wish I could break. "Harrison says it's fine as long as the sides are up and see," she points to the trampoline where Quinn and Peyton are still jumping, "the sides are up. I can't fall out."

"Hmm... what if you got so high that a bird swooped down and picked you up and carried you away from me?"

Again with the eye roll and a shake of her head. "Dat's ridiculous," she says, bouncing back toward the others.

She's right, it is, but the thought has crossed my mind once or twice. The sliding glass door opens and goose bumps spread across my body. A smile breaks out as I bring my iced tea to my lips. His hands find my hips as he pulls me close to him. His lips graze the top of my shoulder.

"What are you doing?" he asks as he moves his hands in front of me, locking me into his arms. I lean my head back and take in his freshly showered, 'Harrison' scent. This man, with all his money, insists on wearing Old Spice and I'm not going to lie, it smells damn good on him.

"Just watching them and trying to convince Elle that she'll get carried away by a bird if she jumps too high."

Harrison laughs. "That would have to be a huge bird."

I shrug. "It could happen."

I feel him shake his head. "He'd drop her after a minute, once he realized that she talks too much and would be worried about how her hair looks."

He's right, of course. Elle is quickly becoming a little fashionista. Not that I mind, she's always been more like me, but Quinn definitely hates it. The many fashion shows he's asked to play music for gets on his nerves, but he's a team player and puts on his game face.

"Are you ready to leave?" I ask, not knowing what their plans are. That was something we agreed on when we started our backwards day. Plans are left a secret, so we have stories to tell later.

Harrison whistles and just like that, all three of them come running. "I am," he says, kissing me full on the lips. I'll never forget the love and experiences I had with Mason, but with Harrison, there's no comparison. He ignites a desire I didn't know I had. A simple touch from him and there's a fire burning until he can extinguish it.

"Are we going now?" Peyton asks. She still wears her football jersey just about everywhere and has it on today, but Harrison doesn't say anything. I wonder sometimes if he cares, but then I remember that he said he'd never replace Mason and that he would always live on in our family.

"I am, kiss your mom and we'll go." I lean down and kiss both girls before they leave me for Harrison. He holds their hands as they bound down the stairs and disappear into the garage.

"Well, that leaves us, are you ready?" I ask Quinn.

"Sure am! Where are we going?"

I shake my head. "What's rule number one?" I ask as I walk back into the house to lock up. Quinn follows, shutting the sliding glass door behind him.

"No questions until we're there."

I ruffle his hair and know my time is limited before he asks me to stop doing that. "Let's go, we have a busy day." He smiles even though I know he wants to pout because I'm not budging.

We drive in silence until he spots the Go-Kart track that just opened today. He's been eyeing this place each time we drive by. I was surprised when he didn't ask if we could go.

"You're so awesome, Katelyn."

"Let's go ride, shall we," I say, as we exit the car. Of course, the line is long and we're given a number. We have about a two-hour wait, but it'll be worth it. "Want to walk around, maybe play some arcade games?"

Quinn nods and leads the way into the arcade. I hand him some money and let him change it into tokens that he hands back to me to hold. I follow him around, never much into video games myself, and watch while he tries them all out.

"What do you want for your birthday?" His birthday is coming up soon and his grandma will be coming to town. This will be the first time he's having a party with kids from school and I want to make it special.

"I want something that probably costs a lot of money and can't have."

I look at him questioningly. His eyes are downcast and the happy kid that I had minutes ago no longer exists. He shrugs and walks away from me.

"Quinn, is this about your mother?" I can't stand the woman, even though I chose to believe her, but if Quinn wants to meet her, I know Harrison will make it happen.

"Sort of."

I take his hand in mine and lead him outside. "Meet me over there." I point to the table that's open and head to the snack counter to get us something to eat.

"Let's talk while we share some fries. Tell me what's going on."

Quinn sighs and sets his fry down. "I don't want to meet my mother or anything like that, but I want... I don't know how to say it, Katelyn."

"Just spitting it out seems to work for the girls, want to try that?"

"I want you to be my mom," he rambles so fast that I

almost miss what he says. He's not looking at me, and I can't tell if he's embarrassed by his request or not. I know I should be stunned, but I've considered him my son for a while now.

"Quinn, can you look at me?"

He does, raising his baby blues that match his dad's, to meet my eyes. "I'm sorry."

"For what?"

"I know you already have kids and probably want to have a baby with my dad."

"So what if your dad and I had a baby, that means you'd be a big brother again."

He shrugs. "They'd call you mom."

"Do you want to call me mom?" He's said it a few times in passing or during sentimental moments, but he's not consistent.

"Yes, but I *want* you to be my mom, like make it real."

I furrow my eyebrows when I look at him. "What do you mean 'make it real'?"

He sighs. "Noah said that before his dad came back, Nick was going to adopt him and his last name was going to be Ashford. I want you to have my last name and I want you to adopt me. Make us a real family."

I sit back as far as I can without falling over. Adoption. It's something I've thought about, but haven't had the nerve to bring up. Adoption might mean marriage and right now, Harrison is dead set against it, saying we can be a family and take care of each other without a piece of paper saying what we already know, that we're committed and in love.

But I want this. I want this boy in my life until I'm no longer here. I want to be there when he graduates and when he is meeting his bride at the end of the aisle. I want to pace the waiting room when his wife is in labor with my grandchild and hold his child in my arms, knowing that I'm a grandma. I want this boy to be my son.

"I'll adopt you, Quinn, on one condition."

"What's that?"

"That from here on out, you call me mom, because when I hear you say that word, it makes my heart soar with so much love. I love you as my own and I think it's about time we make it legal, don't you?"

He smiles so big I can see all his places he's missing teeth. I stand and pull him into my arms, holding him to my chest. I don't know if a son was in the cards for Mason and I, but if he's looking down on me now I hope he's smiling because I have no doubt that I'm meant to be this boy's mom.

CHAPTER 43 - HARRISON

It's backwards day, one of my favorite days of the month. It's a time when I get to be a girly man and hang out with two of my best girls. I've been known to let Peyton and Elle do my hair and paint my nails, but that only occurs when Katelyn takes Quinn to the movies and the girls and I chose to snuggle on the couch, watching Disney movies.

I stand and watch Katelyn while she watches the kids play. Last night, I chose to sleep outside on the trampoline with them. I was hoping Katelyn would change her mind and join us, but she didn't. As Peyton said, she's too girly. I sort of like girly, so I'm okay with it.

To say my life is on path with my dreams would be inaccurate. I never dreamt this. I never thought in a million years that I'd be standing in a house that I own, with the love of my life, surrounded by children that laugh day in and day out. For me, this is perfect.

I slide open the glass door and step behind Katelyn. I can't resist touching her. My skin craves the connection we have. My fingers dig into her hips as my body responds to her. Never will a single moment be enough to quench the desire I have for her and each day, it grows exponentially.

My lips trail kisses from her neck across her shoulder. I love the hot weather we're having. The hotter it is, the fewer clothes she wears. Right now she's rocking these tiny shorts that accentuate her tanned legs and a tank top that's begging me to take it off. She's a walking sin, and I want to be the one she confesses to later.

"What are you doing?" I ask as I move my hands to the front of her stomach. I lock her in my arms, holding her against me. She leans her head back and even though she tries to act coy, I know she smells me. I smile, unable to stop myself.

"Just watching them and trying to convince Elle that she'll get carried away by a bird if she jumps too high."

I laugh at the thought of Elle flying through the sky, screaming her head off. "That would have to be a huge bird."

Katelyn shrugs. "It could happen."

"He'd drop her after a minute once he realized that she talks too much and would be worried about how her hair looks."

Katelyn tightens her arms around mine. "Are you ready to leave?"

I nod and let her go so I can whistle for the kids. It's crazy to see them coming running like their asses are on fire. "I am," I say, kissing her goodbye. The twins each grab my hands and pull me away from their mom. I think they're jealous.

Today it's the park, mall, and ice cream. I need to find Quinn a birthday present. It's a hard task for a kid who has everything, but that's where I'm going to rely on the girls.

The three of them are thick as thieves and they'll know what he wants.

I reluctantly leave Katelyn on the deck and head off with Peyton and Elle. They're both eager to get their day started. As a rule, my plans are kept secret until we arrive at the destination, and while the mall may not be my favorite place to be, I do love watching their faces when we're riding the carousel. For some reason, my horse never seems to catch theirs. I think it's rigged.

The girls pile into our new acquired "family car" and buckle themselves in. We traded in both our cars for an SUV and a luxury sedan. I don't mind driving the SUV; it's fully decked out and completely loaded. These cars have come a long way from the stigma of a "mom mobile". Peyton and Elle turn on the DVD player and start watching whatever movie they left in here. That's one thing I had to grow accustomed to, a mess. Katelyn's not messy by any means, but the girls leave stuff everyone. If I'm not stepping on a Barbie, it's a barrette or I'm tripping over a ribbon. I love these two as if they're my own, but damn do they need to pick up their stuff.

"How long until we are dere?" Elle says. Since we moved in together, her speech has started to falter. I don't know if it's because of Quinn and me or if she's just not focusing. Katelyn and Mason did an amazing job making sure these girls spoke clearly, I hate seeing that she's having this issue now.

"Elle, say 'there'. Can you please do that for me?"

"There," she whispers.

"Thank you," I say, watching her in the rearview mirror. She smiles, but doesn't reply. Frankly, that's good enough for me. The relationship I have with the twins is good, if not excellent, and they know that I'm not trying to replace their dad. I just want to love and be there for them when they need me. And if that means scaring the living shit out of any guy who tries to date them, I'll do it, because I think that's what Mason would want.

I pull into the mall parking lot and earn a 'yippee' as soon as I shut the car off. Months ago, Peyton would've crossed her arms and refused to get out of the car. We've come a long way and I know Katelyn is thankful. I meet both girls at their respective doors and take their hands in mine.

As we walk through the mall, the women gawk. The last time we were here, I got hit on. Katelyn says they were flirting because of who I am. I countered that they saw me as a committed man with twin daughters and that's what they want. She rolled her eyes, but knew I was right. I could've had the upper hand with that conversation since one woman sat down and proceeded to ask if I had custody and what my visitation schedule was like.

"Do you girls want to get lunch first?"

"Yes! Yes! Yes!" they scream in unison as I pull them toward the *Johnny Rockets* for some of the best cheese-burgers and milkshakes around. We're seated right away and in the back, which I prefer.

Once the girls order, I get down to business. "Okay, I need your help. As you know, Quinn's birthday is coming and your mom and I don't know what to get him. So maybe you can help me find him something?"

Peyton pokes Elle in her side with her elbow and nods toward me.

"Quinn said not to tell," Elle whispers.

"I know, but I think we should. I want it too." Peyton counters.

"I don't know, what if he says no?" Elle asks.

"What if I say no to what?" I finally cut in on their back and forth.

The twins turn and look at me. Peyton's eyes are full of mischief and Elle's are full of worry. One is about to spill, while the other wants to keep Quinn's secret, which I can only imagine is going to anger me somehow.

"We're not supposed to tell," Peyton says.

"It's not good to keep secrets though. What if he needs my help?"

"He's not in trouble," Elle adds.

I rest my elbows on the table and lean down slightly so they can look me in the eyes. "What does Quinn want?"

Peyton sighs and looks at her sister before looking back at me. "He wants our mommy to be his mommy and I want you to be our daddy, but Elle doesn't think you want that."

I sit up quickly, shocked by what Peyton just rambled off and say the first thing that comes to mind. "Mason's your dad, Peyton."

She huffs and shakes her head. "I miss my daddy but you're like my daddy now, and Quinn wants mommy to have his last name so we can be a really real family like Noah has."

To say I'm stunned is an understatement and how I can understand anything she's saying is a miracle. "How does Quinn expect to make this happen?"

Peyton shrugs, causing Elle to roll her eyes.

"Quinn said it's call badoption and since he doesn't have a mommy and wants our mommy she can badopt him and he'll get to call her mommy like us."

"And you do the same," Peyton adds.

I lean back against the bench and pull my lip into my mouth. The wheels in my head are turning, but I'd have to talk to Katelyn first. I told her from day one that I didn't want to replace Mason and I'd never pressure her to do anything, but I'm committed to this family. I'm not going anywhere and I'll be damned if I'll let her live with the fear that I'll leave her one day in the back of her mind.

"You want me to be your dad?" I ask, barely able to get the words out.

They both nod. "We want a really real family, like Noah," Peyton says.

"That means your last name will be James."

"And we'd all match," Elle adds.

"I want to match," says Peyton.

"Do you want another brother or sister?" Katelyn and I haven't talked about having our own, but we also haven't ruled it out.

"Let's not go there just yet," Elle says, rolling her eyes.

I can't help but laugh. I see how it is; as long as it's just the three of them, they'll be happy. I thought my life was perfect up until now, but knowing that these little girls love me enough to take my name pretty much defines perfection in my eyes.

CHAPTER 44 - KATELYN

WHEN QUINN AND I GET IN, THE HOUSE IS QUIET. THIS only means one thing: Harrison took them to the mall. It only took a few backward days for me to realize how much he wore the girls out. The mall is Harrison's friend and mine too right now, because I'm tired and just want to curl up in his arms.

After our heavy lunch conversation, we didn't discuss adoption the rest of the day. Instead, we raced Go Karts, bungee jumped and sat at the lake watching all the boaters. Quinn asked if we could get a boat and I said it's something we could probably talk to his dad about.

Quinn gives me a hug when we get to his door. This hug is different. He lingers longer than usual, holding me tighter. I kiss the top of his head and press my cheek there, squeezing him.

"Goodnight, mom, thank you for today."

I fight the emotions building and give him a soft smile. "I had the best day, Quinn."

He smiles before turning into his room. I know that in about an hour Harrison will get up and check on him, find out what he's reading, or if he needs to talk about anything. Their bond is beyond amazing.

I turn the handle to our room and am instantly mesmerized by the sight in front of me. Harrison is sitting up on our bed with a book in his hand. His eyes are closed, his features relaxed. He's shirtless, and the closer I get I can see that the girls had some fun with him tonight. I sneak into the bathroom, change my clothes, and take care of my nightly routine. He startles, but stays asleep when I shut off the bathroom light. I really want to watch him sleep like this, but the urge to be next to him is too great.

"I know you're watching me."

I laugh as I sit down and slide up next him to him, pressing my leg against his. "I see you have new ink."

Harrison shifts, setting his book on the nightstand. He holds his arms out, moving them back and forth showing off the artwork. "I have a new one," he says.

"Oh yeah, where?"

Harrison moves so I can see his side. I gasp when I see Peyton James and Elle James written in their handwriting. "Is that real?"

He shakes his head as he pulls his hand into mine. "How was your day with Quinn?"

I look at him questioningly. "How do you know?"

"The girls; they told me and I figured he asked you by your reaction of seeing their names like that."

I nod. "He did. He asked me to adopt him and I want to Harrison. I want to be his mom. I want that title. If you want me to, that is."

Harrison cups my face, bringing my mouth to his. The kiss is slow, but filled with desire. He's going to make love to me tonight, capping off my already perfect day.

"The girls asked me to badopt them."

"What?" I ask, pulling away slightly.

"Badopt – that's what they called it. I didn't have the heart to correct them."

"Do you want to?"

Harrison grabs my hips and pulls me onto his lap so that I'm straddling him. "I called my lawyer today to find out more information and he said we can do this within a week if it's want we want. We don't have to be married, unless you want to be. We can be just like Brangelina. We can be our very own Karrison."

I lean forward and kiss him quickly. "You're a dork, but you're gorgeous and sexy, so I forgive you."

"I see, using me for my looks?" he asks as he shifts, pushing into me. He's such a dirty little flirt. "Or are you using me for my son?"

"Definitely your son."

"Hmm, that's what I thought."

"I have a proposal, Mr. James."

"Okay, let me hear it."

"One thing Quinn said to me is that he wants me to have his last name. It was more like him adopting me, but I didn't tell him that. He knows what he wants and I want it too, but I'm not ready to get married. I'm very happy with our life right now, and I'm not saying marriage ruins that, but you're right, who needs a piece of paper to show me that we're in this for life, right?"

Harrison nods.

"Right, so my proposal is this: I adopt Quinn, you adopt Peyton and Elle."

"Baby that solves the last name thing except for you," he says with a smile.

"I want to change my last name to James."

"I love you Katelyn, but I can't let you be the only one

to change your name. So my counter-proposal to you is that Quinn and I change our names too, and you and the girls hyphenate your name. I don't mind being called Harrison Powell-James, and that way we'll have a really real family with matching names, and they get to keep a piece of Mason with them."

"A really real family?"

He nods. "It's what Peyton and Elle want, but as I've said, I'm not here to replace Mason. I'm here to love you and the girls and make sure that you're happy and taken care of. I'm not looking to have the girls forget him or ask that he never existed. All the decisions we make regarding the girls, I hope we're doing with his beliefs in mind. I'd want that for Quinn if I wasn't around."

I wipe a lone tear that falls. "You're seriously the most amazing man I've ever had the privilege of knowing. How I ever doubted your intentions last year, I'll never understand."

"It's simple," he says as he adjusts. "You didn't know what to think when you first met me. I blew you away with my wit and charm." Harrison raises his eyebrows, suggestively.

"Yeah I'm not so sure if that was it."

"No?" he asks.

I shake my head. "No, it was how you treated the girls even after I told you I didn't want to see you. You never wavered, even though I was being an epic bitch to you. You never gave up and never pushed, even when I was hot and cold. I should've never been that way with you, but I was afraid. I didn't want to fall in love, only to lose you like I lost Mason. You've shown me that living with fear in your heart is no way to live and because of you, my girls are loved and we're happy. I'll never be able to thank you for what you've done for us. I love you, Harrison, and this life we've created is more than I could've ever imagined after I buried my husband. I want to take your name, but the fact that you're willing to take ours as well means more to me than words can explain.

Harrison moves so fast I almost fall off his lap as his lips crash down on mine. He pulls me to him, removing my shirt quickly. He holds me against his bare chest as his hands roam over my body. His hands cup my rear, grinding me into him. His fingers move under my shorts, pulling them away from my body.

I sit up and finagle my shorts off while he watches. "Do you need me to undress you?"

"No baby, I'm just watching you unwrap my present."

"Were you a good boy today?"

"I'm about to be."

I look at him, waiting for him to continue, but he doesn't. He moves his hands behind his head and nods for me to continue. I crawl over his body, pulling his lounge pants down and throwing them off the bed. My hands rub up and down his legs, my nails digging into this skin. He flinches slightly, encouraging my movements.

"You're killing me, woman."

"Hmm, well now you know how I feel each time you touch me. You have no idea what you do me. How I feel when I know you're behind me," I say, moving up his body. I places kisses on his hips, feeling his cock twitch against my cheek.

"Fucking hell, Katelyn, sit on me so I can fuck you senseless."

I sit up and look him. His hands come out from behind his head. One cups my breast while his index finger and thumb pinch my nipple. His other hand hits the volume on the remote sending music throughout our room.

"Are we going to discuss what Santa's bringing the kids?" I ask as I center myself over his waiting erection. This has been our code word for adult time, since the incident in the bathroom.

Harrison hisses as I slide down his shaft. His hands find my hips, pulling me to his chest. Our mouths meet as he lifts his hips, slamming into me. His mouth muffles my cries as I cry out.

I push up from him, enough so I can bring his nipple ring into my mouth. It's one of my favorite parts of him. I love watching him come undone with a simple tug from my teeth. He pounds into me harder. His breathing increases as he reaches down and flicks my clit, causing me to cry out. My body shakes as I clench around him. My head falls to his shoulder as he finishes, bringing us down from the euphoric high we're on.

Harrison doesn't let me leave his arms, but rolls us onto our sides. Our legs entangle as he kisses me. "I can't imagine my life without you and the girls, Katelyn," he whispers into my hair, holding me to him. His heart beats wildly, even though he's calmed down.

If anyone ever says you can't feel love coming off of someone, they're wrong.

CHAPTER 45 - HARRISON

I TOLD KATELYN THE BADOPTION WOULD TAKE A WEEK; it's taken a month. I'm not complaining, I'm just eager to have everything settled. What my lawyer didn't count on was a judge asking for witnesses. He wanted one from me testifying that I'm a good parent to the girls and one from Katelyn testifying the same with Quinn. We asked my mom and Mr. Powell who were both eager to help us out.

Now, here we are. Today's the day. I'm nervous, but I think it's a good set of nerves. We're going to be a family recognized by law and that is something that's important to us. Our wills change today as well. If something happens to me, Katelyn inherits most of my estate, with trusts being set up for Quinn, Peyton and Elle. If something were to happen to Katelyn, I'll get the girls. But we're going to live until we're one hundred, so we don't have to worry about any of this. It's nothing but a formality in my eyes.

I dress in my black suit with a white button down. I'm forgoing a tie today. I want to look presentable, but not over-done. I add some gel to my hair, giving it a teased look. I slip my black suit jacket on and fix my collar before leaving my bathroom. When I step into our bedroom, Quinn is sitting on my bed, dressed similarly to me.

"What's up, bud?" I ask, as I sit down next to him to put my shoes on.

"Are you scared?" I cock my head and look at him. He's fidgeting, twisting his hands together.

"No, are you?"

Quinn shrugs. "I don't know. What if Katelyn changes her mind?"

I sit up, leaning my elbows on my knees so he can see me. "She's not going to change her mind, Quinn. Katelyn wants this. She wants to be your mom."

"I'm scared."

"About what? You know you can tell me."

Quinn looks at the photo that sits beside Katelyn's side of the bed. It's of the five of us at my apartment in California. It was our first family photo and you can see how much Katelyn already loves Quinn.

"What if my real mom comes back?"

This wasn't exactly why I thought he was scared, not that I had an idea. I sit back and exhale while rubbing my hands down my legs. We've never really spoken about his mom and there's not much I can tell him. But I can show him. I get up and head into my closet and to the box that holds pictures of her the night that we met. I've only saved them for Quinn because he has a right to know.

I come back in the room and hand him the photo. He takes it from my hand and stares at the two people who created him.

"I know we've never discussed your mother, but I'll answer any questions you have to the best of my ability."

Quinn sighs before looking at me with tears in his eyes. "Can she take me away?"

I shake my head. "She can't. You're mine, and you'll soon be Katelyn's too. When you were born, your birth mother left you at my house. I didn't even know her name. We weren't dating. We weren't even friends. She just showed up, set you on the floor, and said that you were mine before walking out. All I got from her was her name, so when you were a few months old we had a blood test done to make sure that you were mine. I didn't want some other dad out there missing their son, just in case. But when the results came back, I was informed she signed away her rights, which means she has no claim on you."

"She didn't want me?"

"I don't know about that, bud, she was young and not able to take care of you. Not like I could. And that doesn't matter because I wanted you. Grandma and aunt Yvie wanted you. The second that grandma saw you, she was in love. And those three women downstairs, they love you, so I don't want you thinking for a minute that you're not wanted."

Quinn falls into my arms, hugging me tightly. "I love you, dad."

"I love you too, Quinn. Now, what do you say we go find those Powell women and make them James'?"

"I think that's a good idea."

"Me too, bud." I ruffle his hair as soon as he pulls away. I finish tying my shoes before following him out the door. I stop and put my hand in my pocket, feeling for the three presents I have in there. I don't know if there's a protocol for this, but I couldn't let today happen without some gifts.

I walk into the kitchen as soon as I'm downstairs. I stop

dead in my tracks when I see Katelyn staring out the kitchen window dressed in a vibrant red dress. This lady in red is going to be the death of me. She turns, as if in slow motion, her mouth dropping open.

"What?" I ask as I watch her jaw move up and down.

"You're so f'ing hot."

I turn my head down slightly and laugh. I step forward, placing my hands on her hips. I lean down so that I'm almost kissing her. "Say fuck, Katelyn."

She shakes her head.

I rub my nose along her jaw, nipping along the way. "Say fuck, Katelyn. I want to hear you tell me I'm fucking hot," I say as I bite her ear, pulling it gently.

"You don't play fair."

"I'm not playing, baby. I want to hear your dirty little mouth tell me I'm fucking hot."

"You're so fucking hot, Harrison."

I cup her face and reward her with a searing kiss. "Are you ready to become Katelyn Powell-James without getting hitched?"

"You know it!"

"GOOD AFTERNOON MR. JAMES and Ms. Powell. I see you're here to petition the court for adoption of Quinn James, Peyton Powell and Elle Powell. I see that the minor children are present for this hearing?"

"Yes, sir," I say, squeezing Katelyn's hand.

"And your attorney?"

"He's not present, sir. He believes everything is in order and isn't needed."

The Judge shuffles the papers around before looking at us. "I'll start with you Mr. James. Are you prepared to offer financial stability to the Powell children in the event you and Ms. Powell part ways?"

"Yes, sir, I am. In your paperwork you'll find that trusts have been set up for both of the girls."

He looks down at his paperwork and nods.

"Ms. Powell, are you prepared to offer financial stability to Quinn James as well as your children in the event you and Mr. James part?"

"Yes, sir," she says confidently.

"Very well. It also states that you'll each be taking each other's names. Is that correct?"

"Yes, sir. It's a family decision that we combine our names."

He nods and writes something down. "I see nothing further. Congratulations Mr. and Ms. Powell-James, you have three children who," he leans slightly to look at the kids behind us, "are eagerly waiting for their parents." With a slam of the gavel, we're done and now a really real family.

Katelyn and I turn and hug the kids. Of course, she pulls Quinn into her arms and the twins jump into mine.

"Can we call you dad now?" Elle asks.

"Only if you want to."

"We want to," they say in unison causing us all to laugh.

"Come on family, we have a lunch date." We walk out of the courthouse as a family and walk down the street to one of Beaumont's finest dining establishments. We usually take the kids to the crazy pizza palace, but today calls for something a little more upscale.

I open the door of *Whimsicality* to cheers and a lot of clapping. A banner saying *Welcome Powell-James Family* hangs on the wall, making this feel almost complete. Everyone is with us today, including my mom and Mr. Powell, but it's Josie that's there to meet us as she hugs the kids with tears in her eyes.

We make our rounds before sitting down to a catered meal. This is how we wanted to spend our first day as a really real family – with the family that brought us all together. I stand, clinking my fork against my glass.

"I just have a few things to say. First, we want thank you all for supporting our decision. I know a lot of you asked why Katelyn and I didn't get married, and the simple answer is that marriage isn't for us right now. But the option is there if we want to take it. Secondly, I've been blessed many times over since moving to Beaumont and I thank each and every one of you for making Quinn and I feel welcomed. Lastly," I say, pulling out the bracelets I've been hiding in my pocket all day. "I'm going to start with my youngest." I walk over to Elle and kneel down in front of her. "Elle, I give you this bracelet as a token of my love and devotion to you as your dad." I clasp it on her wrist and kiss her on the cheek, earning a giggle. "Now for my drummer girl, Peyton." I repeat the same words I said to her sister and get a high-five in return. When I get back to Katelyn, there are tears in her eyes. I bend over, kiss her lightly and open my palm so she can see what I have for her.

"Harrison," she says as she covers her mouth.

I bend down and ask for her hand. She extends her left hand and it shakes as I slip on the ring I had designed for her. It's a diamond solitaire surrounded by Quinn, Peyton and Elle's birthstones. "This is my commitment to you and our family, from here and this day forward, I'm yours forever."

She cups my face, threading her fingers through my hair. "I love you, Harrison Powell-James."

Not as much as I love you, I want to tell her, but I don't. I let her have this moment.

ACKNOWLEDGMENTS

Yvette – my dedication speaks for itself.

Many, many thanks to: Jodie, Toni, Kelly, Heather, Emily P., Damaris, Sarah, Emily T., Espe, Miller, Jen M., Kelly, my girls at Indie Inked, The Beaumont Daily and the team of bloggers that have been working with me throughout My Unexpected Forever. Your continued support means the world to me and I don't know how I'll ever thank you.

Eric Heatherly: thank you for creating the right songs for my stories. I'm so happy to be working with you on The Beaumont Series.

To my family: Thank you for your continued support. You know who you are.

ABOUT THE AUTHOR

Heidi is a New York Times and USA Today Bestselling author.

Originally from the Pacific Northwest, she now lives in picturesque Vermont, with her husband and two daughters. Also renting space in their home is an over-hyper Beagle/Jack Russell, Buttercup and a Highland West/Mini Schnauzer, JiLL and her brother, Racicot.

When she's isn't writing one of the many stories planned for release, you'll find her sitting court-side during either daughter's basketball games.

Forever My Girl, is set to release in theaters on January 19, 2018, starring Alex Roe and Jessica Rothe.

Don't miss more books by Heidi McLaughlin! Sign up for her newsletter or join the fun in her fan group!

Connect with Me!
www.heidimclaughlin.com
heidi@heidimclaughlin.com

ALSO BY HEIDI MCLAUGHLIN

THE BEAUMONT SERIES
Forever My Girl – Beaumont Series #1

My Everything – Beaumont Series #1.5

My Unexpected Forever – Beaumont Series #2

Finding My Forever – Beaumont Series #3

Finding My Way – Beaumont Series #4

12 Days of Forever – Beaumont Series #4.5

My Kind of Forever – Beaumont Series #5

Forever Our Boys - Beaumont Series #5.5

The Beaumont Boxed Set - #1

THE BEAUMONT SERIES: NEXT GENERATION
Holding Onto Forever

THE ARCHER BROTHERS
Here with Me

Choose Me

Save Me

LOST IN YOU SERIES
Lost in You

Lost in Us

THE BOYS OF SUMMER

Third Base

Home Run

Grand Slam

THE REALITY DUET

Blind Reality

Twisted Reality

SOCIETY X

Dark Room

Viewing Room

Play Room

STANDALONE NOVELS

Stripped Bare

Blow

Sexcation

Santa's Secret

CPSIA information can be obtained
at www.ICGtesting.com
Printed in the USA
LVOW13s1608150318
569991LV00010B/488/P